A. M. Sequeira is currently a medical student studying in Tbilisi. She is from India and enjoys spending the final three hours of her night living in another world through writing. She dislikes the idea of a monotonous life; the very idea that many people hate to visualize. She wishes to wake up every day to adrenalin rush but realizes that life is expensive, demanding countless degrees and experiences. It is through her debut book as a first-time author that she explores the aspects of different lives in a single life.

To Jinish John, Bran Becile, and Andrea Sequeira, who keeps me sane.

A.M Sequeira

ENCHANTERS: ROYAL SECRETS

Austin Macauley Publishers™
LONDON * CAMBRIDGE * NEW YORK * SHARJAH

Copyright © A.M. Sequeira 2024

The right of A.M. Sequeira to be identified as author of this work has been asserted by the author in accordance with Federal Law No. (7) of UAE, Year 2002, Concerning Copyrights and Neighboring Rights.

All rights reserved. No part of this publication may be reproduced, stored in a retrieval system, or transmitted in any form or by any means, electronic, mechanical, photocopying, recording, or otherwise, without the prior permission of the publishers.

Any person who commits any unauthorized act in relation to this publication may be liable to legal prosecution and civil claims for damages.

This is a work of fiction. Names, characters, businesses, places, events, locales, and incidents are either the products of the author's imagination or used in a fictitious manner. Any resemblance to actual persons, living or dead, or actual events is purely coincidental.

ISBN 9789948760160 (Paperback)
ISBN 9789948760153 (E-Book)

Application Number: MC-10-01-5947647
Age Classification: 13+

The age group that matches the content of the books has been classified according to the age classification system issued by the UAE Media Council.

Printer Name: iPrint Global Ltd
Printer Address: Witchford, England

First Published 2024
AUSTIN MACAULEY PUBLISHERS FZE
Sharjah Publishing City
P.O Box [519201]
Sharjah, UAE
www.austinmacauley.ae
+971 655 95 202

My first acknowledgment goes to the one true God without whom I'm not even capable of standing. A lot of love to my parents and my sibling and all of my extended family, close friends – you shaped and formed me as I am. Big gratitude to BTS, who each gave me a piece of their life's teaching through their music. The last unforgettable vote of love and thanks is to my very 'little people', all of you who I do not personally know but play a significant role in changing my life- my readers, my supporters, and even my ill-wishers.

Chapter 1
Entering the Unknown

"Life is a deceiver; it makes you dream of the wonders you can achieve and then shatters them right before your face. But that's not the worst part; your story has already been decided, and no matter how hard you plead, you will continue to remain you."

Somewhere far beyond the limits of our world, the Queen of the Enchanters declared to lay open the truth and mysteries of her life.

"I, Queen Elora Slayholt, stand against what the Enchanter community has deemed me to be: a villain. Although I am not one by nature, I intend to shed light on this matter through my very own words."

In love and understanding of her people, she appointed a writer, Grissa Douglas, a woman in her early twenties. Fame and money followed Grissa at a young age, and she carried a streak of green in her hair, the mark of *Andronicus*.

With every great history of victory, a darkness of pain and suffering is prevalent, but it is we who decide the impact we choose to have after the victory.

The King, his left hand also called by *Aristera*, and the diplomat of Prielvar took it upon themselves to investigate the illegal presence of Monojacinth recovered from three men traveling through a security checkpoint from Lacoyara to Prielvar. It was during such moments that the royal duties of the King were temporarily handled by the Queen.

Grissa wore casual formals on the first day of the appointment, and, as customary, greeted the Queen with the *honoris* at the large gold doors of the palace, a traditional form of greeting done by making a cross of the right hand and a small bow. A curtsy is added in the presence of a significant person. The palace was located in Lunare, the province of the King.

"Welcome to the palace!" The Queen wore a wide grin that shone against her golden beige skin. She was dressed too simply for the title she carried, with minimal accessories—an off-white dress, turtle-necked and long-sleeved—and beige stilettos. Her brown hair was tied up with a red streak evident, the mark of *Eromen*.

The palace carried an overall tone of gold and red, looking extravagant, turning the young writer distant. Her shoulders slumped a little because even though 'glory' was not a new word to her, the richness of the palace was far beyond what she had seen in her life.

"Your Highness, with all due respect, we could do this in the royal office too. I respect your privacy here—"

"Grissa, isn't it?" the Queen questioned, sounding superior. The halt on the stairs made the hair on Grissa's neck rise.

"Ye…s," the woman stammered; she had offended the Queen. With one hand on the railing, the queen turned to look at her, and despite the cool temperature of the palace, her skin was turning red. She shouldn't have spoken out of turn. Was the queen indeed like the rumors of her past, rumors of heinous crimes? Or was she like what the morning papers displayed, the face of a sweet, affectionate mother toward her children? The Queen tilted her head to one side, squinting at the countenance before her.

"I acknowledge your concern, Grissa, but…" The light, watery tone of the Queen was beginning to sound as hard as stones, and Grissa's eyes were growing wider with each word the Queen uttered.

"The mysteries of our country's past cannot be filled in within a single day, but if you must be this reserved and terror-stricken about me, then I believe I am going to have a hard time, and so are you. I permit you to call me Elora within the walls till we complete our business, and, in this time, you are free to declare your heart to me. Is that understood?"

Grissa looked at the Queen, who smiled wide after playing around. Partially relieved, partially shaken, she returned a smile.

"Yes, Your Highness."

As a protective measure, citizens of the country were not permitted to enter the palace. The newfound exception had boundaries too; a chamber was appointed, the first next to the end of the stairs. The chamber had two armchairs with a small table placed between them, on a large round spotless carpet.

Several paintings, the fancy ones as seen in an expensive place, were hooked onto the walls. At an ample distance from the armchair on one side was a fireplace, and on the other side was a wooden dining set. The room appeared simple, but the paintings gave an expensive finishing touch.

"How shall we begin?" the Queen asked casually.

"I expect a good start would be from the time you came here. I believe you lived with the non-Enchanters before."

The Queen gave gentle nods, contemplating.

"Before I begin, let me warn you that a lot of what you hear may contradict what the world has spoken of me."

She then began her tale.

"I grew up knowing my real identity, that I was an Enchanter. I spent my childhood with my godfather, Cassiden Anderson, because, like the countless others, my parents died during the rule of *King Maxwell Slayholt-Maldeus*.

Cassiden was a man in his late thirties and always remained vibrant before me. He carried a blue streak, the mark of *Zocia,* on his long black hair, which he tied in a half updo. His black hair was beginning to gray, but he was single and happy with me alone.

I completed my background education in the other world and entered our world on my 17th birthday."

****

Elora Bates

The tall mirror on my wall was just an ordinary mirror, yet the magic that could radiate from it was beyond ordinary. It was a link between us and the magical world—a door, and the key was an M.P. card, without which we would only be crashing through it.

The M.P. card smelled of cellulose acetate and had an electronic print of a blue lily on the back; the front had Cassiden's identity details. He held my hand, pulling me into the mirror, the flow of which I was not acquainted with, causing my eyes to shut in reflex.

"Welcome to Moon City, Prielvar," he said, emotionally stirred. Now that my eyes were open, I took in the glorious view, the smell of metal and iciness that comes from chewing mint prominent in my nose—the smell of magic. I rubbed my nose, refusing to blink at how different this place was from the world I had just left. It was like watching through spring glass, just radiance and smiles and a strong gust of nostalgia.

We were standing inside a huge consulate building; the floor was built of porcelain white tiles, and they reflected the evening light from the half-window walls. Behind us stood five shiny mirrors placed at an ample distance from each other, and from each emerged a person every minute or so.

Two large glass doors stood at the center of the wall in front of us, a table before them, and on either side of the doors were fully armed security guards in navy blue, keeping a watch on everyone who entered from the mirror behind. Enchanters that came through the portal progressed through the identity check pass and left.

The woman behind the desk greeted us with a rushed honoris. I followed Cassiden when he reprinted the act, only having heard about it before.

"Pass," she said, holding out the palm of her hand toward us. Taking the pass from Cassiden, she placed it on the glass surface, and the machine inside made a beeping sound, with a green light emerging.

"What about your pass?" she asked me.

"Oh yes, she hasn't got one. We will have to create one," Cassiden answered, the woman raised her eyebrows, growing suspicious.

"And I assume you are her father, yes?"

"No."

She picked up her radiophone and called into it. "I'll need assistance here for security check-in."

We were asked to step aside and allow the remaining travelers to pass because we had caused a halt to the flow of people. Judgmental expressions arose from the travelers, making me anxious. Soon, another woman wearing a silver nametag, 'Selina' appeared, and she spoke with the woman at the desk. She then asked us to follow her. We went through the glass door, moving to the right instead of the left where all the other Enchanters went.

"And is your identity registered?"

"I believe not." Selina halted at Cassiden's words, her lips pressed against each other. "And her birth?" She pushed; he shook his head. She tried to suppress her suspicion, but it slipped through her expression.

"I'm not sure, to be honest…" Cassiden tried, thinking hard.

"How old are you?" The woman then turned to me.

"17… as of tonight."

"Why, is there a problem?" Cassiden asked, tilting his head.

"Do you have any particular reason why—" She looked at me, trying to make it sound as polite as possible, but a hint of curiosity seeped through her tone.

"Her family died during the war, and I wasn't an active resident here. So, I had to take her away, and the whole registration process did not strike me as important at that moment."

"I'm sorry, sir, but who are you?" She folded her lips. "Elora's current, legal guardian." He stretched.

She paused, scanning the walls above us. "So, what we're going to do now is check if her identity is registered, and if it is, then that's great, but if it isn't, then there will be quite the legal procedures."

We continued walking, passing by several rooms: conference rooms, lavatories, and the legal rights room, until we reached an open square area with front desks made of cherrywood. Each desk stood a few feet apart, partitioned from the public seating area by a transaction window. Most of the desks had a door behind them, but only some of the desks were open. Each Enchanter in that room had streaks on their hair, some red like mine, others blue like Cassiden's, and still others green.

Selina walked to the woman sitting behind the desk that read 'Assistance' and said, "This is Miss…?"

"Elora Bates," I replied to her when I noticed her waiting for an answer, while my eyes roamed the area.

"Please check if there is any database on her identity and help them out with the procedure to create an M.P. pass. And if there isn't, follow the legal procedure." Selina added a quick bow to us and left.

"Welcome to Enchanters International Cooperation. Do you have any form of identification that could lead me to her database?" She spoke monotonously, executing her words without a pause. Cassiden then pulled a white card from his pocket, an M.P. card having an electronic print of a yellow chrysanthemum.

"Will this do?" he asked the woman, bending a little to speak through the hole in the glass.

"Yes, absolutely," the woman said in delight, knowing her task was somewhat lessened.

"Scarlett Bates," she read. "I assume her mother?" Cassiden bobbed his head, smiling at me.

"You must renew these once every ten years and when your mother's card had expired, she gave it to me, telling me, 'Should you ever get lost in this world. Here! Find me.'"

He scoffed at the thought.

"Delightful dimwitted woman, I tell you. She assumed a grown man like myself would lose my way."

"Hey! That's my mother!" I counter-joked, folding my arms and playing along. The woman behind the desk looked at the card and then typed in her information on her computer screen.

"All her documents seem to be in order; she is registered."

She then turned to me, handing me a slip of paper with a stamp from the M.I.C., granting me exit for a week without the M.P. pass.

"You are only required to come in tomorrow for your imprint."

She then turned to Cassiden, who was leading the issue, "Would you like us to reprint her documents and get them stamped by the Cooperation?"

"Yes, please. Thank you," Cassiden said, taking my mother's card that the Enchantress had returned. He tucked it into the inner pocket of his jacket, and I watched him. Seventeen years later, he still kept it, even after my mother had passed away. Sometimes, I wondered if their relationship was 'only friends' or something more. It wasn't just about keeping the card; the way he spoke of my mother even now, the light that shines on his face when he says 'Scarlett' is quite different from when I say 'Max,' my best friend who went to Heidelberg last week.

"We apologize for any discomfort caused. We often come across cases that are illegal and are of such storyline. Thank you for your time and patience," the woman bid us off.

We traced our path back to the identity checkpoint, where we were cleared to exit. After passing through the declaration of self and goods, our journey in the consulate building had come to an end. The latter was not required since we walked here empty-handed, making me question Cassiden's intentions of coming here.

"We could always return, you know. I'd be happy to stay with you there," he played, covering the look of hurt.

Beyond the main arched double door made of pinewood and ornately in silver was a flight of stairs into what seemed like, I halted at the view, Heaven. Before I could realize it, my hands were around my neck in awe and my mouth gaping open. A trail of soft city lights glowed all along the endless road. The bright lights of its stores and buildings reflected the emptiness of the emerging night sky.

People with different fashions, young and old, some in groups, some alone, walked along with their invisible plan. I was so engulfed in the sight that I had to occasionally jog to keep up with Cassiden, who was leading the way. The marketplace had different shops; some sold paintings, some shoes, and some stationery, other tiles, and another endless list of goods. The lady in the bookshop welcomed her customer while she wiped the door frame with a piece of wet cloth. The bottom edge of all the buildings and shops was covered with ivy, wisteria, silver fleece, and many other types of vines that I couldn't recognize, but one among them that particularly stood out was a pink bell-flowered vines that glowed.

"Moon City is known for its liveliness during the night," Cassiden beamed at the awe he saw on my face.

"Here," he said, indicating a graphite-colored shiny surface on one of the walls.

They call it the Spenua. Cassiden told me about these immediate means of teleportation. He held my wrist, and the same old bronze bracelet tattoo on his wrist that my hands had wrapped around ever since I was a child came into view. It was a very common type of tattoo here; the people in the corporate building and the people in the street—they all had them. It came in two colors, silver or bronze.

Cassiden muttered something, and an image began to take form. It kept swirling round and was not clear.

"You know the drill," he said, and we started walking toward it.

The ground we stood on was the sandy edge from where the roads to the residential area began. It had houses with similar blueprints. The moon was already out; the area was dark, making even a little difference indistinguishable.

Behind us was the Spenua, and behind the Spenua was a wide ghosted highway road, lit only by streetlight. They had cars here, but they were rare, extremely rare.

Cassiden scanned the surroundings. The gates of the row of houses had black iron electrical torchlight, guarding their guests and guiding the strangers. The road was silent except for the sound of crickets or the footsteps of a mere passerby. He led us straight, walking confidently, and then halted at the gray gate of house 9.

From the dim lighting, I could make out that the bottom of the gate was rusted, and it creaked loudly when Cassiden pushed it open, like it was wailing. I wouldn't have been surprised if the entire neighborhood woke up. It seemed like nobody lived here, but the plants in the garden seemed well-tended.

Standing at the front door, Cassiden began touching his jacket, probably to take out the keys to his house, but on close watch, he was straightening his clothes, giving large huffs of air, and then, at last, closed his eyes to brace

himself. He gave two light knocks and waited, but nobody responded. He then tried again.

It was likely that no one would open the door, but then a croaky voice sounded, "Hold on, hold on."

The lights of the house were switched on, falling straight onto me through the door window, blinding me for a few seconds. I blinked hard, adjusting to the sudden light. The door lock clicked, and the woman's low muttering continued to be heard. She sounded annoyed at her late-night intruders, but what was more confusing was that Cassiden was fidgety, wringing his fingers, giving out a feeling of tightness.

I wouldn't deny that for a moment I had a feeling that Cassiden was married, and it was here that his hidden wife lived. But the woman sounded twice his age, so I had to eliminate that thought—unless his wife lived with this woman. The old lady opened the door slightly to look at our faces.

"Yes?" her sleepy voice questioned, like she was about to break hell loose if this wasn't serious.

"Mum?" Cassiden's brittle voice came out so low that for a moment I thought I had misheard. The woman opened the door a little more, trying to see the face that spoke, squinting her eyes, trying to focus on the man who claimed to be her son.

And then cried out in a broken voice, "Casey, is that you?"

"Mom!" I shouted, on the realization of his words, so loud that the two of them paused to look at me.

My hands splayed at the emotional scene, at the hunched-back woman who was now crying in Cassiden's arms as though she had just found her long-lost son. Cassiden too hugged her bone-crushingly.

Once they were apart, Cassiden introduced me to his mother, Isabel Anderson. I continued to look at him, gleaming with disbelief and loved-filled hatred.

"17 years, Cassiden, and this…now!"

"Hello, Mrs. Anderson," greeted her with a smile and then stomped into the foyer; it was warmer than outside. After the foyer, there was a large hall and a staircase near the entrance led to the first floor.

The hall was spacious, featuring a well-built sitting area with a television, a dining table, and its own kitchen. Cassiden belonged to well-off families, but not among the excessively rich ones.

I continued to give him my so-called deathly glare with every step I took, causing him to finally raise his hands in defeat. He smiled at me, as though I were still that kid who needed assurance that I was the best. But I was not a kid; I was 17, legal enough to be here on my own. I hid my smirk, knowing I had won.

Mrs. Anderson was a stout woman; her face was sunken, and her chin showed signs of sagging. I watched as she struggled to walk due to her age.

"I want to know—" she started strongly, her eyes shining. But Cassiden knew what she was going to say and dismissed her with the excuse that it was too late to be catching up. The pleasantness that he first wore when he saw her eroded off. "But… Cas…"

"No, Mom." The authority of being the man of the house suddenly seemed dreadful.

I woke up the next morning to raucous sounds issuing from downstairs. "What do you mean the girl was the one?"

It was Mrs. Anderson, her voice was loud, clear, and high-pitched. There was another muffled voice, low and unsteady, presumably Cassiden. I went down slowly, trying to make no noise, listening to them, strongly feeling that *the girl* they mentioned was me.

"Does she know?" Mrs. Anderson questioned it as though her life depended on it, but the conversation stopped the moment I stood next to the kitchen door, like it never began in the first place.

Cassiden was sitting at the kitchen table silently sipping on his tea and reading the newspaper. Isabel was sitting opposite Cassiden, stirring her tea.

Behind her, in the sink were two creatures about the size of my palm washing the dishes; they were pink in color. The front side of their body was covered in scales, but their face had normal human skin, and the back of their bodies was covered in hair extending to their head.

Their skin was much paler in color than their hair, and their hair had a red-colored zebra pattern. However, it was not zigzagged; it consisted of uniformed circle lines breaking at the point where the skin began. Even though their hands and feet were covered in foam from the cleaning, I could see that their fingers were so thin that they resembled the end branches of a tree with their nails clawed.

The large cicada wings shined as they fluttered in the air, keeping these creatures off the ground during their cleaning. Long, thick, antenna-like structures protruded from their heads with the color and texture of their skin. They had no visible ears, and their eyes were large and only black.

"Ahh, Elora…What is it, dear?" Mrs. Anderson pulled my fixed gaze toward her for a moment.

"I… I don't know where the bathroom is…" I squinted at the creature, trying to decipher whether they were real, "and… I've got no clothes."

"The bathroom is on the opposite side of your room upstairs. You head up, I'll be there. I'll hand you some clothes."

"Pixies, Elora," Cassiden said, his eyes making saccadic movements with the text, reading with raised eyebrows.

"Huh?"

"The creatures."

"Oh… umm… yeah… yeah…"

Keeping my thoughts aside, I tried to keep a check on the cultural shock from such drastic differences between the two worlds. If I wanted to fit in, I would have to accept this world as my own and live in the surroundings. I pulled the gray curtains, allowing the brightness of the sun to fall on me, and perhaps that was the only home-like feeling I could feel even here.

I sat on the bed, observing the room. The floor was built of hardwood, and the ceiling had flush-recessed lights. Cassiden told me back then that 'Enchanters don't use electricity for everything; they manipulate energy to make it glow like light,' and indeed when I looked deep within, I could see that there were balls of energy glowing within.

The walls were matte white, and a painting of a woman was hooked on the wall behind the bed. The woman in the painting had mustard-brown skin, and strands of blue streak from her blond hair fell onto her face due to the strong gust of wind, but she sat proudly on a flat rock despite it. A smile of superiority valid and a world of unexplored curiosity in those sky-blue eyes.

"That is Zosia, the one after whom our tribe is named Zocians."

I startled at the sudden voice after the silence, but Mrs. Anderson comforted me, patting my shoulder.

"Here you go," Isabel unfolded the dress in her hand.

"It's the only one I have for you. It was mine when I was young," she compared the yellow knee-length flare gown to my body.

"Yeah, should fit you. You can head out and buy some more clothes."

"If you don't mind me asking, what's with the different streak on our hair?"

I knew they were our groups, but Cassiden never bothered much with history. He always had a hesitation when it came to talking about anything about the past.

"They are the marks of the three tribes; Eromen, Andronicans, and Zocians, upon which our side of the world is built."

Chapter 2
The Curse of Eneas

"Thank you," I whispered to the pixies that placed my breakfast on the table. Their wings fluttered in the air, shining red and pink.

A week had passed, and the sight of magic and unusualness was beginning to look normal to me.

"Here, this came in, this morning," Cassiden handed me a brown envelope.

"What is it?" I questioned, taking the envelope.

Silverstring Academy for Enchanters

My breath caught in that moment, the four words sinking one by one. I tore open the brown envelope like I had only a moment to live and scanned the letter.

"Accepted!" I squealed.

"Shopping it is, then…" he sang, growing excited at the idea.

Cassiden had the best sense of fashion; he was always trendy and had all types of clothes in his closet—from bucket hats to no-show socks, you name it, he had it. Even in his late thirties, he was well capable of enticing a woman such that she would forget the age gap between them, but he still pushed the topic of a relationship away whenever it came up.

"Mom will meet us there. She had business to tend to with the bank." He then justified, "They've deducted 2 bronze coins."

I looked at him wide-eyed, believing that two bronze coins must have been a lot.

"Oh, seriously, it's not big of a deal it's almost… maybe… equal to… maybe a dollar… My mother just… No, it's all mothers, they like to dig into matters deep until the red flaming core can be seen."

I forcefully curved my lips, knowing that this would be something I could never relate to.

We took the same path to the Spenua. The street filled with little children running and playing, but the most peculiar event I'd witnessed was of a man wearing an apron with a large spoon in his hand, running behind his son who refused to drink milk. Such publicity from the father-son duo! I must say everyone stopped to watch them before realizing the whole issue and then carried about their tasks.

Two women were standing and laughing wholeheartedly, one of them wore an apron, holding a cloth bag of green leaves hanging from the side. A man with formal attire hastily ran toward the Spenua carrying an office bag in his hand. Women with floral dresses were a very common sight here and long overcoats on working Enchanters, too.

The crowd in Moon City was nothing compared to Crystal Valley; it was far more packed and had double the drama, gossip, and giggles. A group of little girls were eating ice cream of weird colors, teenagers were traveling on rectangular boards, like skateboards except that they didn't have wheels and were broader, moving in the air. Some were about 1 foot high while some were about 6 feet high. The slates glided with such smoothness, it felt like oil spilling on a surface.

"What are those?" I pointed at one of the boards coming toward us, amazed. "Those are slaters, they're used for covering short distances. Spenua open portals, a direct connection between two places. Slaters are more preferred because Spenua are present only in certain developed areas and… *oh little people*, these models are a kill for models," he said, his gaze fixed on the steel slater, having blue wings protruding from the back, that flapped slowly regulating the speed of the board.

"Back then, when I was a teenager, these slaters would move with energy coming from us but now they are fully automatic… You see those wings, they weren't there before, and… now… they seem much more advanced and glorious."

He took in a large breath, controlling himself.

"Stop fan-boying over a board that flies in the air, Cassiden," I stated with hooded eyes, not understanding a word or even having the simplest idea of his craze for these things.

They were cool but from my point of view, why not just walk the distance? A fall from those would probably be bed rest for days.

"You need to get a license for those…"

"You read my mind well…" I said, impressed.

The first task of the day was to get my pass card from MIC. We climbed up those same familiar stairs, 'Magaime International Corporation' carved boldly above the double door. The card was supposed to be procured the day after I entered here but the man on duty had taken sick leave.

"What's a Magi-ai-ma?" I asked, trying to pronounce what sounded like an ancient word. Cassiden followed my line of sight, tracing the origin of the question.

"That was the older form of what we use now. Enchanters."

The inside of the building was just as I had seen it before, but the main reception area had an adjoining space connecting to another area, something I hadn't paid attention to before. The corridor to the left of the main area was where we came from that day.

Cassiden walked up to the 'help desk cum reception' informing her of the purpose of our visit, the lady dialed to a stout man, Henry, and asked him to assist us. He was balding from the front, but a few strands of green could be traced.

"You'll need to wait; I will get your documents. We have three people today in line so would you be Elora Bates or Avery Khelane?"

"Elora Bates," His eyes went to my red streak, and a bitter look took over his face, "Okay, we'll proceed to the Imflow basin for your card imprinting in a few minutes."

And then left.

"You might have to keep a watch out for Andronicans. A bunch of indignant people," he complained while gluing his sight to the man walking away, pointing secretly at the streak on his hair.

"So, why are there these marks on your hand and hair? What do they symbolize? When can I tattoo the bracelet too?"

"You must have understood by now that there are three types of people," he indicated his hair, "We are three divided communities: Andronicans, Eromens, and Zocians. Eromen and Andronicans don't go well together because of some unhappy historical moments and Zocians are a neutral community. You will get the power mark very soon." He pointed at his wrist, reading the desire on my face, "And you need to stop looking for ways to fit in, Elora. That's not the summary of life."

I rolled my eyes, "Is that why you don't stay here? Because there is a lot of hate?"

A strong deep silence prevailed, he was contemplating hard, "No, because the woman I loved, and my father chose to serve the King and died in the process. I promised never to return to this world until the King was dead."

He jutted his jaw.

"And what's wrong with working for the King?" I scrunched my nose, waving my hand at his excuses.

"The very same King that killed your parents, Elora," he declared, and that was enough.

Henry returned with a few sheets of paper and asked us to follow him. This time we went through the adjoining passage and then turned right, straight into a corridor, passed by many doors carrying nameplates – bragging success.

At the end of the corridor was the door we were walking for. Henry placed his hand on the doorknob and waited moments, turning his face to inform us with a look of laced pride.

"Magic print access! Only a few can access here."

The door clicked, and he then pushed it open. From the way he mentioned the tight security, I was already filled with wonder. But the room within was dark and empty except for a small square stone basin from which glowing light filled the room. We approached the basin and the man continued to speak roughly like he had done the introduction a hundred times and no longer found it fascinating.

"This is the Imflow basin."

We gathered around the basin; its depth was about half a foot, filled with water. The base was covered with pebble-like structures and seaweed surrounded the sides. All the pieces in it glowed.

"These stone-like structures that you see are enchantments. They each identify the magic print you carry; they cannot be deceived. The submerged weeds that surround the basin are anti-potions. In other words, this basin prints your true form."

He then pulled out a card from his overcoat pocket and gave it to me. "Please identify if any corrections are required to your name."

'Elora Scarlett Bates Pass no ES21205.' "It is correct."

"Using your dominant hand, submerge the card. The blank side facing down."

Even though the blue water seemed ordinarily beautiful, there was a feeling of dread that arose from such beauty, especially after the way the man had described it. Because it is mostly beauty that deceives. My hands trembled lightly as I raised to submerge it.

"There is no need to worry," Cassiden placed his hand on my shoulder.

But even after his comfort, my anxiety did not settle because even though I claim that I am in control of my emotions, most of the time it's my emotions that are controlling me. But at this moment, all I could do was try and steady my hand, go with the flow, and allow the event to finish. The first few seconds my skin touched the water, nothing happened.

Then suddenly, an explosion of color took place within the water, causing me to reflexively curl my body away. The color started forming a whirlpool around my hand and then moved toward the card as though a magnet was sucking it. The unceremonious imprint was done before I even knew it.

"You can now pull your hand," the man stated. It was done, maybe I did panic unnecessarily.

"Go on, check it out," Cassiden pushed. I turned the card toward my face.

The electronic identification image was of a brown rose. I didn't know what to feel, so I looked at Cassiden. He and the man both stood frowning, allowing me to draw one conclusion: they were both not expecting this.

"Brown?" Cassiden questioned, his lips twisted.

"Impressive, how very Eromen-like! Never in my 7 years of service have I come across such a strong connection between a person and their tribe."

The man admired and smiled, which was unlike his behavior so far. I didn't know what he meant, but my face glowed. I finally felt accepted here.

Henry registered the pass card and handed over the documents. After all this tedious boring work, we decided to sit down in a café and call Mrs. Anderson to split up. Cassiden would get the books, stationery, and other supplies where my presence was not required while I and Mrs. Anderson would go for uniform, shoes, and all the other requirements.

An Enchanter soon approached our table, "What would you two like to have?"

"Two black fizzes, please," he said, and then suddenly remembered, "Oh, and a dispatcher too."

The waiter turned while on his way back, "And which class would you like?"

"Class?" Cassiden's gaze moved side to side.

"Yes, Class 1 or Class 2?"

"What is the difference? I'm sorry. I just came back to this world and..." His face turned red.

"Class 1 is used for short-distance communication; it can get destroyed on the way, while Class 2 is also called indestructible. It's a better-quality version that can pass even through fire or water, so it's ideal for any occasion..."

"And then how does the second get destroyed?"

"Sir..." the Enchanter pressed his lips, "The person addressed must sign it, and it turns to ashes on the spot."

He agreed to Class 1 since Mrs. Anderson was probably somewhere close to us.

"Okay, sir, and would you like it to be Echo or normal...?"

Cassiden looked at the man, who sighed. "Echo dispatcher is the one that notes down your spoken words, a voice mail. It reads to the receiver, although that happens only once. The receiver must read it if they did not grasp it in one go. The normal dispatcher is normal; you write it with ink, and the receiver reads it."

"Normal, please."

The Enchanter nodded, relieved, and walked away. "Quite the changes here," Cassiden mocked inanely.

The waiter then returned, moments later with two glasses of black fizzing liquid like the title it carried, a pale green envelope, and a piece of ordinary paper. Cassiden thanked him and wrote it down.

'Mom, we're at Hollow Glass. Waiting for you.'

He then put the paper into the pale green envelope and signed on the place that said *sign* using his pen. Immediately, a pair of white wings emerged. It kept tugging at Cassiden's hand, and when he uncurled his fingers, the envelope departed, blending in with the movement of birds in the sky. Would people realize that a paper was flying above them?

Mrs. Anderson joined us after a good fifteen minutes. Cassiden told her the order of things, and we then departed our separate ways. The sun was right above, and the street was overcrowded, a feeling of suffocation took over me as I walked through, but the gentle wind that blew cooled the heat of my body.

We entered Diallo's, an ordinary clothing store making business since 1980. It had a few scattered customers today. We stood waiting for someone to assist us even though there was a sign above a few meters away that read 'Uniform'.

"Oh, mam', this shows off your lovely figure. How is it that you can pull off any dress in this shop?" one of the assistants said to a plump short woman, flatteringly.

"I tell you; young girls nowadays don't take care of their health and figure. Look at me, I'm in my fifties," the last word came out in a low voice, and she then continued, "but attractive enough to lure a boy in his thirties."

The assistant nodded at her words with a gullible expression. I wanted to laugh at the woman but bit my tongue and stood, allowing myself to examine the shop, to look at other customers and their assistants. And indeed!

Business must be blooming by such a façade. It was not just that one assistant; even the one in the men's section on the opposite side buttered the man she was serving.

Mrs. Anderson began getting impatient and called out through the shop. "Audrey?"

It took a while, but somebody finally came for us.

"Oh, Mrs. Anderson. How good is it to see you again!" the vibrant young woman cheered. She was slim and had brown skin, just like any other Enchanter, but crystal clear.

Her straight black hair had a red streak that stood out. Judging from their talking, they knew each other well.

"You haven't been in here for ages. Where were you?" Audrey disapproved, her pitch rising.

They were so engulfed in their conversation that Audrey hadn't noticed her hand placed on Mrs. Anderson, and neither did the latter; listening to each other with ears wide open.

"Oh well, Mrs. Anderson. Our shop is one of the safest. So, what can I get you?"

"Silverstring uniforms!"

"Don't joke, Mrs. Anderson," she playfully tapped Anderson's shoulder, chuckling. The feeling of being distant grew. Did they know I was here?

"No, I'm not," she then turned toward me, catching me off-guard, "Elora is heading for her first level education."

"Goodness girl, I didn't see you there!" she exclaimed and straight after greeting me, led us to the 'Uniform section'.

She made crazy rounds around the clothes hanging on the rack, collecting uniform pieces, and handed them to me, pushing me into a tiny dull room filled with cobwebs, and continued her halted talk outside.

The room was lit only by the basement's windowpanes at the very top edge of the wall. I got into my uniform pieces one by one, but a questionable concern about Audrey grew in me. The uniform consisted of a white shirt, black formal pants, and an ankle-length black overcoat, which was all great, but the size was triple my size.

I opened the door, releasing exasperated sighs, calling Audrey because I had to hold my pants from slipping down. Audrey realized my concern before I could even raise them.

"Don't worry about that," she clarified, placing her hand on the shirt first, causing it to shrink to fit me, and did the same with the pants and coat, causing them to shrink in seconds until they all perfectly fit. It was fabulous magic; this is the very kind of magic that I anticipate living with.

"What do you think? You like them? Are they comfortable?" She inspected the fitting of the pants while placing her hands on her chin. "They always run out of stock during the school season, the most comfortable pants we own."

Her chin rose.

Mrs. Anderson and I waited in line at the main desk counter. The woman in front of us spoke to the Enchantress billing her purchase.

"This shopping reminds me of my time."

"Yes, they do, Mrs. Klein," the lady who was billing held the clothes in her hand, waiting for Mrs. Klein, who opened a tiny purse about the size of a palm to put the clothes in.

At first, their struggle seemed funny and stupid, but then when the clothes went in, I felt ridiculously out of place. The last time I came with Cassiden to buy clothes, I hadn't witnessed this magic. Cassiden carried an ordinary cloth bag around. Why would he do that? All this was good magic.

Audrey returned with a pile of clothes and started folding them neatly into stacks.

"Now, you better give us a good discount," Mrs. Anderson raised her finger toward Audrey.

"Anything for you, Mrs. Anderson. You've got a bag?" She continued multitasking.

Mrs. Anderson pulled out a similar small cloth purse from her pocket. It had a simple 'I' stitched over it. One by one, Audrey began stacking the clothes within.

"This is your blank tie and here are your blank socks," she said, placing them within. "That's going to be 3.3 gold coins."

"I hope it's the best you can give me. Here you go."

And she handed 18 silver coins to Audrey from the very same purse. "Thank you, Mrs. Anderson, and do visit again," her voice echoed, and the

entrance bell chimed.

"Now, we've only got shoes left, and the best place would be *sole*," Anderson said to no one in particular.

While paying at the counter of the shop, we found Cassiden standing through the heat outside the shop, trying to hold everything in his hand through the pushes of the crowd.

"Mom, I forgot a bag…" He mouthed when he noticed us inside the shop.

"I cannot believe you've raised a child, Cassiden," she taunted, holding open the same tiny purse for Cassiden to stack books and other stationery.

Darkness had settled when we reached home. I sat by the dinner table, watching Mrs. Anderson lay the plates.

"Where are the tiny creatures?" I asked, looking left, right, and then up at the ceiling.

"I've given them some sugar cubes and asked them to retire for the day. They must've been tired," Mrs. Anderson explained.

The newspaper named 'Morning Lodestone' that Cassiden was reading this morning lay in front of me. The front-page headline read:

His Highness Crown Prince Riordian Slayholt has once again denied taking over the throne.

Curiosity got the better of me, so I picked it up, beginning to read the article.

His Highness Prince Riordian Slayholt, last night denied the proposal presented by the Magaime International Cooperation regarding his taking over
   the title of King, stating that taking over the throne would be a violation of centuries-old tradition.

"His majesty, King Maxwell Slayholt, still lives. Taking over the throne means overthrowing the King, my brother, and that is something I would certainly refrain from even speaking about."

"Cassiden! Dinner," Mrs. Anderson yelled, her voice trailing off the walls.

Indeed, even though it has been about 16 years since the King has collapsed and lies in the silence of his royal chamber, the sound of his name still terrorizes families and those who lived in his conscious presence.'

"Hey… Mrs. Anderson? If you don't mind me asking, who is the king?" The woman froze, almost opening her mouth to speak. She wasn't expecting the question.

"Maxwell Slayholt is a murderer. During his reign, he wanted full control over the Enchanter's community opposing to what his ancestor declared." But it was Cassiden who answered, his nostril flaring.

"Cassiden! Do not speak like that. If he—"

"Why not! He is what he is. He killed him, and why are you so calm!" He curled his fist, piercing a stare at her.

"It wouldn't take a minute for him to kill you," she warned cautiously.

"What?" My mouth blurted; eyes trailed from Mrs. Anderson to Cassiden and back to her.

"You shouldn't bother…" He barked, refusing eye contact.

When the realization hit him, he merely sighed and watched me in deep thought.

"You make me feel that time does fly fast and maybe it is time you learn these matters."

I didn't know what and why all this pained Cassiden so much, but I tried hard to empathize with him.

"Look, Elora, I know that this part of the world seems beautiful, but the truth is that it is shattered from its roots. King Maxwell Slayholt has been lying in a deep sleep for over sixteen years. No one knows why or what had happened, ever since he collapsed no news about him has emerged from the palace. Suits him, the 10 years he ruled when he was conscious was a terrible reign."

"Terrible—" Before my question could emerge, he cut me.

"Murder. Torture. Pain. Suffering would be the only emotion one would remember on hearing his name, Maldeus; God of evil. The world has lost a lot since then. Partitions between Andronicans and Eromen spread to the worse, and Zocians had to pick sides for the second time in history."

"Why were their partitions to begin with?"

Mrs. Anderson picked up the conversation, sliding onto the chair building the pain of the story, "We Enchanters lived in unity before being cursed by *the Great Eneas*, the one who created this part of the world. King Andronicus, the great Scholar Zocia, and Eromen who went by Aristera, or the left hand of the King when together were powerful. But then Andronicus killed Eromen, eliminating the years of friendship the King had since their education."

"A king, studying with ordinary?" I raised my eyebrows at the idea.

"There is a tradition for princes to be hidden, they live lives of ordinary people away from royal life, completing their education with their false identity and then reveal themselves afterward," Cassiden filled, "This is to allow them to experience life out of the riches."

"Then why did he kill Eromen?"

"Many stories go around but history says the queen had an affair with Eromen in secret and when Andronicus came to know…" She stopped, rising to bring the pots to the table. Outside, the night screamed in agony.

She opened the lid of the pot and the smell of potatoes wafted through the air, "Enchanters picked sides then, Andronicus or Eromen. Those who picked no side stood by Zocia; those who believed neither was at fault. When Eneas got knowledge of this, he cursed us, because he created this part of the world in the hope of unity among Enchanters. This side of the world was created because the ordinary killed us, they saw magic to be evil."

I narrowed my eyes, twisting my lips. We're living in an era of acceptance. "Elora, when people see that you are out of the ordinary. They persecute you," Cassiden added to my skeptical face.

Would people still kill us? Does acceptance only revolve around what is ordinary?

"And what is the curse?"

"This is the curse," he pointed to the blue streak on his hair, "We carry the mark of our tribe. Blue for Zocians, Red for Eromen, and Green for Andronicans."

****

"Is this Cassiden Anderson... The same Cassiden that..." the writer trailed, afraid of the question.

"Yes, the same Cassiden Anderson that died by my hands."

A wave of guilt appeared on the Queen's face. Grissa nodded, trying to hide the look of surprise on her face, avoiding the Queen's eyes. The room was soaked in silence, devoid of her questions.

"Don't worry about that."

The Queen placed her hand on the writer's knee in reassurance, but she knew the Queen was suffering in silence.

Chapter 3
Silverstring Academy for Enchanters and Enchantresses

"What did he mean? When he said I had a strong connection to Eromen?"

The joy and acceptance returned to my face, the man's voice from the MIC lingering in my mind. I sat down on the sling chair next to him, the chilly wind hitting my face on the balcony.

"Eromen is associated with roses," he watched me, "Rum?" He had downed at least four glasses if that bottle was new. When I shook my head, he scoffed, "You're legal already."

He smiled sadly, "You'll be great one day, written on the pages of history. But I won't be there." I didn't know what to make out of that; Cassiden turned into a philosopher whenever he drank. It was his system getting depressed like alcohol did to everybody.

I watched him gulp down the glass without flinching, his hair flying. He sighed, "Tomorrow I'll be having dinner all alone."

"You won't be staying?" my shoulders fell.

"Of course not," he said like it was obvious.

No one said anything for a long time; we just sat in each other's presence. We were always used to having each other next to us. He was my first best friend, and he loved me like I was his only daughter, in fact, like his only relative.

"Elora, I must… tell you…" his words wandered, the alcohol beginning to take its toll on him, "When you go to the academe, have fun… make mistakes. But one thing I would not tolerate would be you messing with two types of boys; one…" he looked at the stars in the sky, his neck muscles loose so that it just hung.

"Men who are complete workaholics. Two, men who want royal jobs. Okay?"

His head rolled forward so that it now hung down, his eyes at the edge of its socket looking at me.

He was drunk, I made no move to place my argument and just nodded without meaning but still questioned him, "But, why?"

He sniffed twice through his red nose, suddenly looking sober. "Our world is a living place for three creatures."

He raised his forefinger to the sky, "One, us. We live on land," raised his middle finger, "Two, the forest, spiritual beings live there," and then raised his ring finger, "Three, the residents of the sea. Before Maldeus fell into his sleep, he challenged the Queen of the Soul Forest, the most powerful being known to exist, second to Eneas; because he knew he wouldn't be able to defeat King Rayan of the sea."

Slashing his hand, he continued, "The Queen had his back. He stood with a legion of over 6,000 royal soldiers. The Queen stood alone with her long holy white staff; one of the triumvirate staff. She saw the men and warned 'Leave or Perish' but none of the men could leave, they were under their King's orders. So, they stood. The Queen merely raised her staff and struck the ground."

He paused, pained, "All perished. She then vowed to him if he tried to invade her land again. He would perish by her hands."

"And your father and *she* were among all?"

He nodded; his eyes red but not watery. "Why didn't she kill the King?" "Maybe as a warning," he shrugged, "The truth is, I don't know. Her Majesty, Queen Frigga, is said to not interfere with affairs of the living unless it puts her people in threat but months later the king went into a deep sleep."

He said rising to go to bed, "But that was after we went to the ordinary world."

I slept with these thoughts in my head and probably, so did he. The only difference was that I felt nothing because I could not relate to war but I'm sure memories of the past haunt him even today.

The following morning was much different from the night, Mrs. Anderson did not forget to fill me with hugs and kisses despite only a few days of acquaintance.

"So how do we get there?" I asked, taking gradual steps to the Spenua. "The school is located far from civilization, within the Soul Forest."

"A forest? You mean the place where there are trees and wild animals live…" I stopped dead, waiting for him to declare this to be a joke.

He only chuckled and said, "Well, it is protected by Her Majesty, Queen Frigga."

"That doesn't make it any better…" I rolled my eyes.

At the Spenua, Cassiden inaudibly muttered 'Silverstring station' and a swirl began to take form. The next step we took was in a gigantic station that had glass panels in place of a ceiling and the same sun above the glass roof shone its homely radiance. The tiles were brown with several benches lying in an orderly manner, the station had no means of transport, with only light laughter and distant conversation all mingling to form noise.

"Good afternoon, I'm Aldroy. Silverstring new batch, are you?" "Yes, I am."

"Please follow me, Collect your identity card. The spirits of the forest will be here any moment now."

He then led us to a desk that looked like a miniature compared with the extremely tall metallic walls of the station.

Suddenly, the station grew silent. The small crowd of students and parents watched the door keenly for the sound of the wind. The sound of my anxious heart began syncing with the wind growing louder and louder. The air in front of us started twirling, and we took slow steady steps backward, unifying with the crowd. The leaves joined in with the gale that was forming. It paused midway, and so did my heart, and then from the wind, a long piece of cloth flowed onto the floor.

From it emerged a translucent green woman. She wore a green sleeveless A-line dress, the torso of the dress was formed from leaves woven together, with flowers randomly fixed over it. From below her waist, green fabric flowed continuously. It was cut in the front, which showed her pale green translucent legs with the breeze.

She was barefoot but wore a crown of flowers upon her emerald hair, and behind her came into sight an army of creatures alike, they looked less majestic as compared to the lady onto whom my eyes were fixed, wide open. She caused fear to build in me, but at the same time, her beauty moved my spirit.

"I am Frigga, guardian and Queen of the Soul Forest. I am here to escort you to the academy."

The moment she said *'escort'*, the hall presented with echoes, love-filled goodbye, kisses, and parents giving last-minute precautions and advice for their journey ahead. But my eyes remained glued on her, such dangerous beauty. Her mere presence radiated power and glory.

The King should have been out of his mind to challenge her. Her eyes fell on me, watching me carefully before she narrowed them, and my contact faltered after a few moments of blinking.

"So, I guess it's goodbye here. I…" Cassiden smiled, which didn't reach his eyes.

"I'll send you messages in whatever way possible," I said in a pacifying tone, wrapping my arms around his shoulders and tiptoeing.

"There's no contact with the outside world—"

"One of us will now stand beside you, and you shall hold hands with us as we take you away to our part of the world," Frigga stated.

The nymphs and satyrs gladly followed the Queen's orders, taking their place beside me and the others. The rest of the crowd automatically took a step back like they were experienced.

"I'll be right here when you return…"

I turned to give Cassiden a final glance at his awkward goodbye. Cassiden was never bad with goodbyes, but this farewell was a long one, and perhaps he was just trying to hide his sadness, pretending like this was awkward. As I stood just a few steps away from him, the weight of the impending separation hit me like a ton of bricks. I wanted to ditch this, to turn around and go back with Cassiden. Now that I was here, the reality of leaving him behind felt almost unbearable.

But deep down, I knew he wanted me to complete my +2. He had always told me I was his special little girl. But he was more dedicated to giving me away, believing that the world would need me more than he ever would.

A girl with a blue streak and freckles almost shrieked in excitement, breaking the solemn silence. All eyes in the room, including the queen's, turned toward her. The unexpected outburst seemed to momentarily startle everyone, but the queen dismissed it, nodding to the satyrs and nymphs

"Hi, I'm Ziva… woo…"

Her voice disappeared, the escorts pulled us along the airstream, toward the door, and into the greenery, the people behind us growing distant with each passing second.

We traveled at the speed of light, and whenever it felt like a tree would strike me, the nymph would immediately pull me away from it. We moved with such precision and speed that, in no time, I could only see green and brown colors around me.

After quite some time, we halted before a black wrought iron gate, its double door carrying the written words 'Silverstring Academy' in eye-catching silver. The nausea and headache that followed seemed unrealistic; our bodies were not made for such movements, and I could hardly grasp what had happened. With great difficulty, I managed to keep my feet straight; my bones felt replaced by jello. One of the boys puked at the back, breaking the breath-taking silence, but the satyr beside him comforted him by rubbing soothing circles on his back. "Sorry about the bad introduction," the same girl began again, "Hi, I'm Ziva," she raised her hands toward me. I looked at her, finally taking her hand. "Elora."

A satyr soon joined us from behind the gate; he genuflected at the sight of the Queen. He wore a simple tunic made of leaves that extended till his knees and was tasked with checking our identity cards and noting down the number so that when the luggage came, it could be sorted easily.

"We must have caught the stars for the Queen to be escorting us today," I whispered into Ziva's ears, who tittered and warned, "She can read your mind, be careful."

Those words caught my gaze at the Queen, despite the new surroundings. She walked with unusual, majestic ease, with the rest of us following behind her. She was scary yet welcoming. The only time my gaze broke was when we came across a two-tier fountain. The top tier held the view of three women with hands raised toward the sky together; their expressions looked rather pleased, and their hair waved with the non-existent air.

The second tier had nymphs and satyr surrounding them with joined hands raised toward the three women. One of the nymphs facing the three women had a crown of flowers and was taller than the other mythical creatures. They were sculpted from clay and were detailed finely, with only the mark of the curse radiating color; the three women were from the three significant tribes.

Surrounding the fountain, a few meters away in a clean circle on the ground, were alternate purple and green fountain grasses. Beyond the fountain, a tall mansion loomed. Its huge glass doors were guarded by two pillars on each side, looking like a modern built version of the pantheon in Rome.

The walls were covered in cheerful white, and the floor was made of gray glazed porcelain tiles. It was tall enough that when Ziva tried to look at the roof, she almost fell back.

"This is where I leave you all," Frigga said, right at the start of the stairs that led to the door.

Everyone was too awed to take note of what Frigga had to say to them—everyone but me, lost in the presence of this all-powerful being. How I would kill to be her—an unknown thirst lurked within me. She turned to me, as if she knew, watching me with those partially closed eyes of superiority. The longing to embody her strength and command echoed within, a desire so palpable that it felt like a magnetic pull toward an unattainable force. My eyes faltered away; her aura was unbearably strong.

Ziva, the girl with freckles looked at me, "Ready?" she asked, joyfully.

I felt eyes on me, and it made my throat feel thick. It wouldn't be right to challenge her; she could read my thoughts. My hands instinctively went to my neck.

I swallowed, managed a smile, and replied to the girl with the blue streak, "Yeah."

I turned my head for one final glance at her, even if it might be her eyes on me. But she wasn't looking at me; she was engaged in conversation with one of her own. I kept cautioning and reminding myself that I would have to learn to control my greed in her presence. If she could read minds, she could access my vulnerabilities without any barriers and use them against me, although that didn't seem like something she would do.

We entered the entrance hall, standing in front of the partial glass door of the academy. Another flight of stairs divided into two, leading to the 'Magic zone' and 'non-magic zone,' right in front of us. Two large doors were present at either side of the entrance hall from where we stood.

From the door to our left that read 'Hall of Bonding', a man called at his peak voice, "In here, children."

The hall was bright, resembling a spring day, as the light from the painted mosaic windows mixed with the glow of the ceiling chandeliers. A single long wooden dining table covered with a white table runner, lined with gold lace, was present in the center of the hall. The plates, glasses, and cutlery were sparkling clean, laid out with meticulous etiquette. The table faced a raised platform where another table was placed, adorned with three royal chairs where two men and a woman sat.

The Enchanter sitting in the center was stout, had a heart-shaped face, and brown curtain hair with a band of red. His beard and mustache were stubble, he had amber eyes, and was in his late 60s, wearing a white shirt with a black overcoat.

The Enchanter sitting next to him had a square face, his shoulder-length hair jet black with a streak of emerald. It was braided to the back, forming a half-crown of emerald and black, a strand of hair fell over his skin. He had a long nose and a well-defined jaw added to his sharp features. He was dressed in a black turtleneck top with a black overcoat.

His face looked familiar. His face looked familiar. I watched as his eyes drifted across the room, dully taking in the students, passing over me, and then stopping at the boy standing next to me. The boy was tall, at least a good 6 feet, considerably taller than me at 5'2. I had to bend my neck slightly to look at him. He was well-built compared to any other male student present, with a diamond-shaped face, a wide jaw that made people question whether his face was rectangular or diamond, defined cheekbones, and downward-facing lips. Very beautiful. A quiet sense of warmth began to flutter within me.

But then his green streak came into view, and his gray eyes locked onto the professor with a penetrating gaze. A smirk played on the face of the boy, rebellious and seemingly unkind, a demeanor quite unlike my ideal type. The flutter seemed to have died in me.

The professor maintained a neutral expression, locking eyes firmly with the arrogant boy. His gaze then shifted to me and back to the boy before suddenly returning to me, scrutinizing me with intense eyes. To sidestep the escalating tension of uncomfortable eye contact, I turned my attention to the only woman among the men. The Enchantress stood tall and had a triangular face with her blond hair tied into a sleek ponytail, and a band of blue shining through. She wore a white shirt and black-fitting skirt with an overcoat.

"Come on in, children," the man in the center welcomed us.

We moved toward the table, breaking the silence, and began eating whatever the nymphs and satyrs brought without waiting for any invitation. We didn't even need one; after such a journey, we could pig away.

I sat there, watching everyone talk and mingle. Occasionally, I joined in to offer my opinion in open discussions, but mostly, I zoned out, still new to this world and absorbing everything around me.

"…my father works at the SAC."

"What's that?"

"Science approval committee." He looked rather proud.

"And what's that for?" The girl next to him asked.

"I believed Zocians were actually smart!" he fell back on his chair, "Where do you think the facts in textbooks at basic level education come from?"

The girl shrugged; her lower lip upturned.

"Why can't you at least pretend to be from your tribe, you foolish girl. SAC approves scientific facts not discovered in our world," The rebellious boy, who out-stared the professor interrupted, and the girl released hot air, turning away.

A boy with a round face caught my eye in a deep stare. It didn't seem like a coincidence, but I continued to look at him. Did he know me? How could he? His face glowed, and his bushy eyebrows and dark brown hair accentuated his soft features. As I observed him, a subtle warmth began to stir within me. I noticed the green mark on his hair through my peripheral vision, a wave of consciousness blocking my way, making me increasingly aware of every movement I made. All the good ones seemed to be in the wrong team, I looked away, letting out a sigh.

"Now that you are all done. Welcome to Silverstring Academy, we are your headmasters and headmistress, I am Solomon Sherwood, this is Professor Celestina Orson, and this is Professor Intimus Iving," he said looking at his fellow colleagues. "Let me take a moment to inform you that today evening you will have the official housing ceremony at 6 pm.

"Your presence is highly requested at 5:00 pm, in your respective uniforms. The other students will be arriving in a few more hours from now. You may eat, freshen up and get familiar with the academy grounds, sleep…" He waved his hands, "Usually, the first-timers do not feel great after the speed. Do not, however, leave the academy grounds. You are now dismissed."

He paused, remembering.

"Acacia, the academy's caretaker will show you to your houses, and should you need anything our offices will be in the magical zone on the third floor."

Acacia, a brown nymph, emerged from the door to the far right—the kitchen, presuming from the noise of clashing and clanging that came along with her when the door opened. We rose, chattering continuing in our midst, all excited to see our new academy and home for the next few months.

The brown nymph led all of us out of the main academy building. We descended the stairs and walked past the fountain, veering right to follow a roughly made concrete road. On both sides of the road, a low-built fenced garden stretched out. These gardens were adorned with flowers and plants so abundant that they reminded me of the deepest parts of an unexplored ocean, where the possibility of finding something unusual was high.

Near the boundary walls of the academy, there stood a small plant house. Its glass was hazy, hinting at a sanctuary for various forms of plant life. The only possible entry was through a locked door, adorned with a sign that sternly read *'keep-out'*.

"Plants that are illegal in the land kingdom are grown there,"

I distanced myself from the voice that whispered in my ears, turning back to look at the boy. His black quiff-styled hair, curlier than the curliest of hair, framed his diamond face, evoking a stalker-like feeling.

The moment I noticed the curse of Andronicus on his hair, a thin, disinterested line appeared on my face. I was going to take Cassiden's advice very seriously and keep an eye out for Andronicans, annoyed by their presence crossing my path.

At the end of the garden were three paths, divided like a fork, separated by cleanly trimmed hedges that were so high that one wouldn't be able to peep at what lay along the other paths.

"So? Both your parents are Eromen?" Ziva asked me.

"Yes, maybe…" I hesitated at the question, bending my neck at the overgrown plant blocking my face.

"Maybe?" She checked, clearly taken aback by my answer.

"Yeah, they're… umm… dead. My mom was an Eromen, and my dad worked at the palace and died with an identity that cannot be revealed so, I don't really know. War tragedy. Don't."

I added when I saw the horrified look of grief on her face, "I haven't ever met them. There's only a certain amount of time you can grieve for the people you don't know."

The unblinking look in my eyes deceived my words, causing us to continue walking without any conversation.

"Only Eromen will follow me now."

The nymph stated with the same smile that never faded. She led us through the path on the right. It had recessed floor lights that were closed with a metallic shutter, but otherwise, the path had nothing worth mentioning.

At the end of the path was a double-door gate, a miniature version of the main academy gates, but with *'Caritas'* written. Guarding the gates were two satyrs, dressed in white tunics, keeping a watch on all who entered.

"This is the Caritas House," the nymph said in her sweet melodious tone, opening the gate with just a sway of her hands.

"These glow at night…" She pointed at the ordinary-looking large pebbles fixed on the pathway, like floor markers.

House E was like those luxurious cabins, built of wood, having an attached veranda, and a large swimming pool next to it. The balcony had pink bell-flowered vines twirling over its wooden railing, like the ones marking the edge of the buildings in Moon City. The remaining plot of land was grass with swings at one end, tables, and chairs, like those placed within the balcony and a small camping area, and a whole load of plants, making it look like a tamed forest.

The hall of the house was basic, with a set of armchairs and settees near the huge fireplace—it must be freezing here during the winters. And despite the expectations I had while walking into the academy, it had a twist of its own. I was expecting a set of huts when I first heard it was in a forest, but this place is a dreamland in its own way.

The nymph pointed at the room toward our right, "Snacks are placed in the kitchen for timeless hunger."

Straight ahead was a large stair that led to the upper floor, leading on either side were two long corridors.

"The left side is yours; the right side is where the professors live. Each housing unit has two rooms so you may go and find your nameplate fixed to the door."

She then turned to face us and pointed behind us.

"There's the balcony for any time you need a break from your daily routine." The banister continued to flow along the wall, leading to the balcony from both sides, leaving the floor hollow in the center from where the main hall could be seen. The balcony was open, it had no door; just an opening in the walls, and a faint sound of insects stridulating, and a sibilant buzz filled the inside. "This is where I leave you," she said, leaving us to ourselves.

I walked into all the rooms just like everyone else, looking for my nameplate on the doors, and found mine in the third housing unit from the stairs. I turned to look at the nameplate next to mine. I should make a good impression if I were to spend this year with her comfortably; she was 'Bexley Weber'.

The door to the housing unit opened. A girl with soft facial features, wide green eyes, and long brown hair entered. She looked very feminine and classy.

After reading her nameplate, she turned to look at me and then at my nameplate. "Ms. Bates?" She pointed her finger at me with raised brows. Her voice was soft, like the grand piano to my ears.

"Oh. Oh, I'm sorry... Yeah," I closed my gaping mouth, at the girl that made me realize my insecurities.

I smiled; we all have insecurities, don't we? I took her hand, welcoming her into my life. My smile faded the moment our hands broke apart, I shut the door, standing against it. I was going to have a hard time with such a perfect person before me.

Maybe, she was just pretty, maybe she was unintelligent and fragile on the inside. She would be those girls who walked with pride because she had her looks to brag about. What a great start! I hope I almost never run into her.

The baggage arrived in another few moments, and I began placing everything accordingly. In the end, it was already around 4:30 pm. I had spent over an hour just fixing things, and now I couldn't leave for the Hall of Bonding with sweat and muck all over me from all the traveling. I saw my less-than-ideal reflection in the mirror.

Oh, dear. I took a quick shower, shampooing the sand out of my hair. As I watched my strands fall with the roughness, I began readying myself and ran down the stairs like Cinderella—only with wet hair, a partly untucked shirt, and uneven socks on my feet. What a great start!

I made it to the fenced garden when I spotted another boy walking hurriedly toward the main building. He saw me too, grinning widely. It was the same boy who had whispered into my ears, the one with curls that fell onto his face. We paused, looking at each other, a gleam of the same notion visible in both our eyes.

If I made it before him, I'd seem less miserable in front of him. With that, we both began running, tugging, and pushing, which only made us delay more. We sprinted up the stairs, but his long legs allowed him to skip steps and overtake me. I was going to lose.

He stopped abruptly at the main door. "Together is better."

He watched me take the last few steps. "Why?"

The streak was the only part of him I could see. What plots did he hold in his mind?

"Trust me," he said, and we both stood outside the Hall of Bonding neatening ourselves up, walking in together.

Professor Iving had already begun speaking, we were late. "Oh no," Bran muttered.

"Well done, the two of you are much disciplined," Iving quirked. "I'm sorry—"

Iving raised his finger at me, "No time for that."

The hall was already decorated for the evening. The wall behind the dais was covered with white curtains adorned with balloons in three colors: red, green, and blue. The balloons seemed attached to the curtain, but they made subtle movements, creating an illusion that they were tethered to an invisible roof.

The ceilings were adorned with gold hanging swirls, and three large flags suspended above each table danced lightly. The tables, each with a white runner, were laced with the colors of the flags overhead.

"There are three houses, Caritas, Imperium, and Prudens. As you can see the flags." He pointed at them, and we followed his fingers, turning to look at them.

The first flag, pale red in color with a crown of roses, adorned the table to the far right of us.

Iving explained, "The symbol of Caritas is a crown of roses, representing the crown of Eromen."

The central table displayed a pale blue flag with an open book and a bulb of light emerging from the rib of the book, resembling the sun.

Iving continued, "The symbol of Pruden's is the book of Zocia... Lastly, the symbol of Imperium is a dragon, derived from the green dragon stone that lies within the staff of Andronicus," he said, gesturing to the last pale green flag to our left with his eyes rather than his hands, which were now placed behind his back.

"When the academy was first founded, students were sorted based on what they personally believed to be of the highest order: Power, Love, or Wisdom. But now, sorting is based on which tribe you belong to, and the ceremony remains to uphold the tradition of the campus. So—"

"If you don't mind me asking, sir, why was the older system changed?" Bexley Weber interrupted, her chin pointed at Iving, who rolled his eyes before speaking.

"The former system was created for the sole purpose of uniting the three tribes, but such eye-bleeding scenes would occur between the students of Eromen and Andronicus in the same house because they were raised with their tribe's stereotypes. In order to prevent such catastrophic events, one of the previous headmasters renounced the former ways," he explained in a single breath, allowing air to fill his lungs through his mouth. "Anything else, Miss…?"

"Bexley Weber, sir, and no," Bexley replied. Iving nodded, keeping his eyes on her as if she were a little bug to be squished for interrupting, before continuing, "Today when you get sorted, which will be in about thirty minutes from now, you will be put into the houses based on your tribes. Eromen go to Caritas, Andronicans go to Imperium, and Zocians go to Prudens."

"During the officiating, you will have to pick up the fluff. The fluff will officiate you entering your house as its color changes…"

Iving then spoke about the classes we were to take and handed us a set of papers that included the timetable: Enchanter History, Planta Concoction, Defensive Magic, Basic Law and Health for Enchanters, Skill Magic, Power Magic, and Creaturology. Behind that was a pinned sheet listing the rules of the academy and a list of other housing instructions, including curfew at 11 pm, no littering of the grounds, no graffiti, avoid overcrowding Silverstring Street, library book time limit—2 weeks maximum, and so on.

The discussion concluded a few minutes before the start of the officiating ceremony, and our seniors and professors began to pour in. We were seated at the same table as in the morning, laid horizontally compared to the tables of the houses that were laid vertically. The crowd took a while to settle, after which Professor Sherwood rose to speak. He gave a brief introduction about the housing ceremony, its history, and stressed the importance of unity despite differences.

I was too anxious to listen to him; my thoughts kept slipping to extreme ideas, even though I was confident of my fate. Given that Bexley was wringing her fingers, I knew I wasn't alone. The officiating ceremony began as Professor Orson started reading from a list, and I couldn't help but notice that when Sherwood stood to speak, a sharp silence prevailed among the crowd, no matter how dull his talk was. It wasn't the same as when the other professors spoke.

"Bexley Weber."

She went forward, tottering a bit on the steps. Once near the tank, she began submerging her hand slowly into it, which was filled with something that resembled water. She lifted the hairy fluff from the bottom of it, and the moment it came in the air, it turned dry like the sand in a desert.

Orson then handed her a needle to prick her finger, and when a drop of blood was visible, she was asked to wipe it onto the fluff and drown it back into the liquid along with her hand till her elbow reached the level of the fluid. Nothing happened, and then suddenly, a suppressed explosion took place, limited to where the water was without disturbing its stillness. Bexley flinched. The liquid had turned red, leaving us all first-timers caught off-guard. The liquid then climbed up her hands and body, wetting her hair until she was all red. She looked horrified, as if this was a terrible prank, breathing through her mouth with her eyes blinking rapidly, ready to cry.

The crowd laughed at her reaction; Sherwood raised his hands to silence them. Orson then motioned for her to leave the fluff and pull her hand out of the liquid. The fluff dissolved the red dye in the tank, like charcoal's adsorbing action, turning it transparent. The moment she pulled her hands out of the liquid, she was dry, with only her tie having the red symbol of Caritas and the lacy outline of her uniform and socks in red.

She broke a laughing sigh of relief and wiped her watery eyes, now grinning widely.

It was wonderful, nerve-wracking but eye-fixating. I released my held breath. "Caritas," Professor Iving said, congratulating her.

The students of the Caritas house cheered as she approached them with her already existing pride.

"Bran Becile."

The boy with curly hair went forward and held the fluff in his hand; he seemed to be carefree and didn't have a single ounce of worry within him. The liquid turned green and then drowned him in green.

"Imperium," Professor Iving stated, congratulating him. The Imperiums cheered as he walked toward the table.

"Ziva Anson."

She seemed to tremble when she drowned the fluff in the liquid, but it exploded blue.

"Prudens."

The Prudens cheered her entry.

Orson took several names, including Maurilio Iverson, the boy who stared Intimus Iving down at first sight, and Liam Sprague, the boy who caught my eyes at the table. Both landed in Imperium, as expected. One only had to see the face of Maurilio to see his true nature; he wore a smug expression and seemed despicable for the attitude he walked with. Liam, on the other hand, was completely the opposite. He wore a smile, walked with confidence, and seemed well-mannered and well-brought-up.

"Elora Bates."

I looked up at the woman who called me and then at the man standing beside the fluff, but he happened to be already looking at me, looking at me with the same look in his eyes as when he first saw me, thinking deeply. I walked up, stumbling like I was about to be skinned alive by Iving's look, but his stare didn't break, not even for a moment, even when I pricked my finger and drowned the fluff. This made every inch of me uncomfortable in addition to the already existing nervousness. I looked at Orson all the while, waiting for her next words to follow, with a heart beating so loud that it wouldn't surprise me if someone claimed they heard it. But Orson's face turned expressionless, she squinted, and her face then turned white. Her eyes grew as wide as her orbits would allow her to reach, and my eyes automatically followed to where her eyes were pinned, I was already breaking a sweat without even knowing the crime I'd committed, and then I saw green. The liquid had turned green.

There was a solemn silence as though someone had died, and reality dawned upon my soul as the color drained into my uniform.

Chapter 4
The Three Tribes and the Academy

"So, the rumors were true? You were indeed put into Imperium. I take it that none took it well."

"None. But one"

"One?" The writer leaned forward.

"Yes, Sherwood. His reaction to this event seemed like he knew it." "Are you indicating that this could have been Sherwood's plan?" The Queen shrugged, cleverly.

****

Elora Bates

I woke up earlier than the rest of the academy, pausing and looking at the roof, trying to remember which part of the night was a dream. The events replayed in my mind like a movie.

Iving was white, angry but not shocked. He turned to Sherwood, his face asking for advice, but Sherwood maintained a calm gesture, giving only a slight nod. Iving's jaw hardened, releasing his final verdict, "Imperium," with clenched teeth. I turned to the crowd that gave an automatic response of gasps and whispering.

I didn't fit here; it was written on every single face. I climbed down the steps slowly, the sound of my heels announcing my conflict. I looked at Caritas and then at Imperium, not knowing where to go. Bran Becile came forward; I curled, waiting for something bad to happen, but he held me by my shoulders, taking me to Imperium's table. There was quietness, even though Sherwood declared celebration not a single ounce of happiness reflected from the ocean of students. I was a buzzkill, and I dared not look at anyone's face. I was petrified, confused, and wanted to run away because I was a loser. I wanted to be a part of this world, but I don't, and never will.

The celebration ended, but I sat at the table, waiting even after students began emptying the hall, throwing disgusted peeks at me. Hoping I would wake up any moment and this would all be a nightmare, but nothing happened. Bran continued to remain seated beside me, and I didn't know why, but I wanted to rewind all this, go back to the moment I received the letter from the Academy, and tear it before Cassiden, telling him that I wanted to stay with him in the other world.

"Let's go, Elora. There's no yield here," Bran whispered. I turned to look at him, the redness in my eyes prominent. Professor Iving then appeared from nowhere when I rose to leave. His mood didn't seem to change throughout the ceremony, and even now he spoke stiffly.

"If you'd excuse us, Mister," Iving turned to Bran. I was the only student in the hall now.

"Let us go," Iving released a tough statement. "As you are aware I'm in charge of Imperium, don't expect kindness and worry to bloom for you, Ms. Bates." He took my name, as though poison was stinging him. We walked to the gates of Imperium, and I could do nothing but wipe the tears off my waterline.

I stood in the shower, the stream from the hot water drifting me back.

Two brown satyrs were walking in front of the gate, guarding the 'Imperium' house, as I read it. I read it again and again, trying to sink into the reality of what had happened. Iving spoke with the satyrs about me, and then we entered through the gate.

"We didn't see your rebellious side coming, Ms. Bates..." Breathe, breathe, I reminded myself. "...so you will be in the same housing unit as Mr. Maurilio Iverson." Maurilio Iverson? The name echoed.

"No," I blurted, but Iving didn't stop in his tracks, and neither did he seem surprised at my tone. "No?" He questioned like he didn't know such a word existed; his anger diffused away from his body except for those black cold eyes.

"I'm not taking that for an answer. You should discuss this with Sherwood tomorrow. I'd be most pleased to see you out."

The hall had a few students scattered, and they stopped dead, witnessing their newfound gossip walk past them. Breathe, breathe. I told myself. Iving opened the door to the last housing unit.

Maurilio was wiping his wet hair with a towel, my gaze inadvertently drifting over his form. His muscular body bore a large, rugged scar in the form of a straight line. The light from the window played gently, revealing the curves and subtle movements of his breathing. I quickly averted my eyes, attempting to shake off the unease that settled within me. My eyes returned to him, and I observed a droplet of water glistening on his pectoris as it made its way down. A pang of guilt washed over for allowing my attention to be drawn to seemingly inconsequential details, especially given the gravity of the recent events. I tried to convince myself that it was a trauma-induced reaction and nothing more—there couldn't be any other reason.

"Perhaps, you could knock, Professor!" It sounded like he was demanding, rather than requesting.

"I brought a guest, Maurilio." Iving lacked interest in his attitude.

Boiling with frustration, I ignored them, feeling myself break, a sob escaping me.

"I thought I made it clear to the headmaster that I'd like a housing unit to myself." *Why did the conversation between the two of them sound personal?*

"Maurilio, there wasn't any room left." Iving calmly said, hands raised.

Maurilio looked up at me, taking in the shape of my face, his eyes gliding down my seamless neck, and in a charming voice spoke, "Hello beautiful." One of my eyes squinted harder than the other, I tilted my neck, shocked at his audacity.

"Bastard," I muttered under my breath, but he heard it. I was tired, messed up, and just wanted to be comforted. The least he could have done was keep his attitude to himself. A tear escaped my eyes, and though I pretended like it didn't happen, I couldn't hide the frustration and anger that burned within me. Glaring back at him, I fought to maintain composure, refusing to let him see the impact of his cruel presence.

"How dare you do that to yo-" He began, completely ignoring his sight. He was utterly inhumane, a despicable figure devoid of empathy or decency.

"Mr. Iverson…" Iving stressed, "It would be no good to threaten girls around the campus on the first day." He gave a long pause, the two of them exchanging serious glances.

"A word, lest you forget your place in this campus."

Iving turned to me, and I took the hint, walking to the room without a nameplate, slamming the door onto their faces.

I quickly put on my socks and fixed my pants, wanting to leave before the other students arrived. The excitement of being special, of having magical blood, had disappeared. I wished to go back to where I truly belonged, or even go back home. The feeling of thrill had vanished, replaced by a desperate plea to wake up from this confusing nightmare. Somebody please, turn on the lights, wake me up.

Despite the early hour, I set out for Sherwood's office, the entire walk filled with self-reassurance. I convinced myself that Sherwood was a wise man who would empathize with my pain and help sort out the chaos that had unfolded in the Hall of Bonding. My thoughts clung to the hope that he would understand, bringing a semblance of positivity to the situation.

I couldn't walk with my head up. Sherwood's office was on the third floor in the magic zone, just as he had mentioned.

"Come in," he answered from the other side of the door.

I pushed open the door, pausing as I took in the aesthetically designed office. His desk was placed in a corner, right in front of the window, and the other corner had words written hugely: 'Love, above all.'

There was a glass cabinet and a bookshelf adjacent to each other on the left wall. The table upon which he sat was covered entirely in papers, and he worked through them with his reading glasses, peaking at me through the bridge of his nose. Then he pointed at the seat in front of him with his hand, welcoming me as though he had been anticipating my arrival.

"First week, busy paperwork," he explained the mess, shaking his head.

He continued in a flowing tone, "Now then, speak for whatever you came here," slowly starting to stack the papers away.

Words didn't come out even though I had prepared hard for this. Sherwood watched me silently, waiting.

"I don't belong in Imperium," were the only words audible enough. Why was I scared?

"And why do you think so?"

"They won't accept me. You see, my hair is… um… proof too," I said, swallowing. "And what makes you think Caritas will accept you, after this?"

My facial muscles lost their tone. He was right. After lying awake an entire night, pondering hard on why the events took place in the wrong fashion, I hadn't thought about this.

"I cannot be of any help to you, child," he smiled comfortingly, but it seemed like an insult to me.

"But you're the headmaster, you can change me back!" I pleaded.

"I cannot exploit the power in my hands because you want me to," he didn't break contact, "Without you even trying to adapt."

Silence.

I rose defeated, frustration bubbling within me like an untamed storm.

Was there anyone with me? Or did everyone give up along with my fate? I had questions, countless, but none of them mattered. Because the fact that people stand with you in the richness and then abandon you in poverty sounded true to me.

"I would like to leave!" I didn't hesitate this time, clearly making my statement.

"And what of Mr. Anderson?"

His name echoed, "What of him?"

"He requested to make an exception for you, and that will be the last I'm accepting."

"What do you mean?"

"The deadline for applying for admission was beyond the date." If I could breathe fire, it would be now.

"A year from now, none of this would matter to you." I heard him say before closing the door.

Cassiden didn't raise a girl only to run away in the face of a problem. I should at least try to push through a week here before allowing the thought of resignation to come into my mind. It was the conflicting ideas within me that were draining me of my energy. I wanted to make it through the academy because that was what was expected of me; that is why Cassiden got me here—to choose and be whoever my capabilities will allow me to be, but my spirit feels disheartened.

I believed I had a choice at where I wanted to live, but instead, it was Cassiden who had already decided that I would be staying here and making it through my education.

The academy was starting its first day by the time I walked to the Hall of Bonding. I tried to hide my face by letting my hair cover my face, taking a seat at the shadowed corner of Imperium's table.

"Heyy… I hope you're doing okay?" Ziva joined me at the Imperium table. "Aren't you going to…?" I pointed at her table, making sure that she had a good enough excuse to walk away from me and that if she was here, she willingly wanted to be and was not compelled by circumstances, since we became friends before the turn of events.

"Oh no, that's applicable only during dinners and during any grand fest."

I nodded back, yawning. My body was weak from the lack of sleep. I was not sure about Ziva being around me, because she too would become the topic of gossip if she associated with me. If I were a good friend, I should be letting her go, but I didn't want to be alone.

"Maybe, you should talk to Sherwood about this," she said, struggling to look through my hair covering my face.

"I already did…" I said, stuffing cereals into my mouth like a dead body eating.

"I take, it didn't go well." It was another voice behind Ziva.

"Hey, what's your deal, Mr. Becile?" I finally mustered the courage to ask him. He took a seat next to Ziva, who moved her body away from him, looking equally confused as me.

"I'm just trying to help." He took a slice of toast spreading strawberry jam onto it.

"Well, thank you very much," I rudely answered back, "An Andronican helping an Eromen is quite the miracle the world wanted."

That came out loud, Maurilio Iverson stopped at what he had heard, turning to look at the source.

"Hi, Elora," he played, making sure it was loud enough for the entire hall when he realized I was trying not to draw attention.

"I didn't see you when I woke up, you must have left—"

I covered my face with my hands, attempting to shield myself from the embarrassment and the echoing giggles that seemed to come from all directions. His steps reverberated, growing louder; he was approaching me. As he neared, he smoothly glided his hands around my wrist, gently pulling them away from my face, and brought his face uncomfortably close to mine. The proximity allowed me to feel the warmth of his breath on my skin.

"What's the matter?" he said, feigning concern, his voice carrying a mocking undertone that sent a shiver down my spine.

Bran, noticing how the situation began unfolding, swiftly rose from his seat. He approached Maurilio and, without hesitation, pressed his hand firmly against Maurilio's chest, pushing him back. Bran's eyes bore into Maurilio with an intense gaze, sizing him up and emitting a clear warning. His move captured my full focus. Ziva stood wide-eyed, caught in surprised amazement.

"Stand down," Bran warned, his voice carrying an authoritative edge. "Or what?" Maurilio retorted, his tongue pressing against his inner cheeks in a defiant manner. Despite the provocation, Bran didn't flinch.

"Hahn... your new girlfriend! Congratulations Imbecile." Bran continued to keep his contact with Maurilio. The talks grew louder, and a sense of unease rippled through me.

"See you later, Elora!" Maurilio smirked, winking as he reveled in the chaos he had created.

I bent to face the ground, rocking back and forth with anger.

"Didn't your parents tell you the story of the three?" Bran asked casually, chewing on his bread as if nothing had happened. "I don't even know how the tables turned; it's not fair." He shrugged.

"Loads of times..." Ziva replied. I ate silently, ignoring them.

Bran looked at me, "It's she that said it," he pouted.

Ziva shook her head at Bran, trying to make it as invisible as possible for me. They had just met each other and were beginning to talk through their expressions, like they had known each other for so long; I suddenly felt out of place suddenly.

"What!" I exclaimed, really annoyed now. Bran looked at me wide-eyed and then at Ziva.

"I could tell you the story—"

"I don't want to know," I spat.

He looked at me for quite some moments and then said, "Well, that's okay because we have history first, and we're doing general history based on the syllabus..." his voice grew lower and lower, and his eyes went higher and higher toward, trying to hide his pleased face when I finally turned to look at him with a straight face. Bran stood up for me, a complete stranger. It was a gesture of kindness that I didn't expect, especially considering his Andronican background.

As much as I appreciated his gesture, I couldn't ignore the fact that he might have underlying motives, and I couldn't let my guard down completely.

But for now, it would do me no good to push away those people who were interested in my well-being.

The bell chimed, signaling the beginning of classes. Sherwood's classroom was located on the second floor in the non-magic zone. The back of the class was dominated by a towering bookshelf, and the chairs and tables stood shabbily, creating broken lines. His class seemed disorganized and boring, and maybe he was the same too, like a snake that unveils its new skin.

"Have you all brought your books, *History of Enchanters*, the first volume?" Sherwood questioned the class.

At his words, the class let out discouraging noises, giving out sighs and making cranky noises as though they didn't want to be here. I might have joined in too, had it not been for the unpleasant encounter with him and Maurilio earlier in the day.

Observing the reactions, Sherwood suppressed a laugh and remarked, "Oh, there's no need to take those out. I merely suggested this book. We won't be engaging in the tedious ritual of textbook reading."

The ones who were in the process of extracting their textbooks halted, and some faces even brightened at the prospect of avoiding the mundane routine of textbook study.

"Can anyone tell me why history is important? Yes, Ms. Weber?" I turned my head very slowly, so that by the time her face came into view, she had already answered.

"Because there is no present without the past," I rolled my eyes. She's an all-rounder—pretty with brains.

Maybe Imperium wasn't that bad after all. Having to live with Weber was a constant threat to my self-esteem. I shifted my gaze toward the far opposite, at Iverson, my current housing mate. A vicious, uncivilized human. Weighty options loomed before me.

"That is right…" Sherwood closed his eyes, nodding in delight.

"The graffiti and engraving on these wooden tables and walls speak about the history of the history class, doesn't it?" he chuckled.

"To me, history is nothing but a story, a story to be told in every class." He glided his hands across the tables. "Likewise, sometimes history is not as it appears to be. The basis of forming history is physical evidence and the opinion of a group of people, but it may be more intricate and misunderstood sometimes."

He seemed genuinely good, or was he just good at putting on an act? If he were truly nice, he would have understood me. But what if he didn't change me to Caritas because he knew that my being there would only have been worse?

He was a peculiar person, enticing, and so were the words that came from him. Maybe it was just because he was experienced and knew how to handle students, but his deep sense of knowledge and passion about the history of life intrigued me even more.

"Today, we'll be listening to two stories: the story of the Curse of Eneas and the Story of the foundation of the academy."

I watched Bran raise his hand in a fist above his head, teasing me.

"Before the history of all Enchanters, the earth on this side of the world was divided into three parts; the land ruled by Great Kings, currently under the rule of His Majesty, King Maxwell Slayholt."

The crowd became disturbed, causing him to clarify, "Yes, his actions may instigate fear and terror, but he still remains our King. We must at least respect his role."

King Andronicus was the first-ever King of the land, but this happened over 500 years ago, so we would never know if he was the actual first.

The other two parts were the forest, currently under the rule of Her Majesty Queen Frigga for the past 200 years, and the land of the sea, currently under the rule of His Majesty King Rayan. King Andronicus lived with his Queen, Wesha; her beauty was described to be glorious, her skin the best shade of brown any of us could produce.

The king's second in command, Aristera, was an Eromen, and they were good friends since their school days. Andronicus wanted to be a King who would not just impose his wishes upon the people, so he appointed a leader for the people; the first foundation of the Magaime Corporation, Zocia. She would listen to the needs of the people and officially present them to him on their behalf. She would also go on to advise the King on issues that arose in the country, earning her the title of a scholar.

On one terrible day, news arrived to the King that his wife was having a secret affair with Aristera. History says the King felt indignant and slew him. It was then that the first two divisions were formed; people took sides, and the King, being welcoming, allowed the formation of such partition. Some say it was because he began to feel guilt for his actions of slaying his dearest Eromen in anger.

Zocia was a wise scholar who saw what had happened and refused to take sides. This confounded people because a wise person like her did not pick a side. Questions arose, and that was the formation of the third division. History also says that the Great Eneas, who came about and saw the division, put a curse because, rather than sorting out the difficulty in unity, they chose separation, and there came the birth of the three tribes.

"Any comments from the class now?" Sherwood questioned, a look of expectation in his eyes.

"Could there be another reason why Zocia didn't take sides?" Bran said, glancing sideways at all the eyes pinned on him.

"And what do you believe could be the reason?" A tiny, successful smirk rose at the side of Sherwood's face.

"Perhaps Andronicus did not want to slay Eromen but had to?" It came out as a question.

"But being a King, what restrictions would he have had?" Bran shrugged, momentarily losing track of his argument.

"Impressive, Becile," Sherwood's eyes were filled with appreciation. "You think outside the wall."

"Anybody else?" He looked around the classroom. "Okay then, let's move on to the foundation of the academy now. Has anyone paid close attention to the fountain of the academy? Yes, Ms. Weber."

"The fountain has the representation of three women: Eloise Norman, Cora Primro, and Juniper Yisdora, and surrounding them in support is Queen Frigga and her citizens."

"Excellent!"

Years after the formation of the three tribes, all places of higher education were selective about the tribes admitted. Never was there a place where Eromen and Andronicans studied together.

Three friends, Eloise Norman, Cora Primro, and Juniper Yisdora from three different tribes—Andronican, Eromen, and Zocia—went in search of a location where they could gather a learning place for the three tribes together. They wanted to rebuild what was broken, and the first-ever united academy to be built was in Herlo, far west from the Soul Forest. At first, the community seemed to take the idea well.

The academy opened its doors welcoming all tribes sorting them based on what they looked up to most: power, knowledge, or love. But small arguments led to fights, and then to blown violence, and it was not just limited to the students in the academy. It led to bigger and worse scenes that included their parents and Enchanters of their tribe. The academy had to be shut down.

The three friends gave up the idea of harmony and togetherness until Eloise Norman proposed the idea of opening the academy within the Soul Forest, where Enchanters would lose their entitlement to cause damage. It seemed brilliant to them since the forest was not part of the land. They would have to propose the idea to the Magaime International Corporation, and should the idea get accepted, it would then be presented to the King.

However, the proposal was deemed impractical by the MIC, with a statement that the whole goal of building an academy was for the sole purpose of education, with plenty already available. Two of the friends gave up on the idea, but Eloise Norman walked into the Soul Forest to present and plead with Her Majesty Queen Frigga.

Pleased with her efforts and courage to enter the Soul Forest unaided, Her Majesty made a covenant to protect and provide for the academy so long as it remained faithful to her words.

"So, here you are, sitting in the first and only academy with the three tribes of Ariesque! Please, I welcome comments in my classroom. There is no need to raise hands," Sherwood said to Weber, who lowered her hands.

"Professor Iving told us that the older system of sorting in the academy was pushed away because of terrible fights, but was there anything in particular that caused the academy to change its ways?"

"This happened before I became headmaster. An incident took place within the academy. You should know that the school is allowed to breed illegal plants and even poisonous ones since it is not under the rule of the land. Apparently, two Andronicans poisoned an Eromen because of a foul challenge, and this matter had been taken to King Egbert Slayholt. He had to look out for the safety of his citizens regardless of their location and requested Her Majesty, Queen Frigga, for the matter to be dealt with as a high priority since his citizen was harmed on her ground."

"So, the three friends failed then?" asked Liam Sprague, a boy with busy eyebrows and a beauty like a canvas painted with delicate strokes of elegance.

My stomach churned when I saw that he was sitting next to Maurilio Iverson, who also looked engulfed in the discussion. Liam's eyes faltered away from Sherwood, falling onto me, there was an intensity in his gaze, a depth that drew you in, but then he returned to Sherwood.

"Perhaps…" Sherwood shrugged, then clarified, "Although that depends on the context. The three tribes are separated within the academy, yes. With a few exceptions, of course…" I could feel all eyes on me.

"But they are still united under the same roof," Sherwood asserted, dispelling any misconceptions about the academy's structure. He then delved into the incident, clarifying that the poisoning was not an act of tribal animosity but rather an unfortunate targeting of what the perpetrators perceived as a 'weakling.'

Sherwood then looked at his wristwatch and said, "Okay, before any other questions, let me give you your homework since it is almost time for the bell. One-page essay on the duties of a king and add another on the important progress made by King Andronicus. That's for chapter one. For the second chapter, you will have to research the relation and the foundation upon which the kingdom of the sea, earth, and forest are built and their contribution to this, as well as the non-magic world.

"And once again, a reminder: 50% of your marks come internally. You will have two weeks, as the schedule says, before our next class." The bell rang, breaking the stillness, and Sherwood said loudly as everyone began making their way out, "Don't forget to read the text!"

Chapter 5
Silverstring Street and Defensive Magic

After a good, luxurious break of about two hours, we had Planta Concoction. It felt like the number of eyes on me from the first years had lessened after Sherwood's class, and I was grateful for that. It seemed like he had cast a spell on them—they just didn't care. But even then, I still tried to hide my face as much as possible, lingering toward the corridor walls until Bran or Ziva would tug on me.

Orson taught Planta Concoction; her class, in comparison to Sherwood's, was much bigger, much organized, and much tidier. There were large round tables for four, and the walls at the back of the class were covered in shelves, but these carried instruments used in making concoctions. In the front, next to the chalkboard, was a tiny room that extended to the glass ceiling, filled with jars, ingredients, and equipment.

"Welcome to Planta Concoction," she smiled, but it didn't reach her eyes. Her fingers struck the wooden surface of the table, one by one, on repeat, waiting impatiently for the commotion to settle down. When it was clear silence, she rose, greeting the class and gave an introduction of herself followed by the subject she taught.

"Planta Concoction, which translates to plant mixtures…" She paused, sizing the students in her class, her eyelids partially covering her cornea. A look of disinterest displayed that made it seem like she was either forced to do this or could not stand teenagers.

"…is a combination of your basic science plus magic. It's not a difficult subject if you work your way through it bit by bit." A suppressed laughter sounded at the far end of the class—it was Louis and Iverson—but Orson displayed one strong stare with no emotions, and that was enough to shut their mouths voluntarily. Keeping her eyes glued to them, she spoke to the class.

"If you want to pass my class, you will have to be in my favor even though you may be the most brilliant. I'm in charge here." She inspected every student; I adjusted the cuffs of my shirt when her eyes momentarily fell on me. "Today's class is only introductory, and you will be sticking to the textbook for the first two weeks until you all have some base knowledge to not get your faces disfigured."

Silence was no longer a word. Throughout the lecture, it seemed surreal, but not even a single soul dared whisper in her presence or move their head. Her eyes were the most dangerous part of her; they shot bullets straight to the core. She concluded the day by handing everybody a sheet of paper titled '50 Basic Ingredients.'

"You have one and a half weeks until we meet again. A single-page essay on each ingredient with its importance and precaution underlined. Those who do not hand it over are not obliged to continue my class. Dismissed," she tapped the table, and the crowd of students all piled at the door, clogging it with an attempt to escape.

I spent the rest of the evening in bed, staring at the ceiling, zoned out, introspecting because I never thought, and it's weird how sometimes a single event can drastically change everything you had planned. The hopes I had, since the moment I stepped into this magical world, are just starting to fade. It's like everything is changing, and the magical world I imagined is not turning out the way I thought. It's making me feel disappointed and unsure about everything.

Dinner was quiet, and I went back to my room, not realizing when sleep had grabbed me. I woke up in the middle of the night to weird, embarrassing noises. The sounds were coming from Maurilio's room, and annoyance rushed over me. It's like he won't ever let me live in peace. He's like that annoying fly always buzzing by the ear, disrupting any chance of tranquility.

Bran showed up the next day, nonchalantly placing a napkin on his thigh as he casually asked, "Has anyone from the two of you been to Silverstring Street?"

"Good morning to you too," I responded with a touch of sarcasm, while Ziva simply said, "No."

"Are you always this dull, Elora?" Bran inquired, seemingly unfazed by my response. I met his gaze and replied, "Probably, what do you think?"

Ignoring my retort, he suggested, "How about a trip there today? A little later?"

I firmly clarified, "No thank you," and their faces went blank.

"Oh, surely you cannot remain within that hole of sorrow, Elora. You MUST come. It'll take your mind off this nonsense," Ziva chimed in, nodding in agreement.

Letting out a sigh, I added, "Do you know what we have after the lunch break?" As the realization dawned on them, I nodded, "But anyways, I'll follow you both." It would either be this or anxiety before Iving's class.

Silverstring Street was meant to be a street filled with distractions, shops, boutiques, restaurants, and cafes. It was built behind the academy and run by nymphs and satyrs of the forest. But it didn't pique much of my interest because I expected it to be ill-managed and chaotic. How possibly can one manage to keep a street working in proper conditions in the middle of a forest?

To my surprise, the street was completely different: bright, dazzling, and clean. This was the place where students had to spend most of their time because it was mandatory. Ziva, too, wore expressions of wonder. Who could have possibly imagined something like this within a learning place?

The heavy, bushy trees that covered us from the sun also gave the smell of wet soil and leaves—it smelled like rain. Drops were falling through holes above; it was raining. Winter still had at least a month before approaching. We made it in time to the street, lingering under the roof of the trees before having to run through nature's shower.

"Why, this place is exactly how I'd imagined it to be!" Bran exclaimed. "Let's drink something, shall we?"

His eyes reflected joyful greed, and his question sounded more like a statement. He pointed to a café that looked like a tree, and a simple scan of the street would not be enough to notice it. It blended well with the surroundings, making it the least visited place. The roof had leaves hanging, and the walls were like the bark of a tree.

The door and large window reflected orange light from inside, and upon entering, the sound of insects created a soothing ambiance. The floor was made of wooden planks, but the walls on the inside were made of bricks, although the roof still had leaves hanging, which moved with invisible forces. The cafe was not packed; it had a few students and a professor who sat near the window, sipping a cup of tea and reading a book titled *The Path to Multiple Successes*.

A forest nymph with graceful movements approached us. She was all green, except for the white apron she wore. Her hair swayed back and forth, as if gravity had its favorites, omitting its force on them.

"What would you like to have?"

"Iced black rose, please," Bran made his order. "Same," the two of us repeated after each other.

The tinkling of the bell resonated through the air as the door to the café swung open. Iverson strolled in, his hand resting on the waist of a slender Zocian who appeared somewhat underfed. Her cheeks glowed with a bright red hue, and she exuded a distinctly feminine demeanor. Iverson leaned in, whispering something into her ear, eliciting a playful hit on his broad shoulder from her.

"It's beginning to get cringy," I remarked, my lips curling in a subtle expression of distaste.

Behind him, Sprague followed suit, and I found myself drinking in his sight. As our eyes met, a simultaneous exchange of scrutiny commenced. My heart seemed to pause its beat, my eyes refused to blink, and all I could perceive were sparks of light enveloping him as my brain processed his presence in slow motion.

Suddenly, a voice called out to him, prompting him to turn his head behind him. His round face tightened, and the display of his jawline seemed to pierce straight through my heart. The forest nymph server returned with three glasses of a black liquid, filled to the brim. It was at that moment my delusional state snapped back to reality, and the surrounding noise returned to my senses. What had just happened to me? Why did it suddenly feel like chocolate was melting in my heart?

"I've lived with my parents in the other world. Nothing special about me. My parents, of course, have had high expectations of me because I'm a Zocian," she said, as if it was obvious, and then explained, "But I too want to explore where my capabilities and abilities end."

I blinked at the server placing our glasses on the table until my eyes drained away the tears, bringing my focus to the liquid that resembled a thick ice cream shake and smelled like roses. I took a sip; it tasted like dark rose chocolate with a hint of coffee. It wasn't the bitter kind, and by far, rose chocolates are my favorite type of sweet in this world.

"And you, Bran?" I asked, trying to find a distraction even though I wanted to peep at him.

"I've lived here all my time; you must have heard of the war between 'Maldeus'" He whispered, trying not to bring attention. "And Her Majesty, Queen Frigga? Yeah, my dad died then."

"Oh, sorry."

"Sorry." Both of us blurted.

"Oh, you should get used to hearing the death of people. It's very common here. At least half the students here are sitting with one of their parents murdered or voluntarily dead," he said like it wasn't a big deal, and Ziva turned her eyes toward me.

"My parents are dead too."

"Was it because of a royal secure job?" Bran asked, sipping with his chin supported by his hands on the table. We both looked at him, for the meaning of his question.

"There's a standardized idea here, that royal occupations are the most secure because firstly, you have guaranteed income, whether it be retirement or being fired—the latter being very unlikely. And secondly, to land with a royal occupation, you need to take up royal studies, which are considered very difficult to pass. The honor and fame you get is a completely different story, but the best of these is that the King…" He paused, building suspense, "chooses his left hand, Aristera, from them."

"So, I may be an ordinary person and, in the next moments, I'm second to the King and equal to the Queen?" Ziva asked, amazed.

"Yeah, provided you pass that exam. So? Your parents were in a stable royal job like my dad?" He looked at me.

"No idea. Maybe my father was. His identity was never revealed, but both my mom and dad were murdered."

I then added, "Better to die a righteous death than do evil, don't you think?"

The two agreed, and for once, I didn't feel so bad about not having my parents around me.

"So, what actually happened to the King? Why is all silent now?" I remembered the news article I read at Mrs. Anderson's home. Our talks were so low that they sounded like breathy whispers, and even our heads were forward.

"From what I've heard, he fell into a deep sleep. Probably a punishment from Queen Frigga for the attempt to take over the forest."

Bran then turned to Ziva, giving her a word of caution, "It is mandatory—you address the three rulers of the earth, sea, and forest with 'majesty' even in their absence. It's a form of deep respect. At least when you're in their kingdom."

Ziva gasped and then mouthed 'sorry'. "So have I heard, too," he added.

"So, if he's in a deep sleep and no one wants him to be King, then why not just… you know," I said, tilting my head like 'murder' was an evident option here.

"That never struck me," Ziva muttered.

Bran silently pondered, looking dumbstruck at my idea. "That does make sense actually."

"Somebody must have attempted it. It must have been in the news at least?"

"No. Nothing," Bran clarified.

"You must have missed it…" Ziva reasoned.

"Couldn't have. My father was Chief-in-Command, and he survived the war against Her Majesty Queen Frigga only to be murdered later. I've been digging for a reason since then."

"Urghhh…" Ziva groaned in disgust, looking behind him. "What is it?"

We turned to see Iverson and the girl deep in a passionate kiss. It looked like Iverson couldn't get enough, kissing her with so much enthusiasm that it seemed as if he was devouring an ice cream on a hot summer day. The professor sitting behind them, clearly uncomfortable, tried to get their attention by clearing his throat. The girl attempted to pull away, reacting to the professor's presence, but Iverson continued kissing her even more intensely. The professor, annoyed, stood up and walked out of the cafe. Iverson, seemingly oblivious to everything around him, kept going, and the girl, instead of resisting, seemed to be enjoying every moment of it.

Sprague looked equally out of place, much like the three of us. We decided to leave rather than endure the awkwardness of his romance before us. After settling the bill of six bronze coins, we lingered around the street, browsing through shops, and eventually entered the library that Bran had insisted we visit.

Although from the outside, it appeared small and insignificant, it felt like a mansion from within. Every nook and cranny of the walls was hidden behind books, and I had never seen such an extensive collection in my life.

Each section of the wall was labeled with categories like 'History,' 'Fantasy,' 'Mystery,' and more. We climbed the stairs to the upper deck, which had rooms clearly designated for different purposes—ancient books, rituals, newspapers, and much more.

Bran then guided us into the room stacked with newspapers, reaching up to the ceiling, covering the period from 1800 to 1996.

He pulled out today's paper, and the headline read, 'Two Andronicans imprisoned for 10 years after several charges.' He scanned through the article, then flipped the pages and carelessly returned the paper to the recent papers stand. He did the same for the papers of the past two days. When he was done, he flattened them and placed them neatly, just as he had found them.

"There's nothing special today, and this week's *Morning Lodestone* is not yet out. *Seers Daily* fabricates their information a lot," he said, unsatisfied with what he had read.

We climbed all the way back towards the exit of the library. I wanted to borrow books, but I believe the academy's library would be much better for doing homework. This place was a bit too overwhelming with information and time-consuming compared to the academic books in the academy's library—according to Ziva.

"Could you please inform me when the *Morning Lodestone* arrives?" he whispered to the satyr at the service desk.

The satyr lowered his book to nod, pushing a slip toward him, and then returned to reading *The Red Gift*. Bran filled in his identity number, and we left.

I went to the academy's library alone. Ziva and Bran had already borrowed books the previous day for their work. I did not go back to my room because I knew it would leave me paranoid. Iving's class was in about half an hour, and my thoughts would kill me before Iving could even attempt to murder me.

I collected the books I felt would be useful and sat in the library itself, beginning to mark the pages that had information relevant to the homework Orson gave us. For Sherwood's work, I thought it'd be best to read the text first because the library's history made no sense to me. There were so many new names and boundless information and different versions of the same story since the information dated before the 1800s when no solid evidence was present.

I managed to spend my time fruitfully, even though within every few minutes, my eyes would drift to the overhead clock. Defensive Magic class was on the ground floor of the magic zone, and I had to take the stairs to the magic zone and then take another set of stairs to the lower floor. Today was just the basic introductory class, and everything would be okay. I think I would make it through until next week when we have our first official class.

One of the worst things that could happen to someone having a bad day is entering a depressing, prison-like setting. His class was dull and extremely unattractive, but it was the biggest one.

The lights were switched off, and the windows had dirty eggplant-colored curtains tucked to one side. I couldn't differentiate whether his floor was dirty, or they were just gray tiles.

Iving entered the spacious class from the small attached room in the front. "Welcome," his voice lacked any sort of enthusiasm. "This year, I shall be teaching defensive magic against dark magic, and next year you shall be learning the basics of dark magic."

He bore his black eyes into everyone, finally reaching mine. I saw the coldness his soul held, sending shivers down my legs and already terrifying me, making me look away.

"Defensive magic is not as effortless as dark magic, but once mastered with practice, it becomes child's play."

He turned to me again, speaking brazenly, "According to the schedule, today was supposed to be an introductory class. But after seeing the turn of events from a few nights ago, I've decided to alter the schedule a bit. Without any more boring introduction, we will begin this subject with the most basic defense: resistance to mind invasion."

There was a pause, and he flipped a switch before beginning.

"Your mind represents you. It is your most prized possession. One with the skill of mind-reading will be able to rob you of your possessions, and those with an advanced level will be able to control it." He simultaneously wrote down the three levels of mind invasion—I. Opening of the mind; II. Manipulation of thoughts, feelings, and ideas; III. Gain of control'—onto the black chalkboard. He was speeding with his explanation since we had only a two-hour class that was solely organized for a lecture.

"Now, how about we start with someone from my house," he said, putting on an act of thinking. I knew who he was going to call, but I still closed my eyes, hoping it wouldn't be me.

"Ahh… Ms. Bates," he called out with great pleasure. "You sure seemed to be power-driven enough that you are seated in Imperium."

"How about you?" A fine smirk lined his lips, and that smirk was enough to tell he waited through his career for a day like this. I swallowed the non-existent saliva from my parched mouth and rose. Professor Iving used finger moments and dragged two chairs to the front, sitting mangily upon one of them, with his arms crossed.

He pointed toward the other chair, and with quick, submissive glances at Iving, I took the seat of death. Nobody could save me! This was it.

I turned to look at Ziva who fisted her hands in encouragement, and then to Bran, who just blinked with an unsettling look.

"Now, watch carefully…" he said to the crowd, focusing on my eyes to see what lay within, "I am now about to invade her mind; she should feel almost nothing unless she is fully aware of herself." His face turned slightly toward the crowd whenever he spoke to them to fill them in on the details.

I saw his forehead line waver from my peripheral vision, and his facial muscles applied force.

I didn't understand what he was doing until something began happening to me. I couldn't describe what I was feeling. Something was there, deep within. My eyes kept pacing the floor. I kept turning my head toward away in reflex; to move away from that sensation, it was invading my personal space. The feeling of being violated was congesting me.

Suddenly, I felt a stabbing sensation, the hand pushed deep within the invisible walls, the hands buried within me. I was not physically bleeding, but I felt every inch of it. My eyes stopped pacing. I held my breath because if I released it, my screams would escape too. The hands plunged further in, looking for a safe spot, and then it released its grip.

The pain stopped; I looked at Iving, and I could feel the invisible hole regenerate as pseudopods extended from the wall, covering the wall and refilling it back. But something was left, something felt extra like it didn't belong to me.

"I am now going to attempt to manipulate you," he said to the crowd while looking into me. What? That was only the beginning? "You must resist it, Bates."

There were voices in my head; they sounded like my thoughts, only they weren't. The voices repeatedly asked me to raise my hand; it wouldn't stop, and it kept getting louder, so I obeyed it. I raised my hands until it stopped speaking to me.

"This is what happens if you don't resist, and I gain control."

Something was pulling me apart from within. The room was filled with my screams, it pierced into me and tore my mind. Then it stopped, it felt like a part of the invasion was still left behind in my mind. My nose started bleeding, and my vision was hazy. I dropped my head,

too tired to keep it up. Iving excused me away; I rose and walked back to my seat, falling onto it, my muscles asked me to stop and rest, for about 100 days.

"Ms. Bates here wouldn't remember anything that happened because I was controlling her," Iving tilted his head from the right to the left. "Pity, what a disappointment."

The crowd carried an ominous silence.

"Now, I haven't changed anything within her even though that is possible, but that's exactly what happens if you don't resist." He handed me a cloth to dab the blood off.

"You alright?" Ziva asked.

"Yeah…yeah," I said, trying to get a steady grip on myself. "Now, then how about you, Mr. Sprague?"

I watched the boy rise. He kept licking his lips. Professor Iving reassured him to remain calm and that he wouldn't face the same end as me, but my heart felt heavy. He started with the same, looking into Sprague's eyes to invade his mind.

"Try harder, Sprague…Resist…Push that feeling away with an invisible force."

Iving's brows were scrunched as Sprague's eyes darted around the room. My body remembered the intense invasion experience, causing me to curl in on myself. The lingering sensation of violation and the blood-stained cloth in my hand added to the discomfort.

"What happened?" I asked Ziva.

"You rose, took two rounds around the chair, and sat back onto it."

She was horror-stricken, not breaking eye contact from the scene ahead. The bell rang, and the class had to be terminated.

"Everyone must read the first chapter in your textbook and write me a three-page essay on why defenses are necessary, and another three-page essay based on mind invasion and how to defend against it. Everyone but you."

He watched me, a sly smile forming on his face. "It'll be six pages for you."

"But, sir—"

"The next class will be held as scheduled with a theory and practical class. The key to mastering mind invasion is meditation, and don't forget the homework; no excuses will be entertained."

"How are you feeling?" Bran asked.

"Alive," I grumbled, annoyed. There was this burning anger inside me, like a furious storm. I felt treated unfairly, and Professor Iving's smug smile just made it worse. It was as if he had unleashed a fiery rage in me.

Chapter 6
His Vulnerable Side, the Greatest Power Mark, and Maldeus

"Your Majesty," the royal servant panted in terror, his cry echoing through the air. He collapsed onto his knees, bending completely, his head touching the ground in submission.

I sat upright, the sensation akin to emerging from beneath a suffocating weight. Retrieving the oxygen mask from my face, I inhaled the air of disparity. Surveying the surroundings, I slowly raised my hand, observing the whiteness of my skin as I flexed my fingers, witnessing the stiffness dissipate. I had returned; how long had I been absent, shrouded in darkness?

With raspy words, I uttered, *"My stick,"* and turned my head, reveling in the sensations of life. Felix, my loyal servant, hastened to retrieve my walking stick from the corner of the room. He presented it to me with both hands, avoiding eye contact in reverence. I scrutinized the polished blackness that gleamed, taking the silver skull into my hand and placing the stick upright.

"Impressive, you've retained the filth of my stick, you filth," I sneered, acknowledging the meticulous care.

I greeted the return to my surroundings with a sense of authority. The familiar atmosphere evoked a realization—I was back.

The door swung open, *"Your Maj-esty?"* He stuttered on the words, the reality of the address feeling surreal.

"Bruh-ther!" I exclaimed, feigning warmth as if our relationship remained affectionate. His stupefaction was evident. *"Long time, brother indeed! Did you miss me?"* I posed the question with feigned innocence, leaving him bewildered and uncertain of the appropriate.

"Of course, I did…" his voice quavered, attempting to play along.

I scoffed, abandoning the act, "Have you forgotten your loyalty?" I asked through gritted teeth. The weight of realization struck him, prompting him to kneel and touch his nose to the floor in a display of allegiance.

"Allow me," he offered.

I tapped the floor with my stick, signaling for him to proceed. He then kissed my bloodless feet, and a smile of satisfaction spread across my face.

"Yes, Riordian, I've witnessed your loyalty. You have not seized the throne yet."

I narrowed my eyes at him. "Oh, Brother, why do you appear terror-stricken?" I chuckled, relishing the sense of power.

"You know I would never harm you. Unless you had taken the throne." My stern expression made him freeze.

"I'm just teasing," I snickered at his evident fear.

I woke up, gasping for air, my top clinging to my skin. It was getting hot, so I flipped the blanket, the residue of the dream replaying in my mind, and looked around the room, grounding myself in the present. Lucid nightmares are the worst! I lingered too much on the topic of the King, and now they were manifesting as my dreams. I need to stop; the King is in a death state, whatever he did to my family is in the past. There is no use worrying over spilled milk.

I pulled open the window, allowing the cold morning breeze to soothe my skin. Life was beginning to settle; two weeks were through. People were getting used to the fact that I was in Imperium; the talks were decreasing, and smiles were appearing.

Even though I share a housing unit with Iverson, I'm facing far fewer problems than I initially anticipated. Most of it is because to have an issue, he must be around—I barely see him. He's always out partying late at night with his crowd, usually making it back before curfew, and that too only if he didn't bring a girl over. It's disheartening to witness Liam Sprague bringing him back to his room when he's out of control, drunk. I like the boy, but I keep having second thoughts about him sticking around with Iverson, even though I anticipate him late at night when Iverson is not back, hoping to catch a glimpse of him as he walks to help Iverson to his room. Why is Iverson such a burden to the world? I believe not all Andronicans are bad; Liam is a good example.

This morning, Creaturology was the first class. It was taught by Professor Danbud, a middle-aged woman with wrinkles creasing the sides of her eyes. Her blond hair was styled in a pixie cut, giving her a youthful appearance with a streak of green. Despite her stern appearance, she turned out to be pleasant and welcoming.

"Today we'll kick off our class with a unique creature. Most of you must be familiar with them…" Professor Danbud paused, as though waiting for an imaginary drumroll.

"Pixies," she announced with excitement.

"I thought she'd say dragons," Bran mocked.

"Where do you get such preposterous ideas? Dragons have gone extinct decades ago," Ziva scowled. Bran responded with a 'blah' expression.

"Turn to page 5 of your textbooks."

The right side of the book featured a full-page painted picture of what looked like a tiny human with wings, similar to the ones I had seen at Cassiden's house. Its clothes were made of leaves woven together, and its wings reflected a shine, like the wings of a dragonfly. The left side of the book contained information about the creature with a large heading:

'PIXIES'
Other names – Noikras, deaf fairies
Size: 3 inches
Identification:
A tiny humanoid.
Has wings with two distinct features: color and shine.
Has 4 pairs of fingers (hands and feet).

The textbook continued to provide information about areas where pixies could be located, their uses to humans, foraging habits, and various percentages and numbers estimating their population.

Professor Danbud often supplemented the text with additional insights. For instance, she shared with us that pixies communicate with a frequency near zero DB, which is impossible for the human ear to hear. This characteristic is why these creatures are said to 'speak to air' because it seems so.

"Professor, I've read that they are able to see the union bond?" Ariel Taylor, a bushy-haired girl with a soft voice, inquired. She seemed to be the 'Bexley Weber' of Creaturology.

"There is an assumption based on research done a few years ago, regarding the wild kind, that they can see the union bond between two lovers. Some claim that it appears to them as a smoke of silver, but there is no confirmed theory as such," Professor Danbud explained. She had a talent for transforming seemingly dull lectures into interesting discussions by engaging with us on various topics. I recall a particularly memorable incident last Thursday when she provided life advice to Mark Dunne, cautioning him about the pitfalls of a superiority complex. However, the discussion took a turn when Dunne asserted that there had never been a ruling Queen in history, countering her advice by suggesting that women's status would only change if the royal family initiated such a shift.

It was a compelling argument. The royal family's influence over public perception is undeniable, and people tend to follow their ideology. However, this is precisely when rumors about the prince began circulating. She playfully suggested to the class that if the prince were present, he should consider amending his views in the future, especially if he were to be crowned King. My attention shifted to Liam at that moment, who seemed to be smirking at her advice.

As we transitioned to the next topic, the creature featured on the right side of the page appeared. The painted picture depicted a collection of oval-shaped creatures with up-slanting, gibbously shaped eyes. Their thin, straight mouths gave them an overall appearance of annoyance. Despite lacking feet or hands, they exuded a cuddly quality, reminiscent of an extra pillow to hold while sleeping.

Other names – Oval, ovalus.
Size-average 19 inches, highly variable.

"Anyone know what these are?" she questioned the class, eagerly awaiting a response.

"Pets!" Taylor squealed.

"Yes!" Danbud exclaimed with delight.

Creaturology had quickly become one of the few classes that managed to capture my attention, thanks to Danbud's engaging teaching style. The textbook, adorned with colorful pictures, also played a role in sparking my interest.

After class, during our customary two-hour lunch break, Bran and I decided to visit the library. Our agenda included returning the books borrowed in the previous weeks, sharing and discussing our homework, and, to some extent, embellishing our papers to create the illusion of hard work.

Ziva, however, wasn't interested in what she deemed 'a fraud.' Engaged in a fierce competition with Bexley Weber for the top spot, she seemed oblivious to the satisfaction that hard work, as shared between Bran and me, could bring. We planned to reward ourselves later with a visit to Silverstring Street.

During lunch, I casually brought up the absence of Liam Sprague and Maurilio Iverson, acting as if I had just noticed it.

"Oh, yeah. I think I heard that Iverson took leave because his mother got sick. I have no clue about Sprague."

"A sick leave, especially for his mother? Do they even grant those?" I questioned, finding the excuse dubious unless his mother was critically ill.

Considering Iverson's family background, it wouldn't be surprising if they held significant wealth and influence. As the conversation continued, Ziva provided additional information.

"Iving's out too," she mentioned, her face following the contours of a thick book as she simultaneously ate and took notes. Since we were unaware of the details, we eagerly waited for her to share more.

"OH! Nobody must have informed you because that was supposed to be his job, but he isn't..." She began speaking rapidly.

"Ziva, slow down. Provide the details for which you halted your labor," Bran mocked, injecting some humor into the discussion.

"Yes!" She breathed. "Orson informed us this morning that all classes with Iving and Sherwood have been suspended for 3 days..."

"Oh no, Iving's class isn't till after 3 days," I sighed.

"Because of legal issues."

"Legal issues, you say?" I asked, suddenly intrigued. The idea of Iving facing legal trouble brought an unexpected sense of satisfaction. I think I would be the happiest to see Iving walk out of the academy. I can't believe I'm praying for something like this; I sound like a pathetic failure.

"Sounds suspicious, don't you think?" Bran added, echoing my sentiments.

"Yeah! It was not just me; I could feel a sly smile almost take form but then..."

"No. I mean, not really. Since the academy is in the forest, someone would have to sort out everything out there about the academy, don't you think?" Ziva interjected, dampening the intrigue.

"But don't you think that should be sorted before the academy begins? We're in the middle of a teaching peri…"

"Don't be a fool; you're overdoing it," Ziva curled her lips, rolling her eyes at him. "Just because you were praised for thinking outside the box doesn't mean you can begin a scandal with your witty brain!"

I groaned loudly, as if carrying the burden of the world on my shoulders, the weight pressing heavily.

The last class for the day was Power Magic, the first time we'd be having it, even though it wasn't the introductory week. Despite the seemingly simple schedule of two classes a day, the workload could be overwhelming for an ordinary human. Our new teacher, Valerie Reika, introduced herself.

"Good evening, class. I will be your teacher for Power Magic. I am Valerie Reika." She had a square face, lion-red hair with the mark of Zocia, and eyes that carried the color of cider with flecks of cinnamon powder. Her hair was in a bun secured with a wooden stick.

"Power Magic is divided into a smaller class—Skill Magic, taught by Professor Martin, where you will learn skills. Here, you will be learning the art of wielding power," she raised her hand for emphasis, revealing the silver power mark on her wrist.

"Power levels are divided into four…" picking up the chalk, she wrote on the blackboard "Diamond, Gold, Silver, and Bronze." She circled Diamond. "Only one person is known to have this, as most of you know, he is the Great Eneas. Her Majesty Queen Frigga shares equal power as the Great Eneas, so you can assume the strength of Diamond. Gold is very rare, with only a handful of people having it. While silver is seen quite often, and bronze is common."

She raised her index finger toward the class in an accusatory tone, "Whenever your power mark appears, to those that carry silver, this is no reason to display superiority over the others. Any questions?"

When no one said anything, she proceeded to write 'Do's and Don'ts' on the board, with the same high-pitched screeching of the chalk resonating in the background. The class ended slower than usual, with Professor Reika dismissing us by assigning over 20 pages of written work. She reminded us that our next class would be on the 1st of November, by which time most students would be carrying their power mark. This also meant ample time to complete the work she had assigned since today was the 2nd of September.

I spent the night completing my essay for law studies, which we'll be discussing tomorrow. Our topic was to discuss how reprimanding centers are used. I made a final read.

'The Magic network utilizes a main correctional center, the Black Heart Correctional Center located in Atlantis. The correctional center employs a stringent technique to reprimand its prisoners. Each prisoner must earn their meal, thereby creating a source of income for the prison to operate independently. Tasks assigned include rock breaking, wood carving, and alloy-making. Currently, it houses over 500 inmates of both genders, posing a challenge to the prospect of moving and establishing an entirely new center, which is an ongoing topic of discussion.

This need for a new center arose when it was discovered that the energy of the Bermuda Triangle matches the frequency of the Black Heart Correctional Center. This occasionally opens portals that cause ordinary beings to enter our world. Although most of the ordinary are returned to their world with erased memories, myths tend to arise, claiming it to be 'the devil's triangle.'-'

The abrupt noise of what sounded like wood striking a surface jolted me from my concentration. Startled, I remained motionless, my ears straining to catch any subsequent noises. But all that lingered in the air was an eerie stillness.

I shifted my attention to the clock on the table – 12:30 am. Fatigue weighed heavily on me, and the weariness had reached a point where my senses seemed to be playing tricks. I shook off the unease. I refocused on the work at hand, attempting to dispel the lingering sense of disquiet that clung to the room. I wanted to complete this before bed.

'A much-debated topic currently, is the method of correction used, whether it takes into account its effects on the well-being of prisoner's health.'

The piece of paper I was holding slips from my fingers, and I freeze in place, the chilling sound filled the air-screams that are tough, hard, and filled with pain. My eyes quickly scan the room, and my heart starts pounding rapidly. Breathing becomes difficult as if my lungs aren't getting enough air. I rose, moving toward the door with the quietest steps my feet can manage.

I reach for the doorknob, turning it slowly, and open the door just a crack. I peek into the hallway, only to find an eerie silence; no more screams. On the floor, a table is broken, one of its legs lying beside it. Something clearly happened here. Maybe there's an animal in the house. I cautiously glance around, trying to see as much as I can through that small opening, and then decide to swing the door wide open, remaining alert.

My grip on the door slipped, the disturbing scream had returned. The hair on the back of my neck rose. It was a boy, and he was, he was weeping, loud sobs escaping from him. Suddenly, fear is replaced by concern, and I rush toward the painful noise. I enter the hall, following the sound to its source in the other room.

"Maurilio," I shuddered at the sight of him, unaware that he had returned from his leave. He was kneeling, his hands tightly gripping a glass bottle. Suddenly, he flung it at the wall, and my hand instinctively covered my mouth as I watched the bottle shatter into pieces. A small shard rebounded, piercing him in the face. I realized that could have been me if I didn't step back. Now.

Despite the danger, I still approached him, lowering myself to the ground. Placing a hand on his back, I whispered his name again, "Maurilio."

He slowly turned his head toward me, and I saw his bloody eyes. Surprisingly, they didn't evoke terror in me; instead, they soothed my racing heart. I felt an overwhelming sense of sympathy for him and his pain. Slowly, I pulled the shard from his face, and he winced, observing me. Then, he immediately wrapped his arms around my back, weeping into my neck.

My initial instinct was to move away, but something held me back. Instead, I held him, rubbing circles on his back as I felt the edge of my t-shirt becoming wet. The smell of intoxication lingered around him. Did he realize that his tough exterior had crumbled, revealing his vulnerable side? Did he realize he was showing it to me? I remembered the reason for his leave—his mother.

"Your mother? Is she okay?" I asked.

He shook his head, and I could feel his nose press against my skin. Pulling away, his eyes were deadpan. "Nobody is."

His tone sent shivers down to my toes. Was everyone in his family sick? Perhaps he didn't realize what he was saying; the alcohol might be speaking for him.

"Come on. It's late. Let's get you tucked into bed," I suggested.

He obediently followed, lost in his own world. I didn't even know why I was doing this for him. He was the same man who had almost threatened me on the first day and argued whenever the chance presented itself. As I tended to his wound, I allowed myself to study his face, memorizing every bend and contour. It was like appreciating the captivating bloom of a venomous flower.

Previously, I had only seen vile emotions in him, but now I saw a human soul cowering under the disguise of a brave facade. He was oblivious to my observations, lost in his sadness.

After ensuring he was peacefully asleep, I returned to my room, abandoning the idea of revisiting my essay. Despite turning off the lights and attempting to sleep, the image of Maurilio's tear-stained face lingered, haunting my thoughts until I succumbed to the realm of dreams.

****

"I hadn't encountered Iverson for several days. It could have been our divergent plans for the day or perhaps a mere coincidence that he seemed to be avoiding me. Regardless, I felt compelled to check on him. Why? Maurilio's troubled face kept flashing in my mind, leaving me uncertain about what to do.

Who would ensure he was okay? I felt a deep sense of pity for him, realizing that in his shoes, anyone would need someone to look after them. Until I had a human heart, I resolved to care for him. The death of his mother had evidently taken a toll on him, evident in his changed demeanor. He often lingered in the corner of his room in the dark with his head in his knees. Barely spoke to anyone outside and didn't bring girls to our housing unit and completely refrained from bullying.

The look of confusion on Grissa's face did not surprise the Queen; she made no remarks about it, and Grissa, not wanting to interrupt the flow, remained still. By the end of October, more than half the students got their power mark.

Weber was the first among us all to get her power mark, which made Ziva uncomfortable because fate had plans other than the way she wanted it to be.

The end of October marked the emergence of power marks for more than half of the students. Weber was the first to receive hers, causing discomfort to Ziva, who had different expectations from fate. Although I understood that it wasn't something within our control, Ziva's envy was short-lived because soon, both Ziva and Bran received their marks—Bronze. While Ziva was fascinated for a week, Bran, after an initial thrill, resumed his routine as if nothing had happened. The mark signified acceptance into the community," the Queen recounted, assuming Grissa could relate.

"It was just me and three others that were left. I still remember the day when Iverson had gotten his, there was an unusual crowd at the Imperium table where he was seated during lunch. Bran had gone to check why such a crowd had gathered, and when he returned, he seemed shaken. 'Silver.'"

The Queen imitated Bran.

"What about your mark?"

"I got it around two days before the 1st of November, it didn't bother me much because I had other things to worry about. We had a defensive magic test up on our list, and we had to prove to Iving we were worth passing, that we could avoid mind invasion purely by resistance and do well on our theory."

"I expect you must have done well," Grissa stated, trying to conclude the discussion, especially over matters that didn't seem important to her.

"Quite the contrary actually. I failed. I still believe that I'd done well, but apparently, he failed me."

"Well, that's absurd now—"

"Not just that, I was the only failed person in a classroom of around twenty-four students."

"Surely you couldn't have been that bad." Her Highness thinned her lips and shrugged.

"I had to attend extra classes. But I wasn't annoyed with Iving for much longer because two great things came my way."

****

Elora Bates

"I don't know what to say, Elora!" Professor Reika tried to find the right words, raising her palm in a display of confusion.

"Never in my entire career! Having the gold mark would not require you as much time as others to master the classes."

She then walked toward the front of the class, pretending like she was over it, and resumed the lesson.

"This year you will be studying four lessons; today your first lesson will be only about wielding energy. This will be followed by the manipulation of fire, water, and earth. Finally, you will learn how to transform your energy into fire, water, and earth."

She began with a brief introduction about energy, its capabilities, and its appearance. This was followed by some mindfulness exercises for concentration, and then a quick mention of the challenges we would face in this class. She stated that she would demonstrate wielding her power by the end of the class if none of us were able to do so.

She then asked us to place our palms forward, facing the ceiling, and close our eyes. We were instructed to self-reflect on finding those thoughts, ideas, and moments that provoked the energy within us, focusing solely on bringing that power into our hands. We spent the entire first period doing this, and by lunch break, everyone appeared mentally drained.

Not a single student was able to wield anything, and by the beginning of the next class, frustration began to manifest in the form of grunts from everyone. Reika constantly offered her support, reassuring us that it was normal and our minds needed more focus. During the past hour, my struggle was mainly to clear my conscience. Thoughts about how everyone looked utterly shocked at my mark and how Iving's face turned red at dinner danced in my mind.

I smiled more often and subconsciously. Besides that confidence boost, there was Liam; he had asked me out, and I said yes. We were going on our first date this weekend. Every time my mind wandered, thoughts of him filled me with unquenchable serotonin.

"Let's take a few minutes break and then get back to work," Reika declared, moving to a group of Prudens, asking them about the variables that caused them not to be able to wield energy. She was understanding and struggled with us.

"Are you still planning on leaving because of Iving?" Bran asked, smiling.

I grinned in return. "Not really, the thrill of carrying this mark is begging me not to leave."

"Everyone seems to want to get to your good side," Ziva muttered. "Yes, I've been noticing the friendly nature too, ever since…"

"Elora," Bran wore a serious expression, "I know things have been going great with you, but I found something about your mom in the news section of the street library. If that's okay with you?"

There was quiet in my mind, it went blank; I didn't know how to react to him.

"Okay, that's enough. Back to work, everybody."

Reika clapped her hands for silence, and I blinked. My mom? On the news? I closed my eyes, attempting to focus on clearing my mind.

Her…her…murder?

My skin flushed, and I could feel the adrenaline begin to pump. The dark silhouette of Maldeus loomed in my mind, just his, and utter silence.

"Look here, everyone, Ms. Bates has done it!" Reika exclaimed in happiness.

I opened my eyes at the sound of my name, only to be met with blazing yellow flames in my hand. It was magnificent, like the sun but not blinding; the energy dulled all other light's presence.

"Focus and try pushing that bottle of water on the table," she whispered carefully, trying not to startle me.

I followed her instruction, slowly turning my hand to face the board while trying to steady them simultaneously.

I pressed onto my hand with as much force as my body could build, and the waves began growing like a long broad cloth floating in the air. The ribbon seemed airy, yet difficult for me to produce and strong enough to make the water within the bottle strike its surface.

It was happening; the bottle was beginning to move lightly. Then I was drained, and the glowing light broke, forming yellow sparkling dust falling to the floor—disappearing.

"Tell me about your source of power?" The crease surrounding her eye and the curve of her lips did not disappear.

"My source?" I was confused.

"Yes, it may be a thought, a feeling, someone… It can be anything, even an object sometimes. Anything that provoked that fuel within to ignite and reveal its presence."

"Ah, my thought…" I dragged on, trying to remember. Reika nodded slowly with her eyebrows raised, waiting patiently.

"Ah… yes, it was Cassiden, my godfather, and the ordinary realm." The creases around her eyes disappeared, but the smile remained.

"That's unusual, the ordinary realm; the key to opening the lock on your magical genes."

Her face grew blank as she walked back. I could feel the eyes of the class upon me.

Reika ended the class before the bell, revealing that the next power class would take place a week from now. The anticipation was overwhelming, and my desperation to learn more about my deceased mother became an insistent tug at my emotions.

As soon as the class concluded, Bran and I rushed towards the street. My eagerness to uncover the truth about my mother intensified. The burning desire to know, which had lingered within me for a long time, was now reaching a boiling point. However, seeking the truth also meant confronting the unsettling reality that my mother's death still held emotional significance for me.

"Has the morning Lodestone come?" He asked the satyr sitting at the desk.

"Ahh, Bran," he looked up at him from the paper he was working on, "Any moment now."

We moved up to the room filled with newspapers, and Bran went to the year 1980, the year I was born, and began digging back through the newspapers, reading the dates one by one by turning his head left-right to match with the alignment of the text. His roughness caused them to wrinkle.

Finally, his eyes grew wild, he picked up one of the papers, and I licked my lips, not knowing what to expect. He folded the paper and handed it to me. I took it, looking at him for a few moments until he nodded. Everything will be fine, I know. I gave one final look at Ziva before reading, Bran went back to look at the papers in that year.

Another victim of King

Scarlett Bates (E), 20 found dead in her residence this morning. The crime scene was found to have 'Aristera' written with blood on the floor. The blood was confirmed to be of the woman who after much struggle during her last breath inscribed the message onto the floor.

The possible speculation of this message could be an indication that she was murdered by Aristera. Her identity was further confirmed by her aged parents, Mr. and Mrs. Bates, who are yet to appear at the Guardian station for a detailed investigation.'

My stunned gaze fixed on the photograph, my lips slightly agape, while Ziva provided a supporting embrace. I felt unsteady, beginning to lose my sense of balance, struggling to breathe as I confronted the image of my lifeless mother beneath the article. The visual portrayal was distressing—she appeared to have suffered a torturous demise. Her eyes were bloodshot, cheeks marked with shades of purple from inflicted bruises, and a grievous wound on her abdomen spilled a ghastly river of blood.

Despite having seen numerous pictures of my mother before, never had an image stirred such intense emotions within me. She beckoned for my aid, and I extended my hands towards her, but they frustratingly failed to reach; a futile attempt as they merely passed through her form.

"Elora," her words faltered as her lungs seemed to collapse, rendering her speech incoherent. Desperately, she attempted to push her hand towards me, the other hand clutched around the knife. Tears streamed down her eyes, an urgent plea for life.

"Elora… Elora!" Bran shook me, bringing me back to reality. I met his gaze, tears still streaming, but not wanting to stop. I needed to know. I snatched the newspaper he had in his hands.

'Mr. Florence Bates (E) and Mrs. Evelyn Bates (A) were found dead an hour before their appearance at the guardian station for the pending investigation on the case of their daughter late Scarlett Bates (E).'

I glanced at Bran before tossing this paper away, to read the next.

'The case of the Bates family was declared closed by the judge later this afternoon after the court had found no concrete evidence except for possible speculations.'

I cast the paper onto the floor in anger.

"They dismissed a murder case and not just one murder but three murder cases, just because they didn't have evidence!"

"It's the same with all cases, Elora. The justice system fears the King." "But why? What is Frigga doing?"

"ELORA!" Bran shot at my tone, "Her Majesty Queen Frigga…" he emphasized, "Cannot interfere in our matters unless it threatens her purpose of existence. Our king on the other hand has the gold power mark. And you should know well, based on how everyone wants your good side that nobody will dare go against him."

"Yes, and if he is able to lift the staff of Andronicus. We all perish, like those who perished under Her Majesty Queen Frigga's staff."

The satyr at the help desk walked into the room, "Big news, it's true. I tell you."

He handed this week's Morning Lodestone to Bran and left. Bran read the title; his hands began trembling as he undid the folding. He stopped dead.

Ziva seized the paper from his hands, and I read along with her.

'The King rises.'

We paused, looking at each other to see whether we read it right.

'His Highness Crown Prince Riordian Slayholt on the 31st of October 2012, announced that His Majesty, the King had first opened his eyes during the first week of September. The King is said to be fit enough to continue his ruling and will take up his responsibilities once he has learned the current matter of Ariesque. The crown prince has declared the 5th to the 10th of November to be days of celebration in honor of his brother, the King.

There is a strict rule that no citizens on land are to work on those days. However, shops with necessities may continue to remain open. If any citizen is found to be working, a punishment of 30 lashes on the back and a fine of 50 gold coins are to be paid. Our reporters were denied the chance of interviewing the King since the royal healer had claimed at least another month of bed rest.'

"Things are to change soon," Bran said deadpan.

Chapter 7
The Date, Aristera, and the Encounter with Real Defense

Despite the immensity of fear on campus since the news of the King, I began preparing myself for today's date, not forgetting to mark November 4th on my calendar. My first-ever date, something I shall remember all my life.

Even though the King was awake, nothing had changed; the world within the forest remained the same, but perhaps the same couldn't be said about the land. It hadn't even been a week, and a vast craze of rumors and stories was spreading around the campus, all centered around the King. According to one of them, the King had a small portion of the Soul Forest and Atlantis within his control.

Creatures from the land, sea, and forest that sided with him lived there in secret. They were betrayers of their kind, giving away tales of their world. The King also seemed to have had a villa built there. They say that any Enchanter who sees the villa never comes out to see the world again; it is said that they are fed to those that live there. The rumors had to be untrue; I doubt cannibalism is still prevalent. The very idea of cannibalism seemed far-fetched, and I struggled to accept such gruesome tales as anything more than baseless gossip, clinging to the hope that such inhumanity couldn't be a reality.

Outside, the wind was strong; spring faded away, and autumn, the season of death, rushed by. The trees seemed to sense the King's awakening and chose to wither rather than confront him. I sighed; meeting the King felt like a distant possibility, and dwelling on it was just a waste of time. Once I wrapped up here, I'd head back to my world.

Cassiden was right; fitting in isn't the only rule in life. Regardless of whether the King lives or dies, I'll return to my place and live with Cassiden, practicing magic in secret. Even though this place had its charm, it wasn't home. I yearned for the comfort of home.

Choosing an outfit proved to be a momentous decision, and a dress no longer seemed fitting. After a considerable amount of time standing and pondering my wardrobe, I eventually settled on a white blouse, blue jeans, and light pink block-heel sandals that I had specially acquired for this occasion from Silverstring Street. Following a comforting warm shower and a touch of makeup, I made my way to the main hall of the house, and soon after, Liam arrived.

Liam, in his formal attire with meticulously gelled-back hair, looked incredibly well-groomed and handsome. For a moment, I couldn't help but wonder if he was perhaps a bit too polished for me. As we strolled together, I found myself awkwardly navigating my movements, feeling an unexpected discomfort now that I was walking alongside a man. Emotions and sensations within me stirred, revealing facets I never knew existed, creating a peculiar desire for his proximity. Those cells had awakened in me that I never knew I had, igniting a weird feeling of wanting his skin.

"You've not lived here, have you?" Liam asked, his voice deep and strong like fire.

"No," I responded with a smile, delicately tucking a loose strand of hair behind my ear.

The destination we were headed to lay at the far end of the street. The trees that formed a natural canopy over the street, casting cooling shadows during the day, were now adorned with numerous fireflies, each emitting a spectrum of colors. Their twinkling resembled the stars in the night sky, only a hundred times more captivating.

A wooden sign marked the spot of the restaurant, directing us towards a trail. Illuminated by standing lanterns in enchanting red, orange, and green hues, the sides of the trail beckoned us forward.

I had never stumbled upon this place before, and truth be told, I hadn't experienced the nightlife of this street. It lacked the vibrancy of the day, yet it held its own unique existence. The destination we were heading towards was nestled within the trees, seemingly on the outskirts of the academy grounds.

The warmth of the night had a soothing effect on me in ways I couldn't fully grasp—the relief of my nagging thoughts, the gentle rustle of leaves, and the tranquility of it all. It felt like a healing balm.

The restaurant itself was an open-air structure, entirely constructed from bamboo. The roof was adorned with lanterns akin to the ones along the path, and the deck railing was outlined with delicate rice lights. These details often made me momentarily forget that I was in a different world, as they resembled the festive lights seen on a Christmas tree. However, here, they weren't powered by electricity; instead, they relied on small energy balls that had a limited lifespan of weeks or months, requiring periodic replacement. Instead of a simple light switch, a shutter was used to control the illumination, acting as a shield for the energy-generated light wherever it wasn't needed.

"Mind if I order for us? I'd like you to try some dishes from Ariesque that I love," Liam suggested.

I nodded, feeling a bit overwhelmed after scanning the menu. "Why did you leave the academy for a few days?" I inquired, my hands supporting my face as I studied his features, committing them to memory.

Liam chuckled huskily; a touch of nervousness evident on his face. "I had family matters to attend to," he explained, raising his hand to summon the waiting satyr and proceeded to place our order.

I observed him as he pointed at the menu, exchanged smiles and nods with the satyr, and engaged in friendly banter. Liam seemed like a character from a fairytale, almost unreal. The satyr walked away with the order. "So, where were we, Elora?" he asked, smiling, a reminder of how opposite we were. Yet, as the saying goes, 'opposites attract.' I loved it when he said my name; it gave me a small dose of euphoria.

"I'd appreciate knowing more about your family," I said, attempting to gauge whether he matched my preconceived notions.

"My family…" Liam began, trying to buy some time. "My father works in the royal court, and my mother is a housewife," he shared.

I narrowed my eyes at him, sensing there might be more to the story. "Royal court?" I asked, my curiosity piqued as I searched for any inadvertent clue about whether he could be the son of the crown prince, who would likely be starting high-level studies around the same time as me. The thought lingered: would our relationship change if he turned out to be a prince? Should I ease up on my detective work and just go with the flow, waiting for him to trust me enough to share?

"Umm… yes. He's a Royal Advocate, you know… presents on behalf of the royal family," Liam explained.

I couldn't quite tell if he was proud of his family or simply sharing information. Nevertheless, I grinned, recognizing a hint of nervousness in him, just like in me. It seemed as though he navigated pressure well, as if he encountered such situations frequently and knew how to handle them.

We made an effort to keep the conversation flowing smoothly, delving into even the silliest questions like his favorite color (gray) or my thoughts on Silverstring Academy. However, Liam's inquiries leaned towards the logical side; he seemed to prefer straightforwardness in his approach.

He even inquired about my parents, and I truthfully explained that they were no longer alive, emphasizing that they had passed away for a noble cause. I sensed a subtle judgmental undertone in his expressions whenever wrongdoers were mentioned, even though he never explicitly commented on it.

The dish Liam had ordered was steak with a violet sauce in a small cup. The sauce had a fruity but not overpowering flavor, reminiscent of the subtle sweetness that hides behind the savory notes of dried fruits. Accompanying the steak were mashed potatoes with winter odde, a local herb, and grilled balsamic mushrooms.

"So, what's your take on this side of the world? Has it been treating you well?" Liam asked, slicing through the meat and taking a bite.

"Well, it has its ups and downs."

"Oh, and Professor Iving's classes. Have you started them?" he inquired, covering his mouth while speaking.

"Not yet, the first one is tomorrow evening."

He then delved into his observations about my performance in defensive magic, expressing his surprise at my proficiency. I could only nod in response because, despite not wanting to discuss the matter, that was the reality. He then shifted the conversation to my power mark, asking whether I felt any different, mentioning an itching sensation he had experienced the day before receiving his own mark. As the date continued, Liam's fascination with the gold power mark dominated the conversation. It became increasingly monotonous, but such twists were not uncommon on dates, or were they? Despite finding it dull, I nodded along to every word he said, acknowledging his enthusiasm for the topic.

When he finally suggested getting ice cream, I responded with a nod, maintaining the pattern of our interaction. He hesitated, rubbing the nape of his neck, and asked, "I'm not boring you, am I?"

I wanted to be honest and say yes, but I opted for a diplomatic "No, not at all," accompanied by a slightly lamenting sigh. He didn't seem to notice, as he was busy placing an order for both of us.

Our ice cream arrived in glass bowls. "Snow honey wafer," he declared, and I eagerly took a taste. The ice cream melted beautifully in my mouth, dominated by the flavors of vanilla, thick honey, chocolate fudge, and crispy wafer bits that made a satisfying crunch with every bite. Liam's choices, it seemed, were crafted to perfection, just like him.

After dessert, we strolled back down the street. It was now empty, and we were running late, nearing the 11 pm curfew. I rubbed my arms, feeling the chill more than I had anticipated. I couldn't wait to retreat to my warm bed, cocooned beneath a blanket, seeking comfort away from the world.

The warmth of my thoughts seemed to seep into my blood, but it was his arms around me, not my thoughts that heated me. He pulled me closer to his chest, and though I felt a bit unnerved, it was reminiscent of hot chocolate flowing down my throat on a cold winter's day. Fortunately, we made it just a few minutes before curfew, avoiding the potential ordeal of facing Iving.

He walked me to my housing unit, standing by the door, watching me as I held the doorknob with longing eyes, causing me to prolong the process. I smiled and waved good night to him, pushing the door open, but before I could enter...

"There are times when I'm able to withhold my emotions, but in times like these..." Liam began.

"I don't understand," I whispered.

Before I could grasp what was happening, his lips pressed onto mine. Initially stunned, I didn't move, my eyes wide open at the sudden approach, and then I gave in, parting my lips for him.

"Liam!" a voice came from behind me. I felt agitated, and Liam broke away.

"What!" Liam sounded annoyed, rolling his eyes at Iverson behind me. "I must tell you something!" he said urgently.

Liam winked at me, awakening the romantic cells within me, and walked along with Iverson toward the balcony, engaged in a deep discussion. I entered my room, pushed the door closed, and leaned on it, holding my breath. It was happening, and I wanted to scream, to wake the entire campus, and announce that I was in love.

Part of me felt relieved that things halted just as they were picking up speed, but another part of me felt disappointed because I craved more. However, I wasn't sure if I wanted 'more' as a temporary diversion from the haunting image of my mother.

Monday evening, after dinner, I moved through the corridors of the magic zone toward Iving's class, the low lighting displayed the odd time when nobody would be around. Iving was waiting, leaning against the wall, hand on his head, eyes closed in contemplation.

Clearing my throat and clutching my sling bag, I made my presence known. "Come in, Bates," he said calmly, his tone unusually casual, which filled me with a sense of dread. This calmness often meant impending joy for him, derived from my inevitable struggles. I was growing increasingly uncomfortable around him.

"Your efforts in defensive magic do not satisfy me," he stated, and for a brief moment, it felt like Iving wore an expression of concern. Yet, that couldn't be possible; I was just an obstacle in his path that he needed to eliminate. Maybe I had misinterpreted his weariness as concern because he didn't exhibit the typical attitude of wanting to crush me. In fact, he hadn't been overly harsh in the past few classes since returning from his brief vacation. Unsure of how to respond, I chose to remain silent.

"I don't see students as bugs to be squished," his voice reverted to its usual unwelcoming tone.

"But …But …but …"

"Now sit down. I'm tired of this, so let's get done with mind invasion quickly. Show me what you've got," he said patiently, his eyelids partially closed.

As he began to invade my mind, his eyes started to grow blank. I tried every method I had come across during my research—keeping my mind blank, honing my barrier skills—but nothing seemed to work. To my surprise, he breached my barriers not once, not twice, but three times in just a minute. It felt like Iving was pushing harder on me, channeling years of resentment into this moment.

Abruptly, he stopped, his breathing haggard, clearly depleted to the worst. I sat there, sweating profusely, but I hadn't tapped out—it was him.

"10 minutes," he called, moving to the window, gazing into the distance. Fatigue was overwhelming me, but I was determined not to give in so easily.

"Professor, I can see that you're exhausted. Maybe we could continue on another day?" I suggested, expressing genuine concern.

"No, Professor Sherwood wanted to see you. Maybe you could pay him a visit before we continue," he replied.

"Why, sir? Is something the matter?"

"I believe you have received a letter."

I headed to Sherwood's office, located on the topmost floor. The letter must have been from Cassiden, which seemed clear, but why was it marked as 'urgent'? During the term, we don't have contact with anyone, and in case of an emergency, letters are typically passed on to the headmaster.

"Please sit down and spare me a moment, Bates," Sherwood requested before leaving, closing the door behind him.

With nothing else to do, I wandered around the room. Sherwood's taste in books leaned toward the historical side, despite the presence of fantasy, mystery, and crime books on the shelf. Playing with the hourglass on his desk, I eventually strolled towards the wide window next to his desk, observing the view from his office.

In the distance, the faint lights of the trees on Silverstring Street could be seen, and beyond that, the black mountains of the night. The clock on his desk indicated an hour left before curfew. The window was still covered in dirt, but a peculiar artifact, a hand mirror, lay on the sill. As I held it, I noticed its unique design, and there was writing on its handle: '*Speculum Mortis.*'

The door opened, and I quickly placed the mirror back. Sherwood paused momentarily at my action but ignored it, shutting the door and returning to his seat. "Child, your guardian requested for you to return," he huffed, gazing at the edge of his table. I waited for him to continue, and when he said nothing, I inquired, "My return?"

"Yes, you must have heard the news about the King?" I nodded.

"I've been receiving quite a few letters recently."

He opened his drawer, pulled out an ordinary brown envelope from the pile of letters, and handed it to me. I extracted the letter through the torn edge of the envelope. The letter read:

'Dear Elora,

You must return home, Crystal Valley, house 9. I now know the reason behind your mother's demand to keep you in the ordinary world before she died. I've re-read the letters your mother would write to me, and it all makes sense. Your father may be alive! He may be looking for you. You must hurry back! We must return. It was your father, he's the killer.

Hurry!
Love,

Cassiden Anderson'

"I'm sorry! What?" I exclaimed loudly, bewildered by his explanation. Sherwood continued to look at me, now raising his eyebrows.

"It seems like your guardian believes that your father may be alive and maybe seeking you."

"No! My parents were killed, and Maldeus did it... he made Arist—and what letters is he talking about? My mother's letters? I never knew he had—Why would he sign out as 'Cassiden Anderson'—what. The. Actual. Nonsense. Cassiden would never write like this to me. He would just pick me up from the station. A killer? My father—what?" Then a thought struck me. "Is Maldeus my...?"

The question sounded bizarre, but I had to clear my doubt before the idea took root in me because he had awakened now.

"No, but have you ever heard of the identity of Aristera?" he ignited curiosity within me, confidently.

"No, but how is that related to..." I halted and looked at him. He gave a soothing smile, nodding.

"Are you saying there is a possibility that Aristera is my father?" When he didn't respond, I stared at him, my stomach sinking.

Anger surged within me—anger I had never felt before. My entire life flashed before me.

"Be you, Elora, that's all you need to survive," Cassiden said. "Look, it's imbecile," the boys chuckled; in the center of them all was Maurilio—the fluff turned green—"What about your father?" Ziva asked. "Elora," the woman in the white gown cried. The king's awake—Liam's face shone, his well-defined jaw and his eyes—

"Elora?" Sherwood called, noticing the stony expression on my face. "You must choose whether you wish to return or continue your studies?"

"Who are you, sir?" I asked, squinting my eyes at him, and adding the 'sir' at the end out of mere tradition.

"I'm sorry?" He feigned innocence, but his eyes betrayed a different story. They gleamed, and I couldn't discern whether they harbored good or ill intentions.

"Nobody knows Aristera or his affairs, and how is it that you know?" I challenged.

"Open your eyes and see, Elora. Having eyes and turning a blind eye is purely thick," he responded.

I continued to stare at him.

"Elora, knowledge is not evil. But I assure you, he is not me."

"And how do I know that?" I couldn't trust anybody; I couldn't do anything without doubt anymore. I had only myself. Maybe.

"Your mother carved Aristera's name while on her deathbed. Your father's name has never been revealed. Doesn't it sound suspicious? Even the best agents, once dead, find their names out. So that leaves the conclusion that he may not be dead, or he was Aristera. But mind you, every past Aristera's name is known. Your father is alive."

I moved back, his words sinking in. "You lie," I scoffed, "My parents were killed because they fought for goodness."

This was not true; this could never be true. "Don't live in denial unless you have evidence. If your father is Aristera, then he is not a witness of goodness only."

"Why do you know so much about my mother? My mother was not the only one who died…"

"Your mother's death was a peculiar case—The only case to prove Aristera's crimes, and if you still question my identity, then know that Her Majesty Queen Frigga would not allow evil to be within her premises," he stated a fact, and I rose, having nothing left to argue or prove.

"Then I shall stay where Her Majesty is." A wild, rebellious attitude grew in me.

He smirked, and before the door shut, he added, "Wise choice, indeed."

I tried grabbing the walls, but they were solid, causing air to slip through my fingers. I fell to the floor, trying to breathe out the suffocation of putting on a mask. I was not sad, but my eyes were teary and warm. I walked back to Iving's class, my body tightening, my muscles readying themselves for war.

Iving was sitting upright with his eyes closed. I didn't have to reveal my presence this time; he just knew and declared, "Back to work." But I was not feeling great; I felt overwhelmed. The huge glass panel that hid me from the truth just broke.

"Can I leave? I have too much on my mind to…" I tried asking him politely, but an unkind attitude still crept up.

He began invading my mind without any warning, but I refused to accept his intrusion. I shut my eyes tightly, attempting to quell the rising anger. After a moment, I opened my eyes, releasing my gritted teeth in a defiant stance. In that instant, Iving found himself backed against the wall, cornered, confronting a formidable golden lion that emerged from my gaze.

The majestic creature roared vehemently, echoing like a resounding trumpet, delivering a clear message: 'NO.'

The intensity of the roar filled the space, creating an aura of authority and strength.

Despite the imposing sight, Iving, though visibly shaken, managed to maintain his composure. He stared back into the lion's empty sockets, displaying a resilience to the force confronting him. As quickly as it had appeared, the golden lion vanished into thin air, leaving a trail of glitter that gently descended to the floor. The room was left with a lingering sense of the powerful stand I had taken against the invasion of my thoughts.

Chapter 8
Andronicus's Day

"Some of the important potions used by the Magaime Corporation and, of course, without objection, the royal regime too, are plants that are illegal to grow without permission, but the academy carries the privilege to conduct teaching practically due to its location. But I do hope the word 'illegal' fits into your egg-sized brain."

Orson carefully scanned us.

"Can anyone tell me what those plants are? Yes, Ms. Anson?"

All eyes turned to Ziva, but I didn't bother because I knew of her potential. "The brew of truth or Dispuverum, strength concoction or Viramplio, weakening potion and…" Ziva tried hard to remember while Orson waited. "The memory-erasing potion, Professor."

"Yes, Ms. Weber, that is correct. But raise your hand the next time," she warned.

Bexley ignored the warning, giving Ziva a sardonic smile who, in turn, rolled her eyes. Nerds, fascinating creatures.

Professor Orson picked one of the potted plants and a picture along with it. "Dispuverum, the plant used to make the brew of truth." The plant was like a stick rooted to the soil, it was stiff and yellow with several thorns protruding. "The brew is made by using the flesh of Dispuverum, which is gel-like after taking the hard outer wall. It is mixed with urchin tears, nymph dust, and other confidential ingredients. The latter, nymph dust, is very rare to get because it comes from the dead remains of a nymph spirit."

She then picked up another plant along with its picture, giving a clearer idea; it was moss floating in dirty brown water rooted to the soil through one single string-like root. The moss was bright red.

"Viramplio is the main ingredient to make the Strengthening potion; the moss is boiled along with quicksilver, lacewing flies, and dragon scales. Again, dragons have gone extinct, therefore this is not an easy potion. Here again, nymph dust is crucial. This potion is almost becoming extinct. Although I must say, experts are trying to replicate dragon scales in the laboratory."

She placed Viramplio down, lifting another image and plant with a hay-like texture.

"Adynamosis. The weakening portion, found illegally very often among criminals."

Orson raised a forefinger toward the crowd and picked the last one, leaving the entire crowd's attention to her actions.

"Memormina…" she said with dangerous calmness in her voice, resembling the odd vibe the plant gave. It reminded me of cattails except that it was a shining green plant with a silver flower.

"Would anyone care to elaborate on why it is dangerous? Anyone, other than Weber and Anson? Yes, Iverson."

"Memormina is a concoction used against X-level criminals without enough evidence to condemn since they are a threat to Ariesque."

"Yes, yes but do you know why…" she sounded demanding, impatiently waiting for the main point. His eyes faltered to mine, and he held the stare for a few moments, the sadness in his eyes creating an unspoken connection between us. His eyes were calling for help, a plea for understanding or assistance. This expression appeared quite often nowadays, and while I pitied him, there was nothing I could do.

"Because," He cut her with his eyebrows raised, "Because it completely makes you unknown to this world."

"Exactly." Orson smiled at him, and it seemed like the first in a very long time. "For it is not the ray of hair or the beauty of one's skin that makes one unique, it is the very memory that lies in your soul that makes you who you are. And losing one's soul is the most dangerous of all."

Within moments, the speck of wisdom died in her eyes, and knowledge began pouring.

"The silveriness comes from the liquid or the blood of the plant; the flower without its blood is transparent, and this is the reason why the stem appears shiny. Beautiful, yes, but a single drop of this mixed with your magical dust, and your memories will be new as a baby about this world."

I raised my hand, "Even if you forget, what of your magical abilities?"

Orson decided to answer my question with her question, "Tell me, Bates. Is magic what makes the ordinary different from us? Do you think you would be able to wield power if you thought magic was a fantasy? Of course, having magical genes is a whole different story. But a lot of people, born with magical genes, never make it to this side of the world because indirectly, they don't believe in magic."

Orson also showed us deliria, susciatin, and soporos; the most common plants found in bars and pubs with illegal origins. These plants are common hallucinogens. We could not brew these concoctions in groups, and neither did Orson display the procedure on her own with the excuse of respecting our laws, and that seeing these plants itself was great.

After this class, we had defensive magic class, and Iving did not seem to be in a good mood, which wasn't new at this point. However, according to most students, Iving's classes were the second-best in terms of interaction and teaching. I don't know how he managed to reach that high place, but it was not true from my perspective.

Iving is a bully to me; he makes me want to curl up in bed and avoid his classes as much as possible. The worst of all was that I could have seen him as the second-best professor in the academy, had it not been for the grudge he held against me for making it into his house without prior notice.

Today's lesson was about methods of defense found in the forest that could be lethal to us.

"There are two most common, well-known displays of fear one can find in this place," raising his forefinger. "The pool of the dead," then raising his middle finger, "and mind invasion as a tactic to introduce fear." The pool of the dead is found mostly in the forest as a trick used to avoid invaders, and yes, it is present within the Soul Forest.

"It is used in such a way that if a traveler invades the protected area and comes across the pool, the outsider will see the near-death body of a living soul dear to him. The steam that rises from the pool at the root of Equis calls upon the invader the moment he inhales it. It is nothing but an illusion, but the illusion presented is so real that most invaders drown."

He lectured us about the creation of shields as protection against any form of matter—liquid, solid, and gas—while looking at everyone in the eye except me. It was because of the event that took place during the extra class that I had no control over.

Even though it made a great escape, I felt like an outlaw, but it was better than having his eyes pinned on me all the time, waiting for an excuse to scold me. Since that day, I've been able to sit in his class with my head up, and the best part was that my extra classes were done.

At dinner, Sherwood presented an announcement that completely grabbed my interest. Andronicus's day was approaching on the 20th of December, the upcoming Thursday, and like every year, the academy was planning an event. "A day in the forest. A flag. No arms, no help, it will be only you and your teammates," he stated.

"But sir…" screamed a boy from Eromen, "What about His Majesty King Maxwell," he forced respect for that name.

"What about him?" Sherwood questioned back.

"The academy has organized this event even before, during his reign when he was awake. If Her Majesty Queen Frigga rules, you have nothing to worry about, and this is something I keep telling your parents and guardians. Unless the king personally seeks you…" he smirked, brightening the mood.

"But that does not guarantee you returning without wounds. The headmaster of Imperium here will take care of organizing the event, but know that life-threatening harm is possible."

I woke up the next morning with the same usual story playing in my mind, a devoid image of my father's act, my mother's dead body. I spoke to no one about it, neither Bran nor Ziva. How could I have told them?

I couldn't even tell Liam about it, and every time he tried to make his move, I couldn't reciprocate. The trust that lived within me has broken since Sherwood gave his conclusion that Aristera, who killed my family, may be my father. The sacred bond of 'love' has shattered.

Even though I was distant and appeared as an uncaring woman to Liam, he was very understanding, but I could see his frustration, which he would pretend did not exist. I would lock up my thoughts in the same box within my mind every day and hide them within the deepest cupboard so that I could go about my day without my insides seething with anger, but during the most intimate moments, I would lose my hold. How must my mother have felt when her husband killed her because of some unknown reason? My father broke that link that keeps all relationships sane, and having that link break at her last breath must have annihilated her.

As requested by Iving, all the Imperium gathered at the house hall. Liam was there too, but I avoided eye contact. Liam had the key to open the door to my heart, but the key was rusty; it broke while unlocking, and a part of it now remains in that still unlocked door, causing the bulkiness I feel.

I knew Bran noticed all this, and he put in the effort to ask me about it, but I just smiled and said, "Oh, you know, the usual couple's nonsense," with an eye roll to make it sound genuine. But his awkward smile said he didn't buy it. "Those interested in taking part in the event, step forward," Iving said monotonously. Maurilio didn't even hesitate, before Iving could even complete his sentence. Kato Lee, a thin girl with a monolid, and Nathan George from level 2 came forward too.

"Is that it?" Iving scoffed. "Come on now, don't be shy!"

Another girl, who seemed to be thinking carefully, stepped forward even though she was blinking repeatedly.

"One?" Iving chuckled, and then his face turned hard as stone. "It's your day, and the hesitation to step up is so in the sky. Such weaklings!" He spat, but nobody stepped up. Everyone looked at each other, waiting for someone to claim the last place. "Hurry up. The event requires five from each house."

Oh, the silence.

The sheer death silence when my feet automatically walked up.

"It's not the time to joke…" Bran laughed nervously at my decision. Even Iving sneered at my audacity, but I was going to do this and prove my place here. I whispered the same back to Bran, and he whispered back aggressively, saying that there were better challenges to life than the forest. The entire crowd silently watched our continuous inaudible argument.

"Are you sure about this, girl?" Iving questioned me, huffing a breath when he realized I was serious about my decision and that he had no other possible option unless someone else stepped up, which didn't seem likely. My eyes unwillingly turned toward Liam, who glared at my decision.

"Why is this even such a big deal? I hold the greatest power among them all," I merely stated a fact with arms open while looking at Iving but occasionally glancing at Liam, to whom I wanted these words to reach.

Iving thought deeply while looking at me and then to the rest, "Very well then. You all have been warned… Lunch break at my room," he dismissed the crowd.

The strategy we discussed during the lunch break was simple. According to Iving, the flag of each team would be placed 30 miles away from the academy in either the north, east, or south direction. So, facing the other team would be very improbable unless one of the teams moves out of track.

There would be no possible method to take a shortcut, and the flag would be placed on the morning of the 21st—meaning we had to spend the night in the forest. Each team will be given a tracker, and any important announcement will be shared by a spiritual being. They will also be given other relevant information such as team elimination, route change, game decisions, etc., through the being.

Nobody will be allowed to pass the 42-mile barrier that will be marked, and given the map in the tracker, it will be impossible to go off track.

Iving advised us to camp 5 miles before the marked location of the flag because if we camped at the location of the flag, then we would have to battle the creature placing the flag there the next morning, which would be an important matter that the other teams would neglect for two reasons. Firstly, the distance to be covered was vast and secondly, a lake was present as an arc around the 40-mile radius from the campus.

Iving gave us a big help when he declared that the entire goal of this event was to test normal skills, not magical. A battle in the forest is something that may not even take place, nor would we be required to defend ourselves from creatures, but there could be a very small possibility, and that we were to be alert and prepare, either way, aiming mainly to hone our defensive skills.

Nathan George, the one with the best abilities and by far the most experienced in a forest setting due to his love for hiking and camping, was appointed leader, and it was the best choice speaking fact-wise. Charlotte Jude was picked to co-lead the group.

After quite some heavy discussion, I left for the final class of the day, Skill Magic, taught by Professor Martin, who had a hawk-like nose, an unusually thin oval face, and wore half-framed glasses. He seemed to have a bit of a hearing problem because whenever a student yelled at the right, he often turned toward the left to find out the source of the noise.

"Now that you are familiar with how to create dimensional storage, dimensional multiplication, and ability to dive and…" every word that came out of his mouth was as slow as a sloth, "…read auras, the art of levitation."

He paused, trying to remember, and then shrugged it off, "Oh well, we'll be learning evocation and liquid transformation today."

Martin's every slow movement, every action, and the very words that came out of his mouth were beginning to ignite irritation in me. His voice was so dull that he sounded on his deathbed. He needed to be replaced soon.

"Turn to chapter fifteen, and start reading. If anybody has any doubt, please tell me."

He sat down, slouching behind his desk, covering his face with a book, but he already seemed to be dozing off. Nobody except Bexley and Ziva, as always, seemed to be delighted at reading the textbook because the moment the class realized Martin was gone.

We decided to utilize this time to talk about the most recent gossip, recent news which was Andronicus Day, the King, winter vacation, and Rita Neuer who had left the academy for good after her parents had summoned her. I was in on it too, but the moment I met Liam's eyes, even I followed in Bexley's footsteps. I was not up for a confrontation, and I knew after class there would be a wild discussion regarding my decision, but I didn't know why I'd decided to take part.

It was just a spur of the moment, and I don't regret it. The rebellious side in me has awakened, and now it just won't sleep.

Basic Skills:
Evocation skill
The ability to summon objects close without physically approaching them.
How to learn:
1. Raise your hand toward the desired object.
2. Picture it clearly within your mind. (To help picture it clearly, you may close your eyes.)
3. Feel the object tugging toward your hand.

"Elora," her voice swayed, she was choking on her breath, "Please..." she pushed her hand further and further toward me, and I didn't try too hard to grab the hand of the woman in the white gown. I knew I wouldn't be able to. I knew this wasn't real. I closed my eyes, standing before her. Waiting for this to end. But then she didn't ask for help.

"Run, Elora," she alerted.

My eyes opened at her words, returning to reality. It was Bran who shook me, "Elora? You okay?"

There was a snow flurry outside, but sweat was dripping down my forehead.

"The same?" he asked, he knew even though I had not hinted anything.

Cold shivers ran down my arm, I nodded. He didn't push; even though I saw his fist form on the side.

"Here," He tossed papers onto my table, "When Ziva heard the news, she spent her whole afternoon for you. You've wasted a bookworm's time…" he grinned, "You've got only a week. Work hard."

I scanned through the sheets on my desk. They contained well-done research on the Soul Forest, its dangers, survival tactics, and all. What would I do without her!

"Wonderful!" I exclaimed and then gave him a scrutinizing look. Why was he doing this? Where did all the yelling go?

"Elora, I know you. You sound normal but you are not."

"What's that supposed to mean? Did. You. Just. Call me. Insane?" I pierced a look at him.

"Oh, no-no." he clarified, sitting up straight.

"I know that things between you and Liam are heated, and I know something's bothering you, and I don't want you to feel pressured to tell me all this. But you need to know that I'm here. The struggles of life are too much for one person to bear alone."

Professor Martin woke with the sound of a book banging onto the floor and started speaking like everyone was performing their task with sheer sincerity and obedience.

"Now then… we'll be practicing the spells you read. Who'd like to go first," he sounded crackly and in half-sleep.

"Ahh… Ms. Weber, com'on up," his voice got less crackly with each new dialogue.

"I want you to stand here and try the evocation skill on that chalk."

Bexley raised her hand and followed the text word to word; extremely light green waves began radiating from her hand.

"No, Ms. Weber, without power. Just by your state of mind."

The chalk stayed in the same place for several minutes after which Professor Martin's fuel of patience ended.

"That's alright Ms. Weber, it's only your first…" The chalk began to rattle, and slowly inch by inch, it levitated off the slate. Ziva's mouth dropped open, but the chalk fell, breaking into two halves.

Bexley looked disappointed at her effort even though Professor Martin assured her that only a handful of people can summon objects without reaching levitation on their first attempt. He patted her shoulders.

After Martin showed us the evocation spell, we tried to perform liquid transformation by transforming water into oil. This seemed much harder as compared to levitation; I had managed to get only a single oil droplet on the surface of the water. But that couldn't be considered as a conclusion since I didn't even attempt the evocation skill.

It didn't take much time for Andronicus Day to arrive. I was equally excited and nervous, sometimes pondering whether this decision of mine was right. Hoping I wouldn't be a liability to the group, but that shouldn't be an issue since I had the gold mark; this level must have some perks.

The competition began on the dawn of 20th December when the sun was on the verge of rising, and the visibility of the forest was almost non-existent due to the fog clouding the opening of the forest. Melted snow covered the ground and the leaves—the weather had clearly been tampered with; it was not cold. Just your average summer evening, with wetness.

We bid goodbye at the academy gates, each carrying a hiking bag, into a haven filled with unknowns to us. The academy had suspended its lessons from now until the end of winter break, so it was not mandatory for students to remain in the academy for Imperium's Day, and such was usually the case with Eromen's Day, which is celebrated on the 2nd of March.

Iving arranged and confirmed with the Queen of the Forest all the possible safety arrangements and precautions to ensure our safety and the welfare of the creatures of the forest.

Sherwood spoke out the rules, some of which included no killing and harming the creatures unless placed in a life-threatening situation, Satyrs would be keeping a hidden eye and passing on information, no tampering with the trackers, and so on.

Slashing through the dense thicket, we made our way into the depths of the forest, carrying a bag filled with necessities—survival equipment, a water bottle, mini-tents, and sleeping bags. We were led by Nathan, the appointed leader who held the main tracker guiding the way. The tracker was a transparent glass-like device through which the soil could be seen if you held it perpendicularly.

The early morning forest failed to live up to my expectations of pleasantness. I found myself drenched in sweat, and the incessant impact of heavy raindrops on my head was becoming increasingly irksome. Despite my discomfort, the invigorating scent of wet soil remained a source of delight, even though I wasn't particularly fond of walking in these conditions.

Our journey continued for several hours, with intermittent breaks to rest and replenish our energy. Our final destination was determined when Nathan and Jude identified an ideal dry spot for camping, located approximately 7 miles away from the flag site according to the tracker.

Having journeyed this far, the most challenging aspect confronted us – the depletion of our magical energy. Even if we had enough, the need to conserve it for potential emergencies took precedence. The expenditure of magical energy in combat was twice as draining as the usual physical exertion. Additionally, the absence of water for the night emerged as an unforeseen obstacle, catching us unprepared.

Acknowledging the situation, Nathan proposed a strategic division of the team. Three members would explore the forest's surroundings, scavenging for essential supplies such as food and water. Simultaneously, Two would remain behind to establish the camp and kindle a vital campfire. The plan aimed to optimize our chances of survival during Andronicus Day in the Soul Forest.

However, as our fatigue became increasingly apparent, I reached a point where I could no longer continue walking. I made the decision to stay back, a choice motivated by both physical exhaustion and the need to preserve my magical energy.

Despite my reluctance, Maurilio also decided to stay back, expressing his intention to help with our preparations. The prospect of being alone with him in this situation made me uncomfortable, but my weariness overshadowed any concerns. I remained silent, accepting the situation and my decision.

Once the others departed, Maurilio and I began on the task of setting up our tent. He skillfully unfolded the tent cloth, while I organized and sorted the various parts. The process unfolded in silence, with both of us diligently following the instructions provided. A sense of accomplishment washed over me as we completed the first tent, standing tall and secure. However, the realization that this was just the beginning sank in, and a sigh escaped me as we began assembling the next one.

As we progressed through the tents, my exhaustion became more pronounced. Numbness crept into my legs, and the onset of a headache added to my discomfort. At this point, Bran's warning echoed in my mind – perhaps this endeavor wasn't such a wise choice. The cozy bed back at the academy seemed far more appealing than enduring the challenges of Andronicus Day in the Soul Forest.

Despite my incessant complaints and whining directed at Maurilio over trivial matters, his silent and patient demeanor towards me was truly impressive. The journey through the forest had drained me, and I couldn't even think of going any further.

"Let's rest for some time," I pleaded with exhaustion evident in my voice.

"Just a little more, Elora," Maurilio calmly insisted, scanning the area for security while I clung to his hands, sitting on the ground and pleading for respite. I felt the warmth of his hand enclosing mine. The firmness of his skin against mine, the subtle angling of his fingers, all creating an unexpected closeness.

I must have looked pathetic, pleading but in this moment, I couldn't bring myself to care about how I must have looked.

My indifference extended to everything and everyone – I don't care about anything or anyone anymore, my life is going to play along with the happiness it finds, doesn't matter even if it meant causing pain to someone else.

"We need to collect dry sticks for a fire," Maurilio gently pulled back on my hands, trying to redirect my attention to the task at hand. His fingers traced soothing lines on my palm, creating a gentle rhythm that seemed to fade the weariness in my bones. The forest sounds faded into the background, and for that brief moment, it was just Maurilio's touch and the palpable connection between us.

His face bathed in the warm hues of the setting sun, his contours defined by the golden glow, he appeared almost immaculate. However, the beauty of the moment became overshadowed by an unexpected awareness, and Liam face flashed before my eyes. Panic seized me, and I instinctively pulled away. Maurilio detected the discomfort etched across my face and took a step back. I purposefully avoided eye-contact.

I observed him as he gracefully approached a shrub of berries that had captured his attention. In that moment, the realization dawned on me that he had evolved from the boy he once was, shedding the layers of his past persona to emerge as someone entirely new. He had transformed into a well-built man, not only in terms of physical stature but also in terms of mental strength.

"Yeah, right!" I rolled my eyes sarcastically, bringing my old self back and attempting to extinguish any awkwardness. "Look at all the dryness around you." My snarky comment, even though was a feeble attempt to mask my current situation did not go unnoticed by Maurilio. "No stop!" I exclaimed, "That's elderberry. Unless you want us all dead, don't take those."

He looked at me, tilting his head in one direction, lowered his brows, and then took in my warning by nodding.

"There," I pointed, "Wild plums."

He watched me point at the tree and followed my instructions. Every time he raised his feet to pluck, I watched his white t-shirt rise reveal the lines on his abdomen.

Finally, he broke the hours-long 'stranger silence.' It seemed as though he was engaged in a mental debate, contemplating whether he should initiate a conversation or maintain the prevailing quietness.

"Where'd you get such knowledge?" he said, still avoiding direct eye contact.

"I read up," I replied, now rising to my feet.

He collected whatever dried leaves and twigs he could find from the ground, and I followed him, inadvertently studying the contours of his face. The tension between us seemed to dissipate when he decided to break the silence with a direct and closed question.

"Is your father, Aristera?"

I stopped dead in my tracks, frozen, staring. How did he know all this? He turned to face me, noting my silence.

"Oh, the night you were drunk. You were muttering that."

The upper half of my body moved forward in confusion. I had to play it smart, my eyes tracking his every move like a predator. I nodded, the memory resurfacing. "Right, that night," I acknowledged, my mind briefly revisiting the intense conversation with Sherwood and the confrontation with Iving that had brought out my fierce side.

He threw his collection on the ground, making the leaves scatter and silently handed me a bottle of water.

"Thank you." I snatched the bottle from him.

"I was drunk, of course," I said, using it as an excuse, "Drunk people spurt nonsense all the time…"

He watched me and then silently nodded, not buying my excuse. After clearing the ground of leaves and building dry soil onto which he could light fire, he gathered large rocks, built a circle, and began throwing the wood he had collected within it, lighting a fire using a matchstick. Even though I could manipulate Earth, he didn't ask me for help. However, my powers were useless here since it required good energy, and I lacked proper breath after such heavy exertion of my body.

We sat down, supporting our backs against a log, waiting, meditating in the silence, listening to the crackling noise of the fire, and feeling nature's affection.

"Yeah, and I'm the Prince," he stated like he was continuing our conversation. He placed his elbow on the log behind so that his broad shoulders protruded forward, displaying his wide clavicle, hidden behind his shirt. I laughed at his words. Lethargy gives you a completely different kind of high. Yeah, right, the prince was sitting next to me. But then he looked at me, with a straight face, and the smile on my face faded, striking a similarity with how the evening had faded into night. "Why? Do I not look like the prince?"

"No, it's not that…" I trailed, attempting to find an excuse. "Well yeah," I admitted, hoping the truth wouldn't hurt him, and tried to divert the conversation. "But why are you telling me this?"

"I saw a paper in your room, 'Reasons why Liam is Prince,' it had 5 reasons altogether…" It was a long time back, but he saw the redness on my face. "And because now we both got a terrible secret that must not get out."

Was he going through my stuff? I couldn't help but feel a tinge of annoyance, but that annoyance didn't last long because he was not judging me. He was blaming himself for that. He hit his hand against his thigh, rubbing them, more like soothing himself, his breathing was loud. He was suppressing his pain, just like that night.

"Yeah, Liam looks more like a prince, doesn't he?" He chuckled, swallowing the bitter truth.

I looked at him, surprised at his comment.

"My dad would always compare me with him, his standard of behavior, and his idea of life… Liam's THE IDEAL ONE. And you see him too, that way, don't you?" He paused, sucking the hurt. "That's how it's supposed to be, isn't it? That's how society depicts a prince to be and that's how you see a prince as too. Not a rebellious, imperfect little bully who seduces wo..."

"Oh no," I cut him off. "You're not imperfect."

Our eyes locked, and his were gray and sparkling. The familiarity struck me; they reminded me of Liam, except his weren't gray. Unlike Liam's, his eyes were not even hooded. He moved forward, his face coming within an inch of mine, and I could feel his warm breath gently caressing my cheeks. His head tilted, and his breaths climbed my neck. The proximity was unsettling; I felt a wave of guilt, realizing I was teetering on the edge of betraying Liam. I had to push him away.

"Elora. Don't. Move." His words came out through gritted teeth, and my body froze instantly. His eyes said it; there was something behind me and it was moving. The rustle of leaves, the mushy sound of the ground, and the tension in the water beneath its feet were all discernible. It moved slowly, and the atmosphere turned terrifying.

"Stay calm, don't move," he whispered with minimal movement of his lips. I strained my eyes to watch his, given how close he was. His gaze followed whatever lurked behind me. From the sound, it seemed to be moving away. Yet, we remained frozen in place, even after the noise had faded, until I could hardly feel my body, yearning for a deep breath.

"Nox-Ingurgito," he said as he slowly moved back. I paused, digesting his words.

"Did you say Nox-Ingurgito? The creature that resembles a black blanket and engulfs any living being it detects?" He nodded, and I forced a laugh to conceal my internal discomfort.

"How did you see it?"

"I was trained… I mean, we are usually trained to keep our peripheral vision open from childhood." His starlit eyes tempted me to forget everything and start anew. Their unending depth was hypnotizing, and I found myself getting lost in them.

"Why do you stick around with Liam if he makes you uncomfortable?" he asked.

"Uncomfortable is a strong word; I feel aware of myself. Liam's my childhood friend."

"Do you…" I hesitated, "know who my father…"

"Yo, ho, we're back!" The voice startled me.

"The area around is secure," he continued, breaking the intense moment. My eyes remained glued to Maurilio, curiosity lingering in the air.

"WE FOUND THESE TOO!" Kato exclaimed in happiness, tossing a round saffron-colored tomato. What was so great about a tomato?

"A tiantang?" Maurilio's eyes grew wide as the fruit landed in his hands.

I watched Maurilio, zoned out, attempting to decipher what he meant to me. It was guilt; I longed to be with Liam, and my suppressed feelings were surfacing in the company of Maurilio. But why? It's not like I did not try to reciprocate Liam's affection, and my body doesn't feel satisfied after just a few moments of intimacy with him. However, it's always after I'm with him, not during his presence that I realise this. I just can't seem to muster the ability to make a move at that time; it feels suffocating. But with Maurilio, it's different.

I wondered what made him disclose his hidden identity, prompting me to revisit the night I got drunk for the first time. After Iving's extra class, with thirty minutes left before curfew, I found myself strolling to 'Another World,' a beverage store that sold alcohol and had a club on the other side. I couldn't recall much, or anything at all, about the night; it was a blank slate in my memory after the heavy drinking.

"Yeah, the very fruit that is said to taste like heaven."

"How did you…"

"Find these? Long story! Oh, we managed to fish!" "What went on when we were away?" The leader asked.

"A nox just passed by," Maurilio informed.

"A nox!" Kato exclaimed; her energy was so overboard from finding tiantangs that she sank onto the ground.

"They're bloody scary, how are they allowed here?"

"But wait," the silent third spoke, pinning everyone's view on her terrorized face, "Aren't nox usually where there are living evil creatures?"

We paused, my heart starting to thump harder. The fire dimmed, casting large shadows, and the leaves jostled hard on the ground. A strong wind was beginning to twirl in front of us, and all of us rose.

And the next thing, my bottom crashed to the crumbly soil, and my eyes struggled to take the view of the white light before me.

A white orb busted into sight before us, my breathing became fatigued, and I was beginning to lose consciousness, but then it said, "Peace." It was a strong, peaceful male voice, and even though it did not calm me, I now turned to look at the others, the reality of unity dawning upon me.

They were all ready, standing in their defense position; Nato with his power sword blazing green, Kato with her blue shield wielded, Jude, waiting to attack with her balls of pink flames, and finally Maurilio with his eyes blazing purple in his orthodox stance, alert for further action.

Compared to them, I felt like an unintellectual being, waiting for salvation. They slowly lowered their guard when they realized it was a royal satyr.

"I bring news; Caritas has lost. Imperium and Pruden are currently in play," it said and then disappeared with a strong gust. The others completely dissolved their power, looking at me with a sense of supremacy. The campfire dwindled to a mere ash glow. Maurilio extended his hand, pulling me to my feet. I dusted off my pants but stopped short, noticing that Jude, who had moved ahead to reignite the fire, had halted as well.

The distant, angry growl echoed not only in my ears but also in the awareness of others. We all stood motionless, fixated on the silhouette of our leader, anticipating instructions. The ominous noise of the approaching beast intensified, widening our eyes in alarm. However, no visible movement accompanied the sound.

A black mist began to emanate from a corner of the camping site, and within seconds, sight became indistinguishable from blindness. Emerging from the mist was a creature—human-faced with gray skin. Its eyes were wide, reminiscent of a beast, hungry, and a deep shade of red due to the burst blood vessels. Inhaling deeply, it filled its lungs, causing its ribs to protrude from its body like it were only bone and skin.

From its waist downwards, it had gray fur, and its feet resembled the hooves of a horse, dragging a wooden tail behind. The creature's teeth were stained with blood, indicating its unsatisfied hunger.

"Run, Elora," a panicked male voice urged.

I quickly wielded my yellow sword as a last resort, but it was too late. Before I could react, I found myself airborne, my back colliding with something hard, and then everything faded to darkness.

Upon regaining consciousness, the surrounding light felt overwhelmingly sensitive. The air I breathed was fresh and clean, and the warmth on my hands felt familiar. The sense of isolation and the despair of living for a hundred years in a cave were gone. As I tried to move my almost immobile lips, a faint murmur escaped, prompting a male voice to exclaim, "She's awake."

The surroundings gradually came into focus—a blend of green, brown, and white. I lay in a state of semi-consciousness for what felt like moments or hours; time had become elusive as I watched vibrant movements around me at lightning speed. My body ached, and my eyes felt heavy. Frustration and helplessness welled up, causing tears to fall.

"Don't try," a melodious voice, tinged with brown, advised.

"You've been given a muscle tranquilizer. Rest. You won't be able to move. All is well."

Chapter 9
The Most Powerful Bond

"Good evening, Ms. Douglas. How are you doing today?" The man behind the desk greeted her without bothering to rise. His hair was slicked back, his beard and eyebrows well-groomed.

He must have grown much more handsome from back then, for he looked two times better than the King himself. His body was a lot worked out on, and he was quite buffed from the dancer body he had as a student. He defined masculinity.

"Very well, sir. Call me Grissa and…"

"How can I help you today, Grissa?" he interrupted, crossing his arms and pushing back into his seat. Grissa's lips slanted, and she released an exasperated sigh.

"Being the diplomat of Criosa must be a tough role, but I was hoping I could borrow some time. You see, the queen wishes to reveal herself to the public."

After listening with furrowed brows, he put on a reluctant smile and exclaimed, "Well, yes, of course. I cannot deny the Queen, even if it means exposing my personal life. Please take a seat," he said, pointing at the chair in front of his desk.

"Let's begin with your relationship with the Queen at the moment."

He swiveled his chair to face the window on his right. "My relationship with the Queen at the moment is solely professional."

"I'm sorry, but if you're uncomfortable with this question, then we can move on," she genuinely said after sensing his tone.

Liam turned toward her with one raised eyebrow and struck his hand onto the table, causing Grissa to freeze and stare at him.

"No, I am not uncomfortable with talking about my relationship with the Queen. I am uncomfortable with the rumors that will follow after Her Highness releases this," he then added, "The Queen and I are in no thorny relations."

Grissa's eyes lingered on the exposed skin behind the collar of his shirt, noticing the partially revealed tattoo of a bent Narcissus flower and the head of a snake looking at the flower with victorious eyes. Liam followed her gaze, rolling up his sleeves, and then turned his neck to face the light outside. The writer cleared her throat when the tattoo disappeared and went on, mustering dominance in her voice to lead the interview.

"I presume you wouldn't have any objection to talking about your past…" Liam stayed silent.

"How about you continue from where I last ended with Her Highness…" she flipped the pages in her notebook, gliding the back of the pen over her lines.

"The night before she left for Andronicus's day."

****

Liam Sprague

What could have led Elora to make that decision? More than anything in the world, I was disappointed in her. The choice to enroll in the competition was not supposed to be hers alone. I walked to her housing unit.

She was a girl, not built to stay on a battlefield. I don't care about other women, but my woman should be obedient to me. Her place was in the house, like my mother—making a house a home.

Things had not been going well between us in the past few weeks, and I didn't even know the reason. Maybe it was because I pushed her too hard, but it's hard being in a relationship with one-sided effort.

I felt hurt, and this wouldn't have been the case if I had at least a glimpse of what she was going to do. Why did she treat me like a stranger? I pushed open the door to her room without knocking, without asking permission to invade her privacy. I wanted answers today. I didn't stop walking even when she started calling my name. She walked back until the wall clashed with her back.

"Liam," she whispered, intimidated.

In that charged moment, my initial instinct urged me to step back, but I resisted the impulse and held my ground.

"What's going on between us?" I asked, the words escaping through clenched teeth. Her eyes met mine, she was so vulnerable, so fragile. She perceived my distress and responded softly, "I need space, Liam…" I acknowledged her plea; I had already given her space for weeks, yet the uncertainty lingered.

"Did I do something wrong? Am I pushing you too hard?" I sought answers in the subtle nuances of her expression.

"No…" she trailed off, fidgeting with her finger.

"DAMN IT, WOMAN," I erupted, unleashing the pent-up frustration. She flinched, but I didn't relent, locking eyes with her and pulling her closer. A gentle push from her hand signaled a breaking point in my composure. "I thought you were supposed to be comfortable enough to share your concern with me…" I fought to control my emotions, taking deep breaths and biting my lips to suppress words that might be regretted later. Finally, I uttered, "I'll give you space," and left without looking back.

****

Grissa listened to him, making a concerted effort to restrain her judgmental expression, and proceeded with the story.

She then went to the forest, it turned out to be mayhem, she woke in the hospital bed with you beside her… "Yes?"

Liam, clenching the armrest of his executive chair, tilted his head, contemplating.

"I wasn't in the academy when she woke up," he revealed, pressing his lips. "From what I'd heard, she had woken up at least 5-6 days later…"

"But she mentioned…" Grissa flipped her page again, scrutinizing her written notes. "Familiar warmth… "

"That warmth was not me."

"And how come you weren't there when she needed you?"

"She didn't tell you what happened in the forest. Did she?"

Liam met her gaze, awaiting a response. She shook her head and replied, "Not yet."

****

Liam Sprague

A significant number of students had left the academy for vacation, and among them, three Eromen and a Zocian chose to abandon their magical lives, opting for a fresh start in the normal world. The main reason for their departure was the influence of the king.

In my room, I busily packed my luggage, knowing that the competition would soon conclude. Prudens and Imperiums would return, marking the end of the event. I contemplated starting anew, hoping to leave behind the tensions with Elora. My plan was to have an open conversation with her, addressing her concerns, and supporting her without being critical.

News had arrived that Caritas had returned several hours ago. One of their team members had been attacked, sustaining a large open wound on his back. The team leader urgently sought help, signaling a disturbance that raised questions. No one, not even the wounded student, could explain how the attack had occurred.

The situation seemed peculiar, especially considering that Queen Frigga, who was known for her awareness of the forest and even the sea, was seemingly unaware of these events. The headmasters and the Queen engaged in discussions about the next steps. However, the injured boy, upon waking up, claimed he had no knowledge of what had happened.

This raised concerns, prompting a decision to cancel the competition immediately. The other teams were instructed to return. The competition was declared invalid, and an investigation was to be conducted to discern the truth from the lies. Once Elora returned, I would bid her goodbye and leave, hoping that the next time we met, things would return to the way they were in the beginning. I didn't want to lose her.

"Liam!" Amelia's urgent voice pierced through the air. She banged on the door of the housing unit.

"They're back," panic was written all over her face, "Elora is knocked out in the hospital and Kato has…" Without waiting for more details, I rushed out to find my girl, but my body clashed with another's – Maurilio.

He was covered in filth and partly limping. Blood dripped from an open wound on his cheekbone, and clotted wounds marked his neck and forehead.

"What happened?" I asked staring into those weary eyes for answers, knowing that Elora wouldn't be able to give me those if she was in a terrible condition. Expecting that she was only unconscious and that it was nothing serious, I braced myself for the worst as Maurilio struggled to convey the events. His tired body pushed forward with each limping step, and his voice cracked as only a few syllables escaped. "A... sangmons... We were attacked," he uttered.

The name, Arasangmons, resonated in my mind. Anxiety gripped me, and my eyes locked onto Maurilio, desperate for more information. Amelia emerged from my unit, bidding farewell to Maurilio and me. My initial plans to leave changed, my focus now on Maurilio's account.

His tired voice continued, recounting, while he himself struggled to understand the horrors of the competition.

"Something went wrong during the competition, and before we knew it... It was there, and I saw it strike her, and she flew in the air. It was angry, and it slashed me. I was in the air and fell into the water; I pushed and climbed out of it and immediately lost consciousness with the pain..." I assisted him onto his bed, the weight of his words sinking in.

"When I woke, the beast was dead on the ground, but nobody was in sight. I assumed that the others had been rescued and began trying to find my way back. But somewhere in the depths of the forest, after walking for, I don't know how long, in water..." His voice faltered. "I saw Elora." My entire being tensed.

"I immediately began..." His voice broke, and my heart sank. "Toward her. Tiny creatures came before me, and I swatted them away; my eyes were glued to the girl before me. I walked, water splattering with my heavy steps. Then they threw something into my eyes, and the girl disappeared. I was alone in a pool of water, with the pixies."

Worry etched across my face, and the pieces of the puzzle slowly fell into place. "The pool was at the root of Equis?" I asked, my voice heavy with realization.

"I don't remember. But I did stumble on a large root, I think," he said. "Maybe... why?"

"The pool of the dead," I stated, the truth hitting me hard. I rose, not wanting to hear more, my mind fixated on Elora.

As I reached the door, Maurilio's last words echoed in my ears. "I thought I was hallucinating at that moment, but it now makes sense... the pixies were there for a reason, not to save me but to save Elora." I stopped, the weight of his revelation settling in.

"They kept pointing in a particular direction, and I followed. I thought they were leading me back to the academy, but they led me to a tree, a dead end. I felt stupid for following them, but then they pointed upwards toward the sky. And I followed their tiny finger to look at a branch that was maybe six feet tall, and Elora was there. I brought her down, and she was totally knocked out but still breathing. Her Majesty, Queen Frigga…"

"The pixies led you there?" my hands fisted to my side.

"Yes, but…"

"You should rest, and I must leave."

****

"I'm sorry, sir! But I don't understand…" Grissa cried, genuinely confounded.

"You don't understand," he sneered, "What are you? Some fool?"

"Excuse me!" Grissa placed her palm onto the table with a low tap, having enough. "If I am talking to you with respect, I expect the same back."

He must have triggered her annoyance. The man looked at her with his chin up and hands steepled together and then questioned her.

"Tell me, Miss. If you were to walk up to the pool of the dead, what would you see?"

"The one I love the most, obviously…" She trailed, suddenly realizing. "And about the pixies, you may not know, but the widely debated area is that they can see the union bond."

"But it's only a debate…" she shrugged.

"Look at His Majesty and the Queen now, does it still look like a debated area to you?"

"No," her voice came out low, she looked away with embarrassment.

"Yes. Exactly," Liam exclaimed with superiority, "The very bond that is said to be the most powerful love bond."

"I'm really sorry," Grissa buried her head in her hands.

"What for? I may have been angry at that time, but I was not heartless. I stepped back without hesitation."

She looked at him, devouring the honesty in his eyes, and something in her eyes changed at that very moment.

"Why are you still single after that relation?" Those words hadn't simply popped out her mouth; she meant every single word that came out while still looking him straight in the eye.

"How do you know I've been single?" He smirked with a fixed gaze, moving his body toward her subconsciously.

"The very man that holds the dearest heart now carries a stone-like heart. It cannot be because he lost trust in love, nor can it be because he is in love. It must be because he has forgotten the very essence of what love felt."

The smirk on his face faded, taken aback, his eyes lost in hers.

"You seem like the commitment type of woman, not the one-night woman…" He moved back, "Miss Grissa."

Grissa crossed her arms at the formal proclamation, rubbing her arm after coming out of her trance.

"I assure you that this meeting is strictly formal within these four walls." After watching his straight-strict face, Grissa couldn't help but feel a mixture of disappointment and confusion at her disappointment.

She bowed her head, almost starting, "I'm really so…"

"Within these four walls, I said." He smiled. She stared at him, shocked at the sudden transition.

He handed her a slip of paper, "You'll be there if you felt that fling too."

"No, I would not want to go out with you, sir. This is all just a misunderstanding. I am a woman who loves the thrill of being independent. Even if I do feel something for you, I can't give up everything for you."

"Time will tell; you'll be there if you feel it." He concluded confidently, and there was silence.

"Then tell me, sir. The queen never tried to confront you about your sudden distance?"

"She may have…" He swirled the pen with his name on it. "But there were two months left, a hectic schedule, and by the end of February, finals were on. I had no clue at that time that she had too much on her mind. The younger Liam believed that she was better off, but mostly because his property was tarnished with the name of another man. I didn't even know whether she knew that they were meant to be and that she was about to marry the King; and that Iverson and she did not have much time together."

"And did you ever expect to be here, as a diplomat of Criosa?"

"No, in fact, none of the diplomats may have expected to be here. After the twelve previous diplomats received their sentence, Ariesque had almost crashed. The king had to appoint twelve people, which was a great task. He didn't want diplomats to turn out like the previous ones. So, he appointed a few from those who did royal studies and personally sent an invitation to me to take up royal studies. But even then, it was not all twelve; we were sharing responsibilities until all twelve came into play."

Chapter 10
The Man behind the Black Mask

"Your Highness, do you, by any chance, know when His Majesty would be available to meet? I've been asking Mr. Leo; he gave me a date yesterday, but His Majesty just seems to keep delaying."

"Very soon. You must have heard the news about Blue," the Queen sighed, "He was amazing! Dedicated himself entirely to Ariesque because of which the King is burdened with another task and so is Ziva of Prielvar along with Bran Becile," she maintained eye contact while rubbing her hands onto her forehead.

"Yes, it's such a shame. But must His Majesty personally attend to the matter?"

She leaned forward.

The Queen nodded, "I was to personally attend their concert as a sign of appreciation and to meet them in person but due to personal reasons, I could not. That makes his murder an indirect threat to me. You must have seen the uproar of his fans on the news. That's just the beginning; our citizens will not remain silent. I too shall leave for Prielvar tomorrow. And hopefully, the King will make time for this after I return."

****

Elora Bates 🍃

This week marked an entire year of hard work, to be judged upon in the form of final exams—an event dreaded by everyone. However, amidst the stress, there was one thing everyone looked forward to: the celebration party of Eromen's day.

The marking scheme for each exam was specific: each subject carried 100 marks, with 40 for the final written part, 30 for the final practical (which happened last week), and 30 for internal assessments on assignments. Passing with at least 50 percent in each section was mandatory. The thought of condensing an entire year's worth of knowledge into a 40-mark written exam felt like a daunting task.

Yet, there was a silver lining—the one bonus question worth a maximum of 5 marks. Optional and often unrelated to the core curriculum, this question served as a potential savior from the fear of failing.

Despite the challenges, my exams went relatively well, including defensive magic, where 'well' meant I would at least secure a 'pass' in a worst-case scenario. The Creaturology exam posed particular difficulty, given that I had the Planta Concoction exam the previous evening, leaving me with minimal time to prepare.

One question stood out: 'Forest cats are excellent hiders. Explain—3 marks.' I couldn't recall details about them, as I had skipped smaller topics in favor of focusing on more critical ones.

"Forest cats are creatures resembling ordinary cats but adorned with green thorn-like protrusions all over their bodies, including their tails. Due to these features, they easily blend into the forest environment, although they are most commonly found among lake bushes," explained Ziva later.

While I struggled with this question, I managed to secure an answer to the bonus question on Glowopus, a topic I was familiar with. Glowopus were small octopus-like creatures with wing-like fins above their entirely black eyes. They earned their name from their translucent derma, revealing greenish or bluish fluorescent innards that glowed in the deep-sea darkness. Within their skin, a pale pink round sheath enclosed their entire organs.

Liam had spoken about Glowopus before, expressing fascination and a desire to see one. The mention of Liam weighed heavy on my heart. I didn't realize that when he said he would 'give me space,' he meant forever.

"Ouch, what was that for?" I hissed discreetly, feeling a stinging pain in my head as we sat in the academy's library. Liam placed the book back on the table, crossing his arms sternly.

"I am going to kill that Bran Becile if he gives his homework to you one more time."

"It's called sharing with my best friend." I stuck my tongue out playfully, but he held my face with his hand, his expression turning sour.

"Best friend, you say? How close are you two?" His voice took on a harder tone.

"Do you do this with him?" Suddenly, he pressed his lips on mine. I looked at him wide-eyed, acutely aware that this was not a private space. I pushed him away, eyeing him.

"What? We're a couple!" He exclaimed, clarifying the nature of our relationship.

We didn't kiss. I never let him get there. He pecked my lips quite openly, but I didn't give him access. It was before our relationship went south, before my perspective on relationships changed. I wish I could turn back time and tell myself to make the most of what we had. He was true to me all that while.

"Elora, you in?" Ziva asked.

"Huh!" I rubbed the nape of my neck.

"Silverstring?" She made an annoyed declaration, "Sherwood's giving off everything for free today… a gift for the end of finals!"

"Don't go all crazy, Ziva. One item from any shop for free. See this, it's the ticket to one item," Bran clarified.

"That's quite the charity…" I gave my opinion for the sake of blending along. "He did say life won't remain the same in the coming year. Many of us won't be here… bla bla bla… true it is, though. Five from our batch left this world for good. Heaven only knows how many more will leave," Bran added in justification.

Liam would not like hoarding free items. He always lived up to a particular standard of life. He would mimic his father, saying, *"You either live with good standards that when somebody remembers you, they remember how sophisticated you were, or not live at all."*

Given that his father had such high expectations, I wonder how he lived. But we never truly did speak of us, of what went through us. I was wrong in our relationship, but I do not wish to go back too. I feel a little free; I was a different person with Liam. He brought out my best side, but that was not me, it was only a part of me. He was great, but it is just too much to handle at the moment. I do agree though, it was sincerely my mistake, and I did not reciprocate back the same way.

"To know Ziva, you must stop looking at two places; your books and Bexley Weber."

Liam stood in conversation among a group of boys while we passed before the fountain. His eyes never made it up to me, like the past two months, and I knew that he knew I was here. But I took in every inch of his face, hoping that one day I'd forget how he made me feel, how he cared for me. But at the same time, I hope I'll never forget how he was among the few who cared for me. I was not good enough for him, but no matter how hard I tried to hide the fact; the truth was that we were just not meant to be or maybe that was just a pathetic excuse for my pathetic life. We talked only about the best when we had time with each other.

We almost kissed; he held me in his arms, made me feel loved, but we never had our darkest moments or worries spoken about. We looked at each other like we were high in love, but we didn't know what pain the other was going through. Liam truly made it feel like he had no worries in life, and I pretended to have no worries when with him.

"Hello, Elora? Are you walking dead?" Bran asked with twisted lips. "She's not over Liam…" Ziva added, looking at my face and reading past my thoughts.

Silverstring Street was the same as usual; crowded, alive, and dream-like. Only I was living the reality of an unhealed conscience.

"It's not that. It's the guilt that eats me," I pushed my lips to curve upwards at their concern. "In my opinion, the best way to get rid of guilt is to shop!" She placed her hands on her heart in eagerness. "Not everyone works the same way, Ziva," Bran stepped forward like a professional. "Pushups do the job for me…" He looked at us, pressing his lips together and then to the location "but I presume yours might be better," he looked away, resigning to Ziva; she flipped her hair in pride.

So, we went to Silverstring Boutique, which was in the middle of the street, toward the left side. I had to be here, buying clothes because Eromen's day was in a day, and if I wanted to stay back for the celebration, I needed a dress.

The shop was silent and had a lot of empty spaces, making whatever we talked about Echo; we had to whisper. But the real problem was when we couldn't spot any gowns. The clothes on display were either casual, shorts, or simple dresses that would make us look overly underdressed.

Bran had no problem since he'd already bought his during the winter gap. Ziva left the academy but forgot about Eromen's day; she was busy working for the finals. It wasn't until a few minutes of us looking and panicking that our lifesaver had come, the boutique in charge.

"Are you all looking for dresses for the party?" she asked, knowing the look of panic on our faces. We nodded, getting fidgety at not finding anything. The nymph left, returning with a load of heavy dresses that she splayed on a large white table, occupying the center of the grand room.

"Here, I'd kept these insides because most of the students were done with their outfits. They began looking for dresses at the start of the year." Shirt dresses, halters, ball gowns, body con dresses—an interesting variety.

She then brought a set of suits—Asian, peak lapel, contrast lapel, and two more types that I couldn't recognize, but one of the suits had a tailcoat-like end. "All of these were made for the royal courts and diplomats, but they were not considered up to standards. Should do it at the last moment. I'll be at the back if you require anything," she pointed toward the door behind the white marbled counter. "Year-end loads to be done. And you," she pointed at Bran, "should you need variety in color too..." She indicated the main counter and then waved, "Take as many as you like; they'll rot in there for another year." And left.

"These were rejected!" Bran exclaimed, looking at both of us while examining the quality of the clothes. "Royal standards are too high; these aren't even defective. They're really good for free." Ziva too exclaimed in disbelief, tossing the dresses to one side after looking at them thoroughly.

After much trial, we decided on our dresses. I chose an emerald-colored dress; the bodice had lace sewn over and extended like drops onto the flowing skirt. It was off-shouldered with a V-neck. The lower part of the dress was plain satin and extended onto the floor like the edge of the sea.

Ziva picked a pink tulle ball gown; it was off-shoulder and had cloth flowers hand-sewn onto it in the ranges of blue. The bodice was pleated, which led to the back, extending over the bare skin of her back like a corset.

"Enticing yet noble." That was all Bran replied at the end, looking satisfied at our choices. He picked a black Asian suit that had silver buttons and tiny diamonds bordering the edges.

The day of the event had finally arrived after much chatter and excitement. Bran waited for both of us near the cross-section of the paths to the houses, and then we left for the academy together. Immediately below the tall stairs of the main building was a long table, divided into two parts. A large sign read:

Pick carefully from one side, your partner for the night is set.
Do not mix.

I looked through the remaining pieces; most of them were silver, gold, diamond, pink, maroon, but then my eyes fell upon a black mask—it was too simple. The region near the head had a crown carving, and right in the center of it was an emerald diamond. It was perfect for me and the most neglected one due to its limited coordination with their dresses.

Ziva picked the silver one with a one-winged butterfly, very similar in design to a venation mask but modern. Bran picked a black half-black, half-silver mask from the boy's side, the silver tuning in with the diamonds on his suit.

The sign now made sense because we had to inform the color of our clothes to Iving yesterday, so everyone's partners were already chosen. And not seeing any black mask similar to mine at all on the table was a sign that my partner was already inside.

The three of us, all set, walked into the opening hall where the stairs were blocked with a sign:

Love is great but not in a classroom!

I could feel my face turn red from the secondhand embarrassment the words gave me.

"Oh no, I was looking forward to those classrooms. Bang, Bang right on those tables of torture!"

Ziva smacked him on the head, and I simultaneously hit him on his back, giving him an eye of warning.

"You dare do something out of the line."

"I'm just playing," he raised his hands.

We then turned toward the left, 'the hall of assembly,' where the actual deal was. Last-minute preparations were still ongoing, satyrs and nymphs kept following the instructions of several professors, altering the position of the décor until the perfect angle or spot was found.

The ceilings were lined with streamers, and the stage was covered with a gold foil curtain, onto which the wording 'Happy Eromen's Day' was stuck. The floor was covered in dry ice smoke, and floating in its midst were red and silver balloons. Somewhere in between all this mess, I caught Maurilio's eyes.

I saw an unclear image of his black mask from the side of my eyes. I didn't know how I had managed to identify him from a whole crowd of men. His eyes looked at me with longing greed, but he must not have realized it was me.

I could feel eyes on me from the person next to him, and my eyes automatically shifted to investigate. It was Liam with his black mask. He bit his entire lower lip, and his eyes were red, watching me with either scrutiny or pain. I couldn't differentiate, despite the long time I'd spent with him.

"I think," I swallowed, "red and silver are the theme colors for the night." My eyes did not leave Liam, but I was outstared when goosebumps arose.

"Watch out for the whites." He slowly pointed to the professors. He sounded like we were about to do something illegal.

"Welcome, to those that still remain," Sherwood said through what looked like a condenser mic, but I could tell it did not work on electricity, since the words that Sherwood spoke radiated away in circles, like the hot air above a fire that seemed to be floating and then disappears.

"Please take your seats around the table; you have a few performances and gratitude to hear, given by your graduating seniors who will be staying for a few more days: for their result, graduating ceremony, and career day."

The crowd went from silent attention to chaotic noise until everyone had settled down. The three of us sat at the table that was at a distance from the center, joined by Samuel Flin and Garry Jason from Pruden and Imperium. Sherwood spoke for some more time, explaining the entire schedule for the night, prohibited acts, and to avoid littering.

This was then proceeded by the cake-cutting ceremony and then the seniors spoke of their experiences. There were two dance performances during which we were all given a slip of paper onto which we had to write our positive and negative experiences about the academy and drop them into the box placed at the entrance of the building.

When the event was getting boring, I looked around the hall to find my partner. I scanned all around and then spotted him a few tables in front of me; I could only see the emerald gem in his mask from this angle, but he still looked familiar.

I then began to search for Bran and Ziva's partner. Bran was paired with O'kera Collins from Eromen, the lady with the best-claimed body according to the boys, and Ziva was paired with Mark Dunne from Imperium, the one who was always with Maurilio and was a complete bully. His face was sunken, and he looked malnourished as usual.

"Now, let's all play. Pair up with your partners," Orson called from behind her white mask. "But let me warn you. Music and all forms of entertainment have been banned by our King so enjoy yourself while you can. MUSIC PLEASE!"

She clapped her hands in the air, genuinely happy at the idea of breaking the rules that Maldeus laid down. The sound of the violin began, playing fast classical music, tuning in with the rush and loud excitement in the room.

"Good luck," I wished them and began pushing my way through the crowd.

It wasn't easy, especially when people kept stepping on my dress and those tall hard bodies acted like walls in my path. But it didn't bother me because adrenaline was already high in my veins.

I looked in all directions, finally spotting his back again. I pushed through the final block in my path and stood behind him, setting myself well, and then with a wide grin tapped onto his shoulders.

"Hi, I'm Elor…" My smile faded, "Maurilio?" My eyes followed up to the crown on his mask to see the emerald, green gem, proof that I was not talking to the wrong person.

"Hey, Elora… I was looking for you," he said, my body sagged. He then looked over my shoulder, eyes growing wide, and put his arms around my waist, pulling me toward him.

"Careful," he whispered, eyeing Arden Duch.

"Sorry," he called, making a small bow.

I stood frozen, at the rough hand that gripped my tiny waist, as if letting go would mean letting me go away for good. His touch was possessive, making me take a huge breath.

"Oh, I'm sorry," he cleared when he realized.

I didn't know how to behave with him because every time I was around him, I remember my actual true life, the one hidden away with a pretense.

The ugly secrets that tear me apart every day in isolation resurfaced in his presence, and suddenly, I wanted to go back home. This felt like turn-off, and in addition to all this, he was a prince.

How was I supposed to treat him, make bows to him? Why did he even tell me that? And then there's all this flirting, did he even know what he was doing? This was the second time he invaded my personal space.

"But he knows who my father is; he must have seen him with his own eyes. Why does he refuse to let me know of his identity with the excuse of the law? I wouldn't tell a soul if he told me. I believe he's finding much joy in watching me suffer. Maurilio is still the same, just wearing a pretense of goodness now.

When everybody had settled, the chaos was less, and the space was more, but it would never be enough between us. The farther away I was from him, the better I felt."

Nymphs circulated, presenting glasses of a vibrant red liquid to everyone in attendance. Professor Reika, now in control of the microphone, addressed the crowd, "To play, you must drink the EN wine, so that anyone who loses will release red sparks above their heads like a mini firecracker, ensuring no cheating."

"Alcoholic drink?" a boy in the far corner queried.

"Oh, I'm sorry, Mr. Kiew. It does contain sulfite. You won't be able to play due to your allergy."

"No problem, I'm used to this by now," he casually waved his hand in the air, visible from my vantage point.

"Now, drink. Unless you don't want to get drunk tonight." At least 2-3 people exited, and their partners reluctantly followed suit. I glanced at Maurilio, who had already emptied his glass.

"She's so lucky... I lost the bet; Maurilio didn't land with any of us," the girl behind me whispered.

"Bates is going to have a tough time tonight."

One of them giggled, and my eyes widened. I didn't want to drink. I didn't want to drink with a playboy. Maurilio held my glass and brought it to my lips after studying me for a moment. Before I knew it, the glass was empty.

I was sober enough to participate in the first game—the mind-boggler. The rule was to defy the instructions. When told to dance, we had to do anything but dance, and vice versa for any other command. I was eliminated after five rounds because I followed the instructions.

The satyr on stage instructed, "Turn away from your partner and smile."

I complied happily, momentarily forgetting we were playing a game. Red sparks erupted a few feet above my head, and I slumped, exhaling heavily as I eyed Maurilio with hooded eyes. How did I end up with him? The game concluded with the second-level winners.

The next game was "Two to Tango on a Paper." Again, we assumed our positions, drank the EN wine, and commenced playing. The alcohol was taking effect, but who cared? I should be enjoying it. After a challenging time with the finals, I had earned a break.

"Eyy…Maurilio, dance!" I playfully slapped his hard biceps when the music began. He observed my energetic dance with a stoic expression. The paper folded and folded, the music guiding our dance into a whirlwind of laughter and movement. Time seemed to slip away as we twirled and spun until the paper folded so tiny that I tripped on my dress, unexpectedly landing on top of Maurilio.

"Hey…" My mouth formed an astonished round, and my eyes squinted at him. "What do you think you're doing? Is this how you plan on winning?" I shot him a playful glare, and he watched my eyes intently, biting his lower lip.

The proximity between us had diminished to mere inches. My face flushed with heat, and a subtle warmth spread through the region between my thighs. The red sparks above us abruptly brought me back to the reality of the public setting.

I pushed myself off the ground, sobering up as the realization hit that alcohol was influencing my actions. Liam's face flashed in my mind, the thought that he might be watching me flirt with his close friend. This time, I had invaded Maurilio's personal space.

"Let's go eat something," I suggested, taking the lead out of the Hall of Assembly and into the 'Hall of Bonding' before things escalated further.

The Hall of Bonding was a feast for the senses, filled with a variety of food—meatballs, potato chips, sausage rolls, chocolate truffles, chicken empanadas, steak, cheese quesadilla, parmesan-crusted baby potatoes, chicken tenders; not an inch on the table could be seen empty. From the kitchen, more freshly prepared drinks and food were continuously being brought in. There were three tables in total—one for food, one for dessert, and the one in the center had drinks. Each table was attended by a cheerful nymph or satyr, contributing to the festive atmosphere. At the far end, near the dais, a few had grouped up, having their own celebration.

"Elora!" Someone called my name, and I turned towards the voice.

"Oh, Bran," I exclaimed, "I'm so done with the night!"

"The two of you…" Ziva interjected, "You both won't believe what happened. That swine dropped his drink on this amazing dress within the first two seconds of our third game, and now he's running around trying to find wipes… There, look at him," her body took a wide stance.

"He's got terrible stamina," she remarked, eyeing him running around with her lips pursed. "He couldn't keep up with the dancing during our previous match. We were almost going to win. Bully, they call him. I could toss him to the ground, and he would succumb. Pathetic fool!"

Mark then came running towards her, adjusting his cuffs, "Here you go!"

Ziva gave him a deadly glare, causing him to stammer, "I'll... do... it," and he began wiping the stain near her ankle.

Bran and I exchanged flabbergasted looks, realizing that getting on Ziva's wrong side was not something we would ever dare to do. Even as Mark wiped her dress, he occasionally threw glances up at her, but she out-stared him every time.

"That's enough. Go get me a Melon Rage, now."

"Yes, Mam," He stuttered and ran to the mini-bar set up.

Ziva turned to us, shrugging off the shock wave on our faces with a laugh. We imitated her, laughing while looking at each other wide-eyed.

"What about you guys?" She tried to change the topic.

Bran pointed at the bar with his eyes, and we followed. O'kera was giggling at a man's comment with a drink in her hand. I sighed looking at Maurilio when it was my turn to talk. They understood; he stood there along with Liam and Owen Figger in deep talk. We stood looking at the ground in silence at our luck.

"Wait here," Bran said and then ran toward the bar, returning with three cocktail glasses well balanced in his hand. "Feeling," he handed both of us the glasses.

"Serotonin boost, ladies," He then added at our curious faces.

"To little people for a little fate change!" Ziva raised her glass, and Bran followed too.

"Little people?" I asked before raising my glass to the toast.

"Yeah," she replied, taking a gulp, "People that you don't know, whose actions change your life." She almost raised her glasses to her lips and then added, when she saw my eyebrows raised.

"You know, like the butterfly effect, a stranger that you don't know does something that affects a change in your life."

Bran now stood with an empty glass, and Ziva gulped hers entirely in the second take.

****

"I followed their actions, and maybe I shouldn't have because the rest of the night continues to remain a mystery in my mind," I admitted.

Grissa moved her head up and down slowly, "You've sounded indecisive on a lot of occasions."

"The young Elora neglected to sort herself; she was filled with conflicting opinions. One moment, she hated Iverson, and the next, she seemed madly in love with him."

"And do you think this was the reason why you and Liam did not work out?"

"I believe so."

"Do you regret not having met Iverson before Liam?"

"Iverson was where he was supposed to be, and so was Liam. No matter how different I could have wanted everything to be, they were designed to shape me into what you see me be."

Chapter 11
Dark Encounter

"Your Highness!" The two men entered and addressed her in unison, making a gentle bow. The Queen, who sat at the far end of the table, gave a slight powerful nod, her eyes carefully speculating their expressions in the dull, empty room.

The man who led every movement was the director of Magnifisoul, an entertainment agency. He had creases on his forehead and had dyed his black hair blond, but the red curse remained as such, standing out like a white sheep among the black. He resembled greed and seemed opposite to the man standing behind him, whose eyes were red and puffy. The dark bags below his eyes made his otherwise handsome face look pale, and the mark of Zocia was the only color in him. He was young, refusing to look above ground level. The two men sat down at the far end of the table, upon command.

"Gifre, tell me. How is your company coping with Blue's loss?"

A few sobs escaped from the tall man sitting behind the named man.

"Your Highness, of course. Blue's loss was not expected, but the company cannot shut down, nor can 'E5' disband," Gifre replied, his silver front teeth sparkling with every word. The Queen remained squinting, silently observing, not surprised by his apathetic answer.

The young male finally looked up; his eyes were filled with pain. He pressed hard on his teeth as if they were heavyweights in his mouth.

"The group will not re-sign the contract," he merely stated.

Gifre turned toward the man, returning the glare, "That is for me to decide."

"Enough," the queen revealed her presence. "Gifre, please allow me to talk with Lev."

"But Your Highness, my brother wanted this company to go on…" his tone turned soft, and then carrying a hint of disrespect he continued, "If you hadn't kill…"

Elora slammed her hand on the table, "I am aware of what had been done and what must be done. You shall follow as your Queen demands, lest you wish to face His Majesty," her tone was not forgiving.

Gifre's face flinched in anger, and his bared teeth were partially visible to her. He rose, forcing a bow, and without parting his lips, apologized. When the door clicked, she wiped the look on her face and began speaking with utmost empathy.

"Lev, tell me what is it that you want?"

"Your Highness... I mean no disrespect, but the five..." He stumbled at the number "Four... of us do not wish to continue entertaining the public as Enigma5. Blue just... he just..." His eyes began sparkling, and his strong voice quavering, but he held himself.

"Died."

He said, before closing his eyes in pain, accepting the truth.

Elora closed the space between her and the table, "Don't you want Blue to get justice?" She tilted her head to get a clearer image of his bowed head, but the man stayed silent. "Don't you want the murderer to be caught?" She pushed on, "I can help you. But I need your help in return." Her eyes pleaded.

Lev looked up at the Queen's hopeful face, thinking deeply. "What is it?"

"I need you to continue with your band."

"But..." He started and stopped after realizing he had cut the Queen. The Queen dismissed the mistake and continued with her pleading face.

"Ariesque has not long come out from its darkest days, and Enigma5 did well in making the people forget and give hope. The people love you, and they spend all of their time reveling in your positive music and shows."

"But Your Highness, the murderer is still on the loose, and it was called Enigma5 because it was a five-membered band. So how can... I don't understand." He searched the room looking for an explanation.

"We will introduce a new member, and there will be no concerts until it seems like all is good. We need to know whether Blue was the target or whether it was someone else."

"And what good is it if we don't keep concerts? And lives at risk?" Lev asked, but the door swung wide open with a forceful push.

A glorious man, rich and royal, entered the room, engaged in conversation with another man who followed him. The queen rose gracefully, immediately bowing in a display of deep respect, while Lev genuflected in a show of deference. The King turned his gaze toward the two of them, an expression of scrutiny on his regal face. A subtle but commanding aura enveloped him.

"Rise, Elora," he said with tired eyes that seemed to find solace, adding, "Get up, Lev."

Standing behind the King was Elora's good friend, Bran Becile, dressed in his finest attire. He greeted her with respect, crossing his right arm and giving a slight bow of the neck. The person who had held the door for the King earlier now exited, and the door closed with a click. Gifre, who had followed the King and Bran, returned to his seat once the King was seated.

Elora occupied the seat to the right of the King, while Bran took his place on the left.

"As per tradition, I'll introduce everyone and explain their roles in this meeting. Elora, seated here, is my Queen, and Bran, on my left, serves as my secretary, stepping in for Ziva Anson, the diplomat of Prielvar."

"I'm Gifre, director of the company Magnifisoul. And beside me is Lev, the leader of Enigma5," Gifre added.

"Now, let's address the matter at hand. What decision has the Company reached regarding Blue's death?" the King initiated the discussion.

Gifre responded, straightening with nervousness, "The Company will continue its operations unchanged."

"Has the family been compensated? And what about the other members?" inquired the King.

Gifre hesitated, his eyes searching for the right words. "The family has received a payment in gold coins, and members have the 'privilege' to renew their contracts."

"Privilege to re-sign a contract," the King spat. "Do you truly believe the remaining four will see it as a privilege?"

Gifre appeared to grow intimidated but remained silent. The King seemed like he was here for business, and any excuse seemed condemnable, but this was how the King usually presented himself when in a meeting. His meetings were usually for important issues. Today was an exception, due to the widespread unrest following Blue's demise.

An ordinary meeting was usually carried out by the Queen, but that had to meet certain requirements and had to be a serious matter; otherwise, the Queen or King may appoint royal heads or diplomats to deal with the problem.

"What about the family? How much compensation has the company provided?" the King inquired.

"A hundred gold coins," he falsely claimed. However, Lev's gaze bore into him, aware that the director hadn't even offered condolences to the grieving family. Despite his struggled response, the King remained unsatisfied.

"A hundred gold coins? The man was their only son; his parents' expenses should be covered for life, including a counselor for their well-being. As for the members, they can decide whether to renew their contracts. If not, the company must support them until they can stand on their own," the King declared.

Gifre's eyes widened, and he swallowed nervously. "This is too much for the company."

"This is how the contract was established," the King responded.

He gestured to Bran, who handed over a copy of the contract. The King flipped through the pages and tossed them toward the director for his reference.

"Clause 5.2, under untimely death, The Company shall undertake full responsibility if the agreed party faces death during work time.

Clause 5.3, The Company agrees to take compensation in such that, it shall comply with the full worth of the memb…"

"But that was the contract my brother created," he protested, feeling unjustly treated. The King tilted his head, glaring at him, and that was enough to bring the man to his knees, begging for mercy. "I apologize for interrupting your speech," he stammered, his lips trembling.

Gifre remained on his knees, and the King turned his gaze to Lev, who was visibly sweating.

"As the leader, do you want your band to continue its role in the Company?" the king asked with the same stern expression.

Lev glanced at the queen, who maintained a composed demeanor. "Ye…s," he stuttered, beads of sweat sliding down his face.

The King then stood, and Lev almost flinched. "It is decided, then. Enigma5 will carry on, but with additional instructions from your King."

He looked down at Gifre on the ground. "As for you, consider yourself fortunate that I haven't silenced your tongue."

Muttering to Bran, he said, "The company matter has been resolved. Inform Ziva. Now, schedule a meeting with the diplomats."

Giving a final glance to his queen, she smiled reassuringly, made a small head bow, and then his presence vanished.

****

Elora Bates 🍁

Silverstring station remained unchanged, even as I stood there almost a year later. The tall walls framed a scene of parents eagerly awaiting their children. In this world, it seemed that there was no greater joy for parents than treating their children to embarrassing displays of love.

The younger version of myself would watch my classmates with envy, but now, those feelings no longer held sway. I wandered around, searching for Cassiden. Standing on tiptoes at each corner, peering over parents when they blocked my view, but he was nowhere in sight. I eventually resigned myself to sitting and waiting. The crowd gradually thinned, and eventually, a worker approached me.

"Can I help ya' with somethin'?" he asked with a thick accent. I shook my head, replying, "Nobody is here for me yet."

I scanned the area once more, growing anxious. The worker continued, "Don't ya know your way back? Parents sometimes… um… forget pick-up day…"

When I only smiled, he pressed further, "Should I get the register for ya, tell ya your address?"

A lingering feeling gnawed at me, suggesting that he might be upset because I hadn't arrived when he wanted me to—back when he sent that urgent letter. But deep down, I trusted that Caissiden respected my wishes. A sense of heaviness settled within me, making me wonder why he wasn't more concerned. Yet, another part reassured me that he would never forget me, even in the midst of war. I believed he would charge through a battlefield just to come to my aid. It occurred to me that he might have overlooked today being the last day of the academy, but regardless, I knew my way back.

"No, I think he must be hooked with something else," I replied finally before heading toward the Spenua.

"Crystal Valley," I muttered to myself, walking through it and struggling to lift my luggage from the ground. Placing it on the hardened road, what I thought was Crystal Valley seemed different. There was an eerie stillness in the air; only the wind blew. It wasn't just silent; it was desolate and lifeless, as if everyone had abandoned this once lively settlement.

I turned back with an odd sense of nervousness and again muttered 'Crystal Valley,' clear and loud. The image appeared, and I lifted my luggage, taking a step into the very same location.

As I began searching for help, not a single soul was in sight. "Goodness!" I exclaimed, scoffing. This place looked exactly like Crystal Valley. I forced a tense smile, attempting to calm myself. However, as soon as the smile took form, it disappeared. The wooden board with the writing of 'Crystal Valley' stood broken, with one part swinging along with the breeze.

My mind went blank, and I began stumbling toward the familiar path, reaching House Number 9. But it was the same everywhere—no sign of life. There were no lights, and the flowers were dead. The glass window was broken, with only sharp edges remaining in its fixed point. I slowly pushed open the gates, the creaking sound and the bindweed below my shoes indicating it hadn't been opened in quite a while.

My heart raced; something had happened here. With sweaty palms, I pushed open the main door of the house. A yellow sword automatically took form in my hands in defense, and I held it with both hands. Even though I lacked experience in fighting and never won a fight, I reassured myself of my capabilities, taking one slow, steady step at a time.

Inside the house, rocks were scattered. "The window," I thought. "Mrs. Anderson?" My voice trembled while examining the dark house, hoping for a reply. But ringing silence was all I received. My eyes caught movement from the kitchen. I swallowed the thickness in my throat and proceeded toward it, alert like prey avoiding its predator.

The kitchen seemed to be in order, and I released a stuffed breath. Then, my ear caught a strangulated low cry, and I began searching for its source. It came from behind the kitchen table, but the moment my eyes fell to the floor, there was blood.

I gasped for air. "Oh… my…" Anxiety began taking over me. There were drag marks. I took deep breaths through my widely opened mouth to calm the rising panic attack and followed the trail steadily, keeping my eyes and ears as sensitive as possible to the surroundings.

"My, my… MRS. ANDERSON!" The sword vanished into gold dust, and my hands went over my mouth. On the floor was Mrs. Anderson, hurt and bleeding through her legs, half unconscious. I shook her, and she struggled to focus on me through her pain.

"You… you must leave. They're here," she warned, terrorized, making quick glances behind me.

"No, you're hurt," I cried, sweat beading on my forehead. "Go!" She let out a wheezy scream. "Now…"

"Who did this to you?" I asked frantically, applying pressure to her wound. "I did."

I froze; it was not Mrs. Anderson who replied.

I slowly turned, my eyes wide and teary at the venomous tone of his voice. He was a tall, shadowy figure, and then it all went black.

My eyes snapped open as though somebody blew life into my lifeless body. My soul felt aware of its presence, and the incidents that took place flashed before my eyes.

My body began levitating from the softness of the bed, waves of yellow energy radiating from me like UV rays of the sun. Energies of fear, anger, and suffocation of the unknown that were trapped within me came out, gushing, overflowing, and filling the room.

I shut my eyes, trying to remember what came after the black, but it was blank, like a dream. How long had it been since this dream? I raised my hands toward the ceiling, trapping all the energy back within me, and allowed myself to slowly drift back down, making a light 'thud' onto the bed.

Something within me felt overloaded. I then observed the surroundings, the curtains swirling through the partially open window, the scent of wet soil and trees filling the air.

It didn't feel new; it was like I'd seen it in another dream, like déjà vu. The truth was that I was aware of every room and corner of this house, like they were memories but not mine because I had never been here.

My feet automatically carried me, cautiously and yet curiously, walking with a sense of pride and ego looming within me. Not a drop of sweat broke out as I walked within the house of my kidnapper. Something had changed with me.

The thin corridor was pitch black, like a haunted house. Stairs appeared, attached to the end of the corridor, to the wall, continuing into a huge lobby. The walls of the lobby on either side were made of glass, and the flooring was done in black marble. A forest surrounded the villa, and the furthest sight was just trees and a mountainous landscape. Beneath the tall stairs was a large door made of hardwood and painted black. It was closed, but I knew what was within it. There was a large half-circle table with a mirror tabletop and silver legs. On the curve were ordinary chairs, but on the opposite side was one royal chair, made of black and silver, and two chairs that seemed less royal but were majestic, unlike the rest.

"Hello, Elora."

I shook at the voice, dark and cunning. It came from a man sitting on the gray sofa right in front of me. His black hair blended with the surroundings, escaping my notice until now. I moved forward, and he sat with his feet laid out on the square glass tabletop that had one potted plant: mint.

The man reached for the plant, plucked a few leaves, and tossed them into the glass he held, twirling through the ice cubes with his long, extremely thin fingers.

"Mint and Ale, fascinating combination. Would you like one?" His voice resonated through the empty hall.

"Who are you?" I asked confidently, even though I knew who he was.

The man turned his head, revealing his pale skin. Hollow cheeks and an empty body made him appear without flesh. The brown skin that an Enchanted carried was gone; he was different from us.

"It is I. Maldeus."

His dry, cracked lips curved into a smirk.

The hair at the back of my neck rose, and even though I only saw half of his face, I knew that smirk would haunt me for the rest of my life.

I paused for several moments; this was the man responsible for countless murders. He was responsible for my broken life, and he was alive, daring to talk to me with superiority. "What is it that you want?"

"To complete our unfinished business," he said, placing his hand onto his black walking stick, clutching the skull on the top with a strong grip, and rose.

He needed support to stand and walk, turning directly to me. The only feature on his square face that made him look alive was his eyes; they shined with sinister darkness.

The jacquard black Indo-western suit he wore emphasized how thin he was, with gray buttons pinned toward the right side like several ants in a line. To put it simply, he was bone and skin. I was conflicted; his appearance was deceiving.

He looked oddly dead, yet undeniably alive. How hard would it be to kill him right here? If I was here, Maldeus had something to do with my dead mother. Or maybe my mother was dead because of him.

"How should you mean? You want to kill me?" I raised fire in my hands, holding them toward him, ready to defend myself from death at any moment he chose to attack.

"Peace. I am not here to harm you," he said, throwing his head back and cracking the stiffness in his neck.

"And why is it that the great Maldeus…" I mocked, "after murdering my family, wants peace?" The flames flickered with my strong emotions. His eyes gleamed with controlled anger, but he merely smirked.

"I was beginning to think that the world had forgotten me after all this time of stillness. Don't you, Elora, wish to know why life has been going downhill for you ever since you entered this world?" His voice was reasonable and calm as he watched me.

"Aren't you an Eromen put in Imperium?" He smiled when he saw my eyes grow wide. "Don't you want to know what happened in the forest or why your mother died?"

For a moment, I flowed with his words, and my head gave small involuntary nods. "Don't you want to know your father who lives and avenge your mother's death?"

My face grew serious, and his smile curved even more. "Unarm yourself, and you shall gain your answers."

His offer was tempting.

I shook my head slowly, in full control of myself. This could be a trap. He watched me in scrutiny while moving his jaw either way, clearly giving the idea that he was having trouble with self-control at disobedience toward him. He placed his right hand behind him, and his suit tightened with anger, speaking through clenched teeth.

"You have my word. I am loyal to only myself. You should know that by now."

He did not blink; I did as he said and lowered my guard instead of attacking. I carried gold, but so did he. I knew I was powerless. Either way, I could be destined for death, but through this path, I might die with answers. I lightly walked toward the sofa, throwing glances at him every now and then while he watched me move, turning his entire body with mine.

He took his glass and gulped it all, his throat bobbing. I tried keeping my eyes as open as possible until they became teary; he could attack me any second.

"Be my Queen…" he said, and that was all I could hear because my body had turned weak, not because he asked me something unimaginable, but because he demanded it of me without reason. I couldn't feel my legs.

"No."

The word slipped out, and before I could return to focus back on the present, his walking stick was pressing against my collarbone. I stayed still, looking at him wide-eyed because even a small movement I made would result in the snapping of that bone.

"You dare defy me," he spat, clearly not trying to hide his anger, and I watched how demonic his face had turned. My chest rose and fell with heavy breaths, his stick following along.

I chose silence because before me stood the man behind the terrible stories that I've only heard of and never witnessed.

"Good," he sneered sadistically. I watched him walk back to his seat, taking immense support from his stick, and poured himself another glass of ale. My heavy breathing did not cease; my body was compensating for the breaths that it would lose after I lay dead.

"Elora," he said solemnly without facing me, "As queen-to-be, the first law for you to obey would be that I do not take 'no' for an answer."

He turned toward me. "So, yes or no?"

I remained silent because I did not want to say yes, and I couldn't say no.

He again solemnly said, "Elora, as queen-to-be, you should be as devoted to me as the sun to the day."

I had to choose my next words carefully, so I asked, "And to what do I owe this great offer?"

The words sounded pleasurable, but they were all I could think of at the moment. My tone, however, contradicted the words—they were cynical.

"Because you are the answer to my existence," he tried hiding his disgust for my insolence. I looked at him. Was he in love with me? How could… What is this…

"Yes, darling, you were sacrificed to me; your father had to!"

He looked proud. "So that I could live eternally, and he could pledge loyalty." Something within me broke, and I had mixed feelings about what he was about to say.

"You are part of the eternity ritual."

"You're lying! Dark magic always leaves a mark."

I rose, roaring at him. He grabbed me by my shirt, tossed me to the floor, and thrust his palm toward me. Yellow waves escaped him. I watched that yellow light touch me, closing my eyes; I was going to die.

Moments passed; I was still breathing. I opened my eyes; maybe death was another life?

His powers were all around me; I was engulfed in it.

He stopped, bending to come close to my face, looking into my eyes, and then pulled roughly on my shirt. The mark was there, on the left side of my chest, immediately above my heart. My eyes did not leave his face, but my expression turned pale with every word I heard.

"As long as I live, you live, and as long as you live, I live."

An awful silence spread through the room. A triumphant smirk lined his face. I looked away into nothingness, and my hands curled in an attempt to gain support from the cold tiles.

He then chuckled, "It is humorous how you believe that your mother was important enough to be murdered without a reason," he emphasized. "Your mother knew our secret, and so your father killed her. And even after reading those newspaper clippings, you couldn't figure it out. Elora, it was so simple."

How lightly those words came out of his mouth and how heavily they weighed upon my chest. How easily he could mock me without even the slightest amount of guilt.

Then it occurred to me, "How…" my lips trembled.

****

The Queen sat silently, holding the climax of her story, and the writer sat making steady eye contact. She was leaning forward, taking every word from her Queen's mouth like a drop of water to a desert traveler.

"Then what happened?" she pushed when the Queen did not answer. The Queen returned a more sympathetic smile to herself.

"You took the crown!" Grissa suddenly blasted, forgetting Elora's title. "But why?" She cried, thinking.

"Because he offered me freedom or death." Painful guilt lined the Queen's face.

"But he said you can't be dead—"

"Yes, Maldeus didn't die too. He was living an endless loop in his world while the real world went on for over sixteen years. No ordinary weapon can kill me. If I bled to an extreme extent, my body would only be breathing air but while living in a loop of my mind."

Grissa tilted her head in confusion, "Grissa, have you seen a plant? It's living but not conscious or aware of its surroundings. Like a state of coma."

"And how can he know things, when he was not present—you put into Imperium—the newspapers?"

Her face was calculating, "The eternity ritual does not grant him that power then?"

"He did not have that power."

Chapter 12
The Union Bond

"After I had publicly declared my vows to Maldeus, and the union bond formed around my finger, things were no longer the same. Immediately after the wedding, I had to take vows for Ariesque, which is usually not the case, as you might know that the two ceremonies must have a gap of at least seven days. All of this seemed to ignite hope among people, and scandalous rumors began that the King might change his ways after what they thought was 'love,' but they had to pay for such thoughts."

****

Elora Bates

My sight lingered on the flickering reflection of the twelve men sitting around the glass table in the room beneath the stairs of Maldeus's residence; they were the diplomats of the twelve provinces of Ariesque, excluding the King's province—the province of Lunare. They spoke roughly and knew only vulgarness, and there seemed to be a dominance of Andronicans in the King's court, for all twelve of them were Andronicans. I was a golden fish in a sea of ordinary fishes, and that made great talk for the country.

When Maldeus took his first step into this room with Aristera tagging behind him—the very man that I spoke to on countless occasions; my father as declared—the room grew even nosier. The diplomats wore pride on their faces; they were not terrified or sad to be seated here, and this made me realize the likemindedness of the King and the diplomats, and the dirty affairs Ariesque was going to face.

I looked up at the King, rising to bow to my husband, and then lingered on the face of my father, my nose scrunching up, hardness spreading over my heart like water on a piece of dry cloth.

The King, pleased with his welcome, took a seat on his chair next to me, and a grim silence spread instantly. Aristera sat on the left side of the King. I refused to look up at his real face, blankly watching his reflection on the table. The three of us faced the 12 diplomats that sat on the arch of the semi-circle glass table.

"Tell me, diplomats! What news do you bring? How has Ariesque dealt with my absence?"

My eyes moved to the reflection of the man who had raised his hand; he wore a heavy gold chain around his neck and had a stubby beard.

"Yes, Diplomat of Largus," the King called.

"Your Majesty, people in my province were protesting against you."

The King tilted his head, listening. "All twenty of them are in prison now," he laughed with great delight. The King watched him with a straight face. I felt like he would condemn him for arresting people, and he did.

"You arrested them!" he spat. The Diplomat of Largus turned quiet, now looking at his reflection.

"Do you think they deserve such sympathy?" The diplomat's eyes went up. "Cut off their food supply to half," he said through gritted teeth, making me swiftly turn to the King.

The diplomat smirked in awe. "Yes, Your Majesty. Absolutely."

Another man raised his hands; he had a few gray hairs and wrinkles creasing around his baby face.

"Yes, Diplomat of Prielvar."

"Your Majesty, the director of Magnifisoul Entertainment has requested the removal of the ban that you placed. How shall I punish him for questioning?" The Diplomat of Prielvar assigned the tone of his question while trying to read the King's face, scared of his response.

"Bring him to me. I shall personally tend to his request." His eyes grew with hateful desire at what he had heard. A tiny sigh of relief was emitted from the mouth of the diplomat.

"Tell me, diplomat, how is your wife doing? I heard you got married," the King asked with cunning eyes.

He immediately responded in a jolly good mood, having nothing to worry about.

"Oh, she's doing fantastic, Your Majesty, and I—"

"Would you mind if I borrowed her for a night?" While the curve of the King's lips grew, the curve of the diplomat's face decreased. He looked upon the King with pleading eyes, and then his eyes grew distant.

"Yes, Your Majesty," he then added a confirmation to himself, "Yes."

I was beginning to suffocate in here; I clutched my dress, praying for an escape. I knew Aristera was looking at me through the mirror. I kept my face straight like none of this meeting's discussions affected me when it was eating me from the inside. Even time sat quietly in a corner and refused to acknowledge my presence.

The very same afternoon, immediately when the King had concluded the meeting with the diplomats, another was held with the royal members of the family. Those included the Crown Prince, Riordian Slayholt, and his wife Galina Slayholt, Aristera, and Maurilio Slayholt along with their present Queen. Me. The meeting had one main topic: the three of our return to Silverstring.

****

"Did they know?" she interrupted the flow, adding, "Know about you, the whole ordeal as to why you ended up being queen?"

"No. Nobody except for Aristera knew the truth. Maurilio had felt betrayed, even though we were in no relationship at that moment. The look of hurt was written all over his face. He thought of me as somebody completely different from the Elora he'd met in the academy. But I was that very same Elora, just compromised."

****

Elora Bates 🌿

The world knew of my identity now, and walking through the gates of Silverstring was another scandalous topic for Ariesque. And not just Ariesque—the academy was in a state of imbalance. Most attendees had hoped to study under the guidance of Her Majesty, Queen Frigga. However, the covenant was on my side, allowing anyone seeking education to be admitted. Despite Queen Frigga knowing my true purpose, she could not prevent me.

While I used the excuse that I wanted to fulfill my education to become a more worthy Queen, I was restricted by the King from engaging with others. Group projects became my sole burden, and I could only attend classes. I couldn't accompany others through the forest from the station, meet Bran or Ziva, nor did I intend to, even in secret. It's not because I didn't care, but I knew they would never expect me to be there. For their safety and mine, it was better to keep the doors closed. Maldeus obtained news from sources I was not aware of, and I didn't want to jeopardize more lives because of this mess.

I did not attend the opening ceremony, and even though Sherwood permitted me to follow the King's wishes, He was not obliged. He agreed to make an exception in my case—so much of an exception that it made me wonder whether Sherwood was on Maldeus's side. Sherwood was never unaware of anybody's lies, and it was always evident in the silence he kept after the lie had been spoken.

He saw through me too, but he permitted me to lie openly. I couldn't have been more grateful for this because I was not here to complete my education. I was here to fulfill Maldeus's desire, the task he demanded of me. Maldeus knew his way with anything, and I was a witness to that.

The corridor of our campus residence was dark, the academy busy with the opening ceremony. Maurilio stood in front of me, leaning on the walls near our housing unit, waiting for the confrontation. Two satyrs walked in front of me and two behind me, following the orders of their Queen to protect me. To keep me away from Maurilio too, unless otherwise asked. He walked toward me, his body stiff.

"Stand down," I whispered to them, raising my left hand toward him, watching him continue toward me, wearing a straight face in the gray darkness.

Before he spoke, his eyes fell to the ring of the union on my left ring finger.

"Your Highness," he scoffed, bowing mockingly. "Funny it is, how money and power deceive all."

I smiled at his words and remained silent. He had a lot to say. He came close to me, I didn't move, and whispered, "I thought you were different. Why?"

I turned to look at him, our eyes watching each other.

He hoped for a reason, but the truth was I enjoyed power, I enjoyed looking Frigga right in the eye, maybe as an equal. Even though deep down, my heart melted in guilt, knowing that I would never be an equal, only a slave to words. The satyrs brought their spears up toward him, but he bared his teeth toward them and walked away. I tilted my head, amazed at how much his words could impact me but still walked with my head held high because a Queen does not walk with the pain of somebody's words. We were going to share the same housing unit, and it was going to be tough but not as compared to getting the Scimitar of Darkness from the Queen of the Forest.

I sat on my bed, my mind replaying and my body reliving what it felt like to be in Maldeus's presence. The chills and numbness of a cold-hearted murderer filled me.

"Sit down," his airy cold voice sounded. We were in the same room that had the mirror table, but instead of the diplomats, the remaining members of the royal family sat at the curve of the table. I could feel a pair of eyes staring intently at me, but I made no effort to look at the person. Instead, I looked devotedly to Maldeus, like the role I was to play.

"It had been three months since I presented my kingdom with a Queen. I was so caught up with handling the affairs of Ariesque that I could not formally introduce her to you. Elora, this is Crown Prince Riordian Slayholt, my brother."

He pointed his hand toward the man with high cheekbones and a face that struck similarity to his son, the very same son that I refused to make eye contact with. Riordian did not carry pride on his face; he mimicked pride, and I knew it because even I wore a pretense before Maldeus. I bowed my head, giving him a serious greeting while he tried to force his nod.

"This is Princess, Galina Slayholt, wife of my brother."

He pointed at the lady, a woman with brown tousled hair and an oblong face. Her face had the expression of 'better here in the riches as an exception than among the poor, suffering'. I could not blame her.

"And this is their son, Prince Maurilio Slayholt. You must know him." He pointed at the man sitting in the middle, his eyes locked in mine, unmoved. I quickly broke away, thinking of my husband, the King.

Maldeus then displayed his true side, beginning to talk with dominance; family was only a title to him.

"Now then, Silverstring Academy is to open in a few weeks. Students will likely return for two reasons: protection and to advance their studies. Mystica's protection is rather feeble being on land, but Silverstring's is strong. The Queen of the Soul Forest makes the forest impenetrable to outsiders, and that is where

the real deal is." He tapped his bony fingers on the table and then slowly turned his head toward me.

"Which is why you will be returning along with Maurilio." I stared wide-eyed at him; his demands were non-negotiable, and I looked at him for an answer. He eyed the crowd, piercing his fire into them, making them tremble in their hearts.

"The Scimitar of Darkness is with the Queen of the Forest."

He again turned to look at me, and my hands were beginning to tremble beneath the table for what he was going to ask me. The scimitar is the second most prized possession to the Queen, second to her ruling staff. It was the only weapon known to destroy the most powerful dark magic spells, with the exception of the three-triumvirate staff's power altogether.

"Elora."

His voice startled me.

It was Maurilio; he was back from the ceremony. I watched him; he dared to utter my name without any title of respect, but I drew comfort from the only recognition I got of my true self.

I shook my head, devastated. "It's impossible. The Queen knows my purpose. She recognized it the moment she saw me."

Maurilio sat down beside me; he was gambling with his life by not adhering to the King's wishes.

"Are you scared of death? Why did you marry the King?" he asked without judgment. I looked right into his eyes, unable to answer, and then turned away, ignoring him.

I wanted the world to know the reason, but the reason was trapped within a small box that nobody would understand, making me appear immoral and dark. I forced a nod, leaving the small box to rust in the darkness. We sat in consoling silence.

"Why did you agree, Elora? Agree to die by slow suffering rather than a moment's worth of pain?" he asked the question he had been holding in ever since I saw him at the table.

"You would've never…" He looked into my eyes, shaking his head, demanding.

"Because I was scared… I don't want to die." This had to stop; he was overstepping his boundaries. "Don't pretend like you know me," I snapped back, now wearing a stony look. "You must leave now!"

He did not move. I huffed a breath and looked into his eyes, piercing my finger into his chest with a shaking fist. "Don't you dare gamble with the King's laws because of your emotions toward me. Keep…" I raised my head to the ceiling, controlling my slippery emotions.

Maurilio knew that the King would torture him to death for even making eye contact with me, but he still stood defiant.

"Elora…" His voice rose to a higher level, and he held my hand. "Tell me… what…"

"Maurilio, what do you think you're doing?"

I wanted those words to come out with anger, but they came softly, like I couldn't care anymore. His touch was soothing, and I wanted his hands all over me to extinguish the fire of loneliness.

I stood, pressing my eyelids tightly, exhaling breaths through my mouth; fear was not letting me feel anything at this instant. I turned to face him completely, releasing even harder breaths.

"We'll leave and go away to the other realm…" he begged. The distance between us began to decrease, and I could feel his breath on my cheeks, the guilt of sinning increasing within me.

"Then what? We hide away until the King hunts and kills us? It's not that easy…" I trailed off, my eyes turning watery. I swallowed the dreams he showed me and said through my clenched teeth,

"My reasons are none of your concern. I am your Queen, and I demand obedience." His hand released at my words, and he bowed, leaving without even looking back once.

I slept that night, but before dawn could break, the night brought upon me my memories of distress.

"Get him," his cold voice called. "The time has come."

I looked at him, my face devoid of any expression. A part of his lips raised. "Time?" I questioned, my mouth going dry at his words. "Time to prove your loyalty."

The union bond was formed, and I was crowned as he demanded, what now? Footsteps echoed through the stairs, and a servant dragged a man down by his white, dirty shirt that was partially torn from all the violence.

His long, dirty hair was clumped into sections by the sweat from his perspiration, and his hands were tied behind him. I could not see his face until he was hurled onto the floor immediately before me. I gasped, my lungs collapsing at the once handsome face that was now bruised and tarnished with grime.

"Elora?" he called, trying to look through his swollen eyes. He mouthed 'What are you doing here?' with creased eyebrows, now breathing heavily.

"Cassiden…" Nothing but a tiny rustle of whisper came from me because a panic attack was taking over, and I held my throat fighting for air.

Cassiden's face was filled with terror, and he looked only into my eyes. I fell onto the floor, my legs unable to keep up with its numbness. Frank pulled out a kopis and placed it in his bare hands, without any command from the King. He knew the King too well, and that concerned me.

"Prove your loyalty to me. Pick up the kopis and kill." Maldeus's words were laced with delightful poison.

I pushed myself away from him, uttering 'No,' and crying tears of pain for what he was asking of me. Maldeus walked with such graceful steps, hands behind his back, and I realized.

"No…" I cried as he fisted my hair, tugging it, making me stand.

He walked up to Frank, snatched the kopis, and played with it before returning to me. He disengaged the kopis from its sheath, tossed it onto the floor, and pulled on my hair again.

"Don't touch her," Cassiden spat.

Maldeus paid no heed to his words; instead, he brought his face close to mine and pierced his stare.

"You. Dare. Disobey. Me." He spoke through clenched teeth and then glided the pointed end laterally on my face down until it reached my neck where he depressed it so that it went through the outermost layer of my skin. I felt a drop of blood trickle down, and I shut my eyes, whimpering in pain at his slow, torturous movement.

"OH!" He played with my emotions. "First kill is never easy; here, let me help you!" His tone was excruciating to my ears. I pleaded with my eyes, but he held my hand and curled my fingers tightly around the handle.

"Please," I cried. He dragged me by my hair, holding my hand along with the kopis. "Please... Please... Please..." I cried loudly, but it was too late. His blood dripped on the floor, and then his lifeless body fell.

The room was shrouded in darkness, and the memories of the dream lingered like a haunting ghost. I tried to shake off the uneasy feeling, realizing that it was just a dream. However, the weight of reality pressed upon me, and I couldn't escape the harsh truth of my situation. An empty soul I was, and my mind reminded me every night through its dreams of what made me empty. I wept for weeks over this evil act of mine, but Maldeus was right; it was only the first kill that made me guilty and sad. Because for a second, a mere hesitation stopped me, but that too was overcome. I was in a 'do or die' situation, and I couldn't be selfless because I had to save myself first. I couldn't help but think about Maurilio's words.

"Now!" He exclaimed in his airy tone, "The director of Magnifisoul Entertainment is going to find my gracious presence in his house." His voice turned rough as a storm at my face, "YOU!" He said, poking his stick at my shoulder, "Cleanse yourself and dress, well. I shall return with a guest." I stood stiff as a stone statue, and he left. My strength left me when Felix closed the door after him.

I fell to the floor eyeing the ring on my hand, the only thing that shone brightly in my life, bright gold. As much as the next few hours felt agonizing and slow, I wanted it to pass even more slowly. I wanted to extend every second to an hour because I didn't want to stand before Maldeus, but time passed as quickly as it takes for the heart to stop beating. I stood before the mirror after a shower, looking at the black dress resembling the dark lines under my eyes from the sleepless nights. I flinched at the sound of the main door. He was here, but there were muffled screams along with him, a male's voice. Even though Maldeus walked around with his stick, he was powerful enough to bring whoever it was here without any kind of protection. He alone was enough, and that gave me goosebumps.

"Elora, darling. I'm home!" Maldeus announced in his angry voice. He demanded that I always walk with pride despite the situation, my eyes were never to cry in the presence of another Enchanter, and my expression should always resemble that of the happiest woman in the world. He didn't just demand this;

he fixed it into my head with a whip whenever it was not up to his standard. I had to always cover up my body because of visible welts, just like how this black dress of mine covered every inch of my skin except my face. Wearing a look of arrogance, I climbed down the stairs, taking note of every piece of information that I could catch. Maldeus splayed on the sofa, facing the man on the floor. The man was drenched in sweat and had saliva dripping through the white cloth tied around his mouth. It had blood stains, and his head was swollen.

"Brief introduction, sweetheart," he said in an amusing tone, with eyes fixed on his new toy. "This is Daniel Belier, the director of Magnifisoul Entertainment. He wants to start his company again; says that it would 'employ and benefit' many. Ever heard of the Glitz or the Starstruck?" I raised the right side of my lip, scoffing, and shook my head. "Yes, exactly, invisible company." He poked his stick at the man who didn't look up. I began hyperventilating; this scene was one I had witnessed before with Cassiden.

"What are his charges, Your Majesty?" I played along with a parched mouth. Every moment was a living lie.

"Disobedience to his King's desires." Maldeus saw me, my expression. He did not seem satisfied.

"And his punishment?"

"Death." The man looked at the King, blinking rapidly. I stopped dead, my feet glued to the ground, and a look of pure white terror screamed all over my face. "What's the matter, darling?" He sang through his bared teeth. "You think death is a cruel punishment for a man who requested to reopen his money-making business against the King's wishes."

"No…" I immediately started, not wanting Maldeus to hold any more reason against me. "But I think a King, oh so great as you, carrying out the deed to kill a man so insignificant…" I was trying to save the man even though it could lead to serious consequences.

"That's why you're here, Elora," he said my name, making me wince at his tone. The smile on my face faded.

Felix brought the same dagger that had pierced Cassiden's heart. I had the same memories flood back to me, but with a cold heart, I picked it up and, with undiminishing eye contact, stabbed the man not even thinking twice. One of us only gets to live, and it will be me. I'm sorry.

"You are finding that happiness in murder. I am delighted, Elora." A smile of surprise crossed his face. The man fell with a thud onto the floor. He raised

his hands toward me, "Come here." I walked toward him, my heart racing, and he tapped onto his lap. I followed his demands, sitting on his lap despite the feeling of discomfort. "Now, it's your turn." I went stiff, the look of glee returning to his eyes. "My whip," he demanded.

Everything in the academy was a new experience for me despite staying here for a year. Satyrs accompanied me to all locations, and I always stayed in my housing unit unless an important matter came up that required my attention. I sat in the corner of the class without speaking. Nobody was allowed within three meters of me, but the truth was that despite that nobody dared or wanted to enter the forbidden zone. I could not enjoy or even have a casual conversation with Bran, despite his desperate attempts to find answers. Ziva gave up on me, but it didn't make me sad; being a disappointment was something I was getting used to. I always kept my head down when they were around because I was ashamed of who I was. Their dearest friend ended up committing murder, as was displayed in the news. Devoid of human contact except for Maurilio, who always insisted on answers that I could not give, and the headmasters, months passed. The workload kept me busy, but every moment of nothingness opened a hidden deep memory and delved further into a world of nothingness. My body had lost its ability to experience life.

"Intimus. She will be living with you until pronounced Queen. You will make sure of her safety. I will summon my allies soon." He ordered at that face that never made eye contact with Maldeus, not out of fear but out of sheer reverence.

I watched every moment that Iving made, and my eyes displayed how pleased I was at knowing that my ideas of Iving were not in the slightest manner wrong. He was a heartless murderer on the King's side, and just like the King, he was pathetic to be alive.

"Now that Elora is with us, nothing can stand in my *way.*"

Maldeus sneered, knowing that death is evitable. He turned to look at the smirk on my face and fixed his eyes on me, taking absolute joy in what he was about to say, "And Aristera," His words wiped the smile immediately from my face.

"Make sure nobody knows our secret." He said, confirming the identity of Intimus Iving.

"Yes, Your Majesty."

Chapter 13
The End?

Sometimes, the thought of ending my own life seemed like a viable option, but knowing that death would always elude me was disorienting. I knew for a fact that I couldn't obtain the Scimitar of Darkness. Maldeus had indirectly pronounced a death sentence on me, yet I had to remain calm. There had to be a solution, a connection I wasn't seeing. Frigga must have had some weakness. I threw the books on my table to the floor, clutching my hair.

A few days before Christmas, during the same week as Andronicus Day, Maurilio, Iving, and I had decided to meet. Even uttering the name Iving made me feel indifferent, as if the human switch had been turned off. Desperation drove me to seek help; we needed to take action. Although this task was assigned to me, they would also be equally responsible for facing him.

Our primary goal was to determine the whereabouts of the scimitar, as we were clueless about its location. Acquiring it posed an even greater challenge; without knowing its whereabouts, the entire ordeal would be futile.

"I believe I know where the scimitar is," Maurilio said, sensing the tension in the room. He unfolded a piece of paper from his left pocket and slammed it onto the table, capturing our attention.

"The Garden of Eden," he declared, looking at Iving and me with concern. The painted image depicted a floating green island, with small land formations resembling steps leading to a vast, endless expanse. It appeared perilous, with substantial gaps between each tiny foothold and an unfathomable depth below.

On the floating land, at a considerable distance, stood a domed gazebo with a balustrade, bright white and surrounded by dense green trees. The painting resembled a scene from a fantasy book.

"That's quite an assumption, Maurilio. The Scimitar has only been heard of but never seen, and if it's there, it poses a significant problem."

"And where is that?" I asked, temporarily setting aside my feelings of abhorrence.

"Within the Soul Forest," Iving answered.

"But the article clearly states…" He flipped the paper.

"'All-powerful pieces of weapons, artifacts that could lead to mass destruction if in the wrong hands are situated within…'"

"And what problem does that create?" I inquired, raising my brows as I continued to read the article.

"Only the first man and woman are said to have entered there. After they were banished, the land has remained pristine from sin…" Maurilio explained, observing my reaction.

Iving added, "It has an invisible barrier, Perit Peccatum. Sin perishes."

As we stared at each other, I broke the silence, "So, none of us can enter there? Even if we confirm the scimitar's presence?"

"No," Iving replied.

I sighed loudly, my fingers digging through my crossed arms. "Maybe a nymph… or a satyr…" The random thought startled me, and I almost shrieked as a light shone through the keyhole.

"Yes, but you would have to make them break their law to get the task done. They would perish, wouldn't they?" Maurilio pointed out.

"They wouldn't break any law just by thoughts now, would they?" A cold joy filled me. "They would be sinless, entering and exiting. Only after they hand it over to me would they turn impure."

"Elora, the possibility of them not perishing is almost zero. The place is not said to be pristine from human contact for no reason…" Iving tried to explain further, "But let's say that you manage to get the scimitar, the spiritual being would then have to face Her Majesty Queen Frigga, and they would cease to exist."

"Are you telling me I am wasting my time with practically impossible ideas? Might I add that this situation itself is an impossible one?" My aggravation grew. "Since when did you, a murderer, care so much about anyone's life?"

The room fell silent, with only the ticking of the wall clock breaking the stillness.

"Elora…" Iving softly called my name, wearing the same expression he had worn countless times when I was ordered to live with him in his house.

"Don't you dare take my name!" I spat, rising.

"I am your Queen," I reminded him sharply. "I do not agree with you mocking me!" My teeth ground against each other with every word.

"Elora, I am not…" He tried to sound reasonable, but it was too late.

I slammed the door, leaving everything incomplete. The two girls who were deep in conversation stopped to look at me, witnessing my glare, which made them bow. Yes, I am a Queen. I shall not be treated as ordinary because I am not the kind and generous Queen that the books talk about.

Entering my housing unit, I smashed the door behind me and stood by the window. Folding my arms, I convinced myself that I was right in my circumstances while staring at the fenced garden, unaffected by the scene I had caused.

My hands were seized roughly, and before I could catch a glimpse of my assailant's face, I found myself forcefully thrown against the wall. The eyes that met mine were only inches away, filled with a seething anger and profound pain.

He ensnared me within a cage of his arms, his words forced through clenched teeth, "Iving, being Aristera can call you by your name…" I shut my eyes, turning away, desperately hoping he would release his grip, but he remained steadfast. "But you tell me, what is going on!" he growled.

"WHAT DO YOU THINK YOU'RE DOING?" I spat back at him, summoning the courage to confront the intense situation.

The mere mention of Iving's name felt like acid on my skin, causing an intense burning sensation. He cracked his neck, a slow bend to the right and then the left, followed by a roll from right to left, all while maintaining direct eye contact. I should have known better from past experiences.

In an instant, his fist collided with the wall, narrowly grazing past my ear and leaving it reddened. I involuntarily held my breath, the air thick with tension and distress. Breaking away from the wall, he turned, pinching the bridge of his nose, visibly grappling with his anger. Then, he pivoted to face me again, pressing against the wall as he prepared to speak once more.

My eyes began to leak tears, overwhelmed by fear and worry. I had thought Maldeus was the only being in the world capable of igniting terror in me, but I was wrong. Maurilio did too, except his presence kindled pain, worry, and an endless well of patience for love.

"Elora," he whispered, his hand tenderly resting on my cheek. He rubbed gently, as if applying a soothing ointment to whatever was broken within me. His warm breath enveloped me, silently pleading for love. My emotions were a chaotic mess.

"Why do you care?" I interrupted, halting him before the yearning for love could slip off.

He closed his eyes and let out a breath of disbelief. "Do you not know, or are you pretending?" he asked. I paused, looking at him, attempting to conceal the look of complete euphoria on my face. "I'm in love with you."

His words left me flabbergasted, the earlier look of passion now fading. "I don't understand. You demand answers that I cannot give you, and even after knowing who I am, you… you say you love me?" I hesitated, and as soon as I concluded my question, I gave my resolution, not wanting him to answer because I feared a 'yes.' "Too late," I showed him my left hand. "I'm married."

I pushed him away at his elbow, causing the cage to break, and started walking away. However, he pulled me back, pressing me against the wall and leaving a trail of light kisses along my ear, jaw, and neck. He bit my skin lightly, playing with the sensations that I desired. Despite the tempting allure, I resisted the urge to give in. It made me feel alive, but I couldn't deny the commitment of my marriage.

I didn't even realize when the passion had escalated, and suddenly my hands were pinned to the wall. I found myself standing in the most vulnerable position a woman could allow a man to reach. His kisses continued down to my sensitive chest, but then he stopped abruptly.

Opening my eyes to see what caused the sudden halt, I realized he was staring at my chest. A wave of shame flooded over me as he stood there, observing the imprint of dark magic on my heart, on my bare chest.

I attempted to pull my hands away, but the grip felt like weights. After struggling for what felt like an eternity, I just stood there, watching him watch the mark with a look of terror. The thought of the mark had been completely erased from my head; my desires had overwhelmed my rational thinking.

He stood without even blinking. I broke at the sight. He mustn't have known… His eyes shifted from my chest to my eyes, and he took a step back.

Pushing him away, I quickly closed my shirt and wiped the tears running down my cheeks. I rushed into the shower, turned it on, and stood below it, attempting to mask away my sobbing with the patterning of the drops. I wasn't aware until he held me from behind, his hand snaking around my waist, pulling me closer to his heavenly comfort, wrapping me in his cocoon of warmth and love. I tried pushing him away, fearful of Maldeus's anger, but Maurilio was strong, and eventually, I gave in.

"Shh…" he whispered into my ears, burying his head in my neck. "It's okay, I'm here."

We stood in that comforting position for several minutes, the water drops gliding over us, unifying us.

"Let me love you," he breathed in my ears after my sobs had settled.

****

The Queen's face turned red, and she bit her lips while looking at the writer. "The people cannot see that side of me and Iverson. It is too open. His Majesty wouldn't mind, but would you please write that less intimately?"

The question disrupted Grissa's focus. "Umm…Yes…Yes, of course," she struggled with her words. "And Iverson was not scared of… you know…? Maldeus seemingly knew deep things about you that he couldn't have known without having access to your mind."

"Oh, we were terrified, but even then, every night I would find myself crawling into his arms, and he would too, sometimes. If I didn't fall asleep, I would stare at the ring on my finger, pondering whether the events would have turned out differently, whether I would have been with Maurilio.

"I would watch Maurilio's face when he slept… not knowing when it would be the last. Maldeus knew of my life before I even met him, maybe it was the bond between us that gave him knowledge… but every moment was scary because if he knew things, then it meant I was openly defying him."

"And did he know?" The writer's face turned grave.

"In January, he summoned the three of us. We had no information about why, and we had to leave. I had to give priority to my King."

****

Even though we stood in a part of the Soul Forest, surrounded by an army of trees as tall as the Hyperion, the smell of the ground outside the black mansion was dirty and unusual, akin to the pits of hell—burnt coal and sulfur. I walked, hidden behind Iving and Maurilio, into the very house that only a handful of people knew because whoever entered never exited alive. The inside of the house remained the same as when I had last seen it, with a sense of brooding evil in every corner.

My hands trembled at the table, and even the slightest of sounds made me recoil. Maurilio looked equally terrified but showed no regret for the time we spent together. He reassured me with a small nod when he saw my pale face. The crown prince and his wife were already seated, and Frank, who opened the door, now stood beside the table. Iving eyed me indifferently.

Contrary to the idea that family time was a period of joyous peace, this one was not, and then the deadliest of sounds came—the clicking of his walking stick with every step. I closed my eyes, hoping to disappear into thin air. My mouth began growing dry, but the moment I felt his shadow on me, I rose and genuflected before him, just like the others in the room. Maldeus' shadow was not ordinary; it was not just a reflection of grayness. Every inch of it spoke anger and an aura of absolute hate.

"My king," I said with the best affection I could muster.

"Rise, all," he commanded, and we followed his orders like dogs. Perhaps even a dog had more dignity compared to us.

"Tell me what news you bring, Elora." He did not wear his pretense, which was more disturbing because his question was direct with a hidden purpose. I did not look at his face all this while; I could not. I swallowed the non-existent moisture in my mouth. "Your Majesty—"

"SILENCE!" He spat at Iving, who shuddered. He then turned and brought his face close, making sure I could hear the stiffness in his breath. Gripping my face with brutal tension, he forced me to face him. I winced but dared not make eye contact.

"Look at me!" his spit flew onto my face through his bared teeth. My jaw began to ache. Summoning energy, I looked up into his eyes. They were pitch black, the darkest of the darkest room, pure evil that made my body burn. I had to look away, toward the King's left, at Iving, who watched the scene with no sympathy at all.

I wanted him to release my face, but he did not. "I-will-not-repeat-twice."

"I have not…" I said, my eyes filled with tears, but I fell silent. His hand struck me across the face, driving it laterally and leaving it stinging red.

"Failure NEVER receives acceptance, only punishment."

****

"So, it was not because of Iverson…" Grissa looked confused, "Then how is it that Maldeus knew, how did he know everything about you so well?"

"Till this day, that remains the biggest mystery of my life. I forgot to mention, you may meet the King tomorrow and Bran Becile, the day after. Should your work not end with them, you may ask for another appointment…"

"Oh, finally!" The woman placed her hand on her chest in relief. "I thought I would never be able to meet them! Thank you, Your Highness."

Elora acknowledged her gratitude and continued to speak about how the King had permitted time only until term end, and if the task was not complete, then he would personally create hell for her. Grissa interrupted her again.

"You mentioned that the king spoke about punishment? Did he use the whip…" her face scrunched, "What of Iving and Maurilio's punishment?"

The Queen shook her head. "No, he took away an Enchanter's identity. Our power." The Queen watched her flabbergasted face and chose her next words delicately, "away from me."

"That's like living with half the supply of oxygen cut to our body… It must have been painful… you could have died, how did…" She cried.

The Queen smiled, "An ordinary Enchanter would have, but I was bound to dark magic."

"He could have done that earlier then why did he not?"

"Maldeus always looked at his benefit; he couldn't have done it earlier. He was not stable. The reason why he had gone into over sixteen years of sleep was not because of Her Majesty Queen Frigga."

She paused, "It was because I was not in the same realm as his; he had bound his soul to mine, and I was not near him. When I returned, he woke. He had his walking stick for support, but later it became an accessory, and that was when he decided he could increase his power without collapsing. But it was going to end soon."

"How do you mean?" She froze, staring at the Queen.

****

Elora Bates

The three of us returned to the academy; Queen Frigga stared at me, deeply contemplating, before we could enter the academy ground. She halted us.

"Queen of the Land," she claimed my title, touching my shoulder with her green hands. "I know what obligation the King has put you under, and I know what he has done to you."

Her voice was comforting, not threatening. But I looked at her with such hatred in my eyes. She was the reason why I wasn't even able to stand properly, the reason why I had trouble breathing because 'she knew,' she knew things that ordinary people did not. How evil and vile my thoughts were toward her knowledge of the known, and I didn't care whether she could read them; nothing could be worse than the situation I am in.

I made no move to reply, but she continued, "I shall help you."

My eyebrows furrowed, "Why!" I automatically hissed, but I took a step back, realizing that she meant what she had said. Her eyes didn't even blink, and her appearance was one of severe concern. "I thought you were not to interfere with the matters of the living!"

"Not everything should have a reasonable explanation,"

"Then what for in return?" Maurilio stood up next to me. I was not the only one shaken to the core. Iving too watched her with one raised eyebrow.

"Nothing," she whispered, "Nothing of my benefit." Something stirred within me; I was more perplexed now. "And how will you…" I hesitated.

"I will give you the scimitar." She didn't hesitate, showing how different we were even though we both carried the title of Queen.

"Scimitar?" Iving finally spoke, almost choking at his question. "You will not benefit anything by giving us the scimitar…" Iving rubbed his forehead, "and you want to go out of your way to give us the scimitar…" His words, for the first time, sounded inferior.

"You have done well, child. The man in Headmaster Sherwood's office will speak to you."

"And who is that?" I asked, bringing my neck forward. She stood silent, as a spiritual being; she always spoke in a much-complicated manner, and so I pushed, realizing that only Sherwood would be in his office.

"You mean, Sherwood?" Her eyes wandered to me, then to Iving, to Maurilio, and finally ended back at me.

"Sherwood has been dead for a year now." We didn't blink, gawking at Frigga. The sound of the whispers of the forest and the response of its creatures filled the dumbstruck silence.

"You must go now. I will meet you there. Hurry, not all of the forest stands by me. Those of his will inform him." Frigga spoke, bringing us back to reality, making us realize that this was not a dream.

The depth of her words had not sunken into us; we were concerned about Maldeus at hand. We followed her partial commands without any further question, rushing into the darkness at the academy's gate. It must have been beyond curfew time.

When the light of the ground came into our view, we began taking hurried steps, but I couldn't. My lungs were aching and so were the muscles in my feet; I wanted to fall.

"Why would the king be mad if his informers tell him that the Queen has agreed to hand the scimitar to us?" Maurilio asked in between exhales, seeing my steps slow, and the question seemed to have struck me too. He came back to support me.

"Because the Queen clearly stands against him."

When we began climbing the stairs, a powerful gust of wind blew, tossing me down the stairs. It was a dark gale, swirling high up in the sky far beyond the ends of the forest, the remnant of its force attacking us. It was so dark that it stood out even in the night's darkness.

"He knows!" I screamed through the loudness of the wind's scream.

Iving and Maurilio caught me by my arm and pulled me up, helping me into the building. The screams of the gale got louder with each moment, and even though it didn't affect us within the building, it showed how bad this was going to get.

"He is two times powerful… My power must have made his power grow."
"We must hurry…. Elora," Iving called my name, causing me to break my contact from the outside to the stairs in front of me toward Sherwood's office. I turned to look at Iving, who was beginning to break a sweat. I then turned to look at Maurilio; he took deep-quick breaths. He was more terrified than worried.

The intensity of the situation hit me. We were going to die; what were we going to do with the scimitar if that King had been provoked? He was capable enough to stand in front of Frigga and probably win.

"Sherwood…" Iving almost screamed, sounding like he was begging for help when he pushed the door open.

Sherwood was standing behind his desk, hands locked behind him, staring at the door, waiting patiently for us. A knowing smile spread across his face when he saw us. Maurilio shut the door behind us.

"Her Majesty Queen…" I began explaining through ragged breath, but Sherwood raised his palm at me.

"There is no need to explain. The Queen has spoken true; she will hand over the scimitar."

"But what of it?" Iving asked.

Sherwood turned to look at me, his gaze intently fixed until I realized what he was asking of me. The idea came as though he had planted it into my barren mind. My eyes grew wide, and I stuttered, hoping that what I was going to say was wrong.

"I die," I stated, knowing that was what he wanted, that was the only possible way. If I died, then all of this would end. Maldeus would lose my share of his power, and he could be defeated, but only if the Queen agreed to end him.

"Maybe, this is the time to make things right…" Sherwood whispered.

I took a step back, rubbing my sweaty neck, still not breaking my gaze. "And what if I don't?"

"Then the entire academy will perish. Every single student and teacher. Every spiritual being, including Queen Frigga. Maldeus will rule the world for all eternity, and you will forever be trapped in your body within an endless loop."

"No!" Maurilio defended me, "You cannot possibly ask her to sacrifice herself!" He clenched his fist, shaking. "Goodness never dies."

Sherwood gave his final words before the Queen entered with the scimitar; 11 inches long, a ruby placed in the center of the hilt covered with diamonds, and on the guard was a black stone, the snake pearl. A white line made of tiny pearls linked the two gems: the pearl and the ruby.

The blade was covered with a sheath made of gold, and a large marking of a cross with triquetra in silver was visible.

"Elora…" Maurilio whispered, making me break my eye contact with the glory of the artifact.

He shook his head, his face had turned red, and he was suffocating. I turned back at the blade, then back at Maurilio, and smiled.

"This option is quick and painless than the slow, torturous death…" Death was inevitable, and I knew it.

"That was not what I…"

"I know, but if I had another option, I would have… Please don't make me think through the situation. I'm fucking terrified," I begged before walking to the scimitar, taking it into my hand from her.

I unsheathed it, unraveling its sharpness through its reflection, sensing the pain before it touched my skin.

"Your Majesty!" I cried, and so did the others come forward to aid her. She fell to the ground, her hand wrapped around her neck, looking at the sky, crying. She then turned toward Sherwood.

"We must move; he has penetrated the border."

Sherwood nodded, turning toward Iving. "It's time to leave, child," and he did the very same thing he did to me.

Iving nodded at the seed planted in his head; I didn't know what it was. The three of them left, leaving me and Maurilio in the room with the watchful eyes of death lurking in the corner. I placed the sheath on the desk.

"You can't… you can't… you sorry… I just…" his voice shook, and he snatched the blade from my hand causing the diamonds to graze my fingers, making blood begin to drip.

"Maurilio, look at me," and I held his face in my hand, "I have to…"

"No," he firmly refused, shaking his head violently. He closed his fingers tightly around the handle of the scimitar, in defense.

"No," he confirmed his refusal.

I looked him in the eye, "You'll make a fine King one day." And clutched his hand; his eyes grew wide at my unguarded move and drove his hand, causing the blade to pierce through my heart smoothly.

I watched his face, taking in every detail. He clutched my head; the events of my life began flashing before me. My neck was losing its strength, and the last thing I saw was a white light toward the sky, and then it went black; the light had pulled me into the vacuum.

Chapter 14
The Remaining Evil

Grissa sat in the chair in the same chamber that she had been occupying for the past few weeks during her meetings with the Queen. Even though she was usually comfortable, today her feet were violently tapping the carpeted floor. After glancing around at the empty room, she allowed a mirror to form in her hand, making sure she seemed presentable enough.

The door opened and shut, and the mirror vanished into green dust, falling to the floor. Grissa rose and immediately knelt without looking at the person who had just walked in.

"Your Majesty!" She bowed her head, licking her lips.

"Rise, Grissa, how are you today?" the King asked, immediately sitting on the armchair in front of her. She frowned at his friendly tone, a side none had seen before.

"I'm fine…" She rose, returning to her seat, still devoid of eye contact. "How can I help you today?" She finally tried to peek at his face, who ruled Ariesque. The image that people would risk all to be blessed with. She would be among the only few Enchanters who had had the privilege of meeting the man who only came to them through the pictures portrayed in the media.

A well-shaped beard, those gray eyes that Elora spoke of all suited up and seated before her, was the King. Maurilio Slayholt. Her eyes warmed with tears. "Perhaps, you could tell me what happened after the Queen died?" She choked in nervousness. "If you're comfortable with…" She began coughing and immediately covered her mouth, looking away in fear of the King.

The King rose, in his elegantly crafted body, walked toward the table, poured a glass of water, and handed it to her.

"There is no need to worry. I am King only when I am needed to be. You may be open to questioning me during our interviews." Her gaze stood fixed on him until he indicated the glass in his hand through his eyes.

"Thank you, Your Majesty," she replied, covering her shock with a smile, and sipping the water. The King waited patiently until the glass clinked on the table.

"Now then, go ahead…" He said, waving his hand.

"The Queen has told me of quite the events with your involvement, but there are some that I would like to personally hear from you, like the ball, how you came to fall in love with her but before all that, I'd like to hear about the changes that happened when the Queen had died."

****

Maurilio Slayholt 👑

Orson appeared out of nowhere when I least expected her. The shock on her face was palpable as her mouth hung wide open. Pausing to digest the scene, she eventually shook me, demanding answers, while the girl in my arms collapsed onto the floor.

In the midst of Orson's questioning, the gravity of the situation began to sink in. I wondered if Orson, along with all the students and the entire academy, knew that Elora had sacrificed herself for them. Would they ever know?

Orson halted and composed herself, realizing the urgency. "We need to take her for nursing."

Other professors appeared at the scene, attempting to take the lifeless girl away from me, but I resisted vehemently. I yelled at their faces, refusing to leave her side.

In the whirlwind of emotions, they pulled me up along with the lifeless form, guiding us toward the hospital. Overwhelmed, I lost track of the moments that transpired during the journey from the office to the hospital—waves of people, gasps, and screams echoed around me.

As we reached the hospital, a nymph held my hand sympathetically and uttered, "She's gone. I'm sorry." I blinked once, twice, and then turned to look at the bed. The truth hit me like a ton of bricks—she was dead.

Orson entered the room, delivering more devastating news. "I know what has happened. The King is dead. Iving is dead," she paused, her voice breaking. "And so is Sherwood. Sherwood's body isn't even there, and now… and now Elora's dead."

"Elora is not dead," I firmly refused.

"Maurilio," she turned to face me, staring into my eyes. "That's Elora…" she cried.

"No! That's not, that's… that's…" My voice cracked, breaking into irreparable pieces. "Your father will be here soon, dear. Pull yourself together; this is an emergency. The students have been dismissed home, and there is to be a meeting in three hours."

What was she worried about, Ariesque? Elora is dead! Her student is dead! My Elora is dead!

"Maurilio!" she bellowed with patience. "WHAT!"

"We must leave, now!"

I rolled my tongue against the front of my lower teeth, anger building within me. "NO!" I glared.

"Don't you dare 'no' me. I am just as wounded as you are. Three innocent people are dead…" She huffed out deep breaths, calming herself. "Look, Maurilio, I know you didn't choose to be who you are." Her eyes sparkled with just as much pain as mine did. "The nation must be before everyone, to you." She pressed her finger onto my chest, whispering "even before your loved ones, and I'm sorry you don't get to mourn in peace."

I had no words left to argue with, and so, I obeyed her, giving Elora one final glance before leaving. I followed Orson, unmindful of the surroundings, the only feeling of Elora in my arms, now cold and without a soul in bed lingering in my mind.

We felt loved together, she loved me too. But we never had a chance together. We could have made it to the happy ending, but it ended before it could start.

Father showed up at the border of the forest where Queen Frigga, Orson, and I were waiting. Even the night was at a loss, the sky was pitch black without stars. The earth was bare and dead.

When father saw me, he held me, cupping my face, the look of worry eased off of him. "Your mother was…" he exhaled, turning to the Queen of the Forest.

"What caused the turn of events?" He asked solemnly, and hesitantly added, "Is he… really…"

"Gone," Frigga completed, "The ground you stand on is a witness, and so am I. We shall testify only his death."

"We should leave then, now."

Frigga observed the diplomats with an air of authority, and the room fell into an uneasy silence. She caressed the polished surface of the table as if drawing strength from it, summoning a brown satyr to her side, a creature that emerged from the very ground itself.

Our entourage entered the royal office building located in the province of Lunare, ascended two floors using a lift, and entered a conference room designed to accommodate at least twenty people. The twelve diplomats and the minister of the Magaime Corporation were already seated around the long table. As Frigga entered, they rose and bowed to their hip level, waiting for further commands.

With everyone settled, the tumultuous talks began immediately. The diplomats appeared disoriented, their loyalties tied to Maldeus, who had appointed them during his oppressive reign. Earlier traditions, where the royal family held diplomatic roles, were overthrown by Maldeus, resulting in the murder of the entire royal bloodline, including my grandfather and the Grand-Queen.

Amidst the diplomats, the minister of the Magaime Corporation stood out as a hopeful figure. Despite being summoned in the middle of the night, he maintained a well-groomed appearance, displaying a sense of professionalism and eagerness.

One of the diplomats, seemingly amused by the news of the King's death, couldn't restrain his laughter. "I was awakened in the middle of the night for such humorous news that the King is dead!"

"Yes, and should the King be here, he will torture the rumorer to death," another added.

Frigga intervened, commanding peace in the room with her formidable presence. "I know of your concern, and I know of what intentions they come from," she declared, scanning each diplomat's eyes with a keen understanding of their vain lives.

"So then, Your Highness, what is the cause of this meeting?" The diplomat from Largus asked, playing with his ostentatious gold chain in an uncivilized manner, questioned the purpose of the meeting, his tone filled with distrust. Frigga, maintaining her composure, prepared to address their concerns. The anger within me simmered, but revenge would have to wait; now was the time for resolution.

The room buzzed with commotion as the diplomats vehemently denied the news of Maldeus's death. Frigga maintained her composed silence, a regal demeanor that demanded respect.

Amidst the chaos, a swirl of water near the double doors drew my attention. Gradually taking shape, a man emerged, holding one of the triumvirate staff made of sanctalbum, also known as the 'holy white' metal. The staff bore the symbol of the scimitar – the cross and the triquetra. Sanctalbum, with its distinctive properties, had three prongs, each reflecting a different color – green, blue, and brown. In the center was an extension of white metal topped with the crystal of Atlantis, encased in an intricately designed cage. The staff was one of three, each held by a powerful figure: the king of the land, the king of the sea (presently entering the room), and Queen Frigga.

This was my first encounter with King Rayan, the ruler of the sea. He defied my expectations, dressed in a golden top extending from his neck to his waist, showcasing his muscular physique. The lower part of his attire, like the top, was a breathable combination of plastic and nylon, complemented by shiny rubber-like shoes. A green fabric tied around his waist added a splash of color to his ensemble.

King Rayan, expressing apologies to Queen Frigga for his delayed arrival, bowed gracefully. The queen acknowledged his presence with a nod, and he proceeded to take his seat.

Amidst the gathered assembly, Queen Frigga addressed the room, confirming, "Now, since we have all gathered here. The news is true. Maldeus is dead," the Queen declared. The diplomats erupted in another uproar of denial, expressing disbelief.

"Preposterous!"

"What's the proof?" one diplomat challenged, facing Frigga directly. The Queen remained stoic, a harbinger of the deathly silence followed.

"How dare such filth question me!" She retorted aggressively.

She didn't like being here, among Enchanters, and would usually not have interfered with our matters. The diplomat, who unintentionally provoked her, began apologizing for his life. But that is the actual question, why did she voluntarily take part in the elimination of Maldeus. She shifted her gaze to me, squinting, before refocusing on the diplomat.

She kept her promise to Maldeus, she had devised a successful plan, but at a great cost – three lives lost. Does her compromise make her good or bad?

The diplomat quickly added, "I didn't mean to provoke Her Majesty. I only wish to pay my final respects to the King's body and offer condolences to his Queen."

Frigga, looking at the diplomats with superiority, mentioned the deaths with pride. "The King is dead, and so are two innocent people. The King's body has been consumed by the earth, and any evil shall perish in the same manner."

She continued, revealing the names of the deceased. "Solomon Sherwood, main headmaster of the Academy of Silverstring; Intimus Iving, one of the three headmasters of Aristera; Father of the Queen of the land…" Gasps arose, and Frigga declared their deaths as sacrifices to save the people.

In response to my father's polite inquiry about her assistance, the accusations began. "She didn't help us. She murdered our King."

"Aristera was involved in this plot too. How dare he betray the King!"

"We must declare war against her."

My father, the crown prince, flatly refused through gritted teeth, turning to look back at the Queen after eyeing every accuser. "I will do no such thing!"

"You must take over the crown," the Queen declared to my father, then addressed the crowd. "Let this act of mine be a reminder of peace and morality for the forest, the land, and the sea."

The King of the sea, finally speaking, added his voice to the conversation. "Indeed. Maldeus has destroyed the land and its people, and you must restore it back."

"I trust your words…" Father hesitated, still scared of the idea of 'Maldeus', "and so I shall hold the ceremony tomorrow. After this, I shall bury the dead with respect, but I must know of their deeds to do so. For the Aristera that I knew was a cruel man by heart."

It is a huge act for a king to conduct a burial, only the greatly honored receive it, and so, Father's inquiry seemed justified.

"I am curious too, Your Highness," King Rayan said, "For all I've heard are about his murders and inhumanity."

The Queen remained silent in response to the queries, turning instead toward the minister of Magaime.

"I assume you will be holding a trial tomorrow after the new King crowns."

"Indeed, it is mandatory to eliminate anything that HE created now that you've said he's gone." Several eyes swirled in the room when 'trial' was announced.

"And what about us?"

"You cannot just kick us out."

"Yeah, we were chosen." The diplomats argued, but the Queen looked at Riordian.

"After the crowning, your presence in the court shall be justified. You shall follow your laws and keep what is good, or you shall perish by the hands of evil. That is all for now, spread the good news," the Queen gave a final nod, dismissing the crowd.

"Rayan, Riordian, Maurilio, and Celestina. I must speak to the four of you," Frigga declared and stopped the four of us on our way out. The remainder of the crowd disappeared, and the voice of annoyance and curses faltered along.

"Intimus Iving and Solomon Sherwood's secret must remain a secret, and I assure you that it is upon their request that their glory is not being declared. But I shall reason with you very soon once I handle all matters. I must stand before the greatest Enchanter before so. After the day that follows," She looked at Riordian, "After your crowning, the three kingdoms will meet again to discuss its affairs."

She then turned to look at me. "You seem devastated, Maurilio. Why?" The three other people in the room turned their eyes toward me. Was it fun being 'knowledgeable'? Why was she acting like she was one of us! Didn't she know?

"Elora is a good woman, Maurilio."

I closed my eyes; I had to correct her. Elora is not there. "Was," I said, looking at the floor.

"Have you ever heard me make an error in my speech before?"

I looked up at her, bewildered. What was she trying to tell me? A fire lit in my heart, and my legs grew wobbly at the idea.

****

"But how?" Grissa cried in frustration. "Hasn't the Queen told you about it?"

"No, not yet." "I must respect her privacy. I cannot tell you what happened then.

You must ask her…" Maurilio leaned back, turning his head up to the ceiling. Grissa looked disappointed but did not attempt to plead further.

"Then, maybe you could tell me about the time you fell in love with her?"

"The truth is, I don't know."

The writer tipped her head forward, "You don't know!" and immediately apologized for her tone.

"Maybe it was the first day of the academy when I saw something unusual in her while she climbed the stairs of the main building, but yes, the moment I realized I was in love was at the ball."

****

Maurilio Slayholt 👑 —*Eromen's day*

I listened to Mark speak about how Ariel Taylor's father, the girl from Pruden—almost died on New Year's Eve when he was blaspheming about the King to the man next to him in an underground secret pub. The man had later claimed to be Aristera. Funnily enough, that news cannot be true.

The man must have been a follower of the King and not Aristera. Because I know Aristera could never be a good man. The Taylor family would have been entirely eradicated or been sentenced to slog in Bermuda.

I scanned around the room. Reika wore a white mask and a pale yellow outfit, like all the other professors in the room. I turned away from Iving, who was wearing a collared shirt quite different from his always turtleneck tops. But someone caught my eyes—an unclear figure began walking forward, her face hidden beneath a black mask like mine but carved more feminine. She wore a lace emerald off-shouldered gown, and the dress matched with the gem on her mask.

She turned toward me, and I instantly recognized her. She was Elora, the most beautiful woman at this moment. I was beginning to tear up, but I refused to blink. Her eyes moved to the man next to me, at Liam, and they grew sad and red. She looked away to the boy standing beside her, telling him something. I continued to look at her. I must be the luckiest man tonight.

"Maurilio?" Liam called, "Are you even listening, or are you too busy with Elora?" His tone told me that he was trying not to display what he felt from within.

The ceremony unfolded with its initiation and speeches, and Katelyn Giovani's graduation speech resonated deeply with me.

"The worst part of all is being out of reach even though you're there, but don't worry, you were written to grab the stars."

I was out of reach in my nation, I felt like an outsider even though I've lived here through my birth. I wish I did not have to live up to certain aspects of manners and keep my personality within a circle of fire. I should probably just shove my stuff down my throat and live with it.

During the pairing ceremony, Elora tapped my shoulder, attempting to introduce herself. However, she stopped abruptly and then called my name. It was evident she wasn't pleased with my presence around her. In a protective instinct, I pulled her into me when I noticed the guy behind her almost tripping onto her.

"Careful," I called out.

There was a desire within me to keep her close, not to let her go. But I reluctantly had to let her go of my touch, realizing that my actions only created discomfort. Elora was unlike any other girl I had been with, and the feeling of wanting to envelop her in my wings and shield her from the world intensified with each passing moment.

I felt strange within me. The royal family's law dictated that I could only marry a woman from my tribe. If not for that, Elora would have already carried the title of 'mine.' Every man in the room might be yearning for royal blood, but I would give anything to be them just to have Elora.

As we played through the games, I watched her become tipsy with just the first glass of EN wine, even though she tried hard to conceal it. She seemed so soft and fragile.

Occasionally, my gaze would shift to her, and the desire to make her mine intensified. Thoughts of Iving, her father, only brought forth the image of a devastated Elora.

I couldn't bring myself to tell her about her father, despite her numerous pleas. It wasn't solely my decision, but I wanted to witness her happiness for as long as possible before the harsh truth confronted her. Iving continued to live up to his terrible reputation in my eyes. Initially, it was just stories, but now I was a witness to his disgusting nature silently keeping watch over his daughter and causing her suffering.

Elora swayed to the beat, clutching her gown—a visible struggle. The paper in diminished in size every few minutes, yet she reveled in her euphoric world. Suddenly, she tripped, and I, entangled in her dress, lost my balance, falling to the floor.

The couple behind us groaned, having lost their paper-space. Elora began whining, oblivious to her semi-babbling state, "Hey, what ya… is bish hou yu plan on winnin'?" I grinned, biting my lip; she was cute.

She shook her head, face turning red. We were inches apart, and her lips were tempting me. Pushing herself up, she gathered her composure.

"Let's go eat something…" she attempted to assert dominance, but it waned when she turned to me. Her words morphed into an inaudible whisper of embarrassment.

Entering the Hall of Bonding and parting ways, Owen Figer, the Eromen, engaged me in conversation in Liam's presence. "Ahh…There's Iverson," he called, and reluctantly, I joined their discussion.

"Like I was saying, I heard it was His Majesty the King who planned the attack on the forest, on Andronicus Day."

This caught my attention.

"No way, you think Her Majesty the Queen of the Forest was not strong enough to prevent it," Liam replied.

"I overheard the satyr talk about it. Her Majesty was not in our realm at that time. She was in the spiritual realm, and by the time those men entered the forest, it was too late… What do you think, Maurilio? You were there, weren't you?"

"Ummm…" I hesitated, contemplating the possibility of his potential explanation for the escalated events in the forest. Glancing at Liam, who appeared unfazed by the conversation, I took a moment to collect my thoughts.

"But that's not the real question here; the question is why did His Majesty want to invade the forest? It wouldn't be for no reason now, would it? And if it was for waging war, two men!" Owen exclaimed. "He sent two men!"

"Why are we having this discussion at least three months later?" My eyes shifted to Liam, hoping none of this conversation affected him because that was when he and Elora parted ways. I wanted to maintain good terms with him.

"We were just talking about Her Majesty, and I didn't realize when things escalated," Owen replied.

Owen Figer's reasoning seemed sound, fitting all the puzzle pieces together except for the last one. Why did Maldeus want to enter the forest? Was it because of me? But he could have just summoned me out of the academy. My attention wavered from the conversation, and my expression twisted when I spotted Elora, who had just downed a glass of 'feeling.'

I groaned inwardly; that fool didn't just give her a strong alcoholic drink after two glasses of EN wine. Now she's smiling like a child lost in their imaginary world. Oh no, fuck! She turned to look at me, a pout on her face. What the hell are you doing to me? She was so adorably sexy; my pants were growing tighter by the minute. I am so mad now.

"Ther yu ar! Les go danc," She stomped while pointing at the 'room of assembly.'

I rolled my eyes at Bran and then went along with Elora's desire, extending my palm toward her. She squealed, jumping with her hands over her mouth, and then took it. I hoped my face didn't betray what my body was feeling as I led us out of the dining area.

Entering the hall, the games were over, and it was almost midnight, the lights dim. White smoke swirled from hip level to the floor, people were already dancing. A group of girls danced in the corner, but it was mainly couples. Some danced with their respective partners, while others danced with their companions.

I placed my hand on her waist, and she delicately rested hers behind my shoulder as we swayed to the rhythmic music. Initially, she avoided my gaze, and I followed her line of sight to Sherwood, gracefully dancing with Reika. Iving, leaning on the dais, observing the festivities with eyes reflecting nostalgia for his own time.

Turning my attention back to her sparkling eyes, I wished to be the sole focus of her gaze.

"So, tell me, am I not handsome enough that your eyes wander to everyone but me?" I teased her, and she giggled nervously.

Playfully, I pulled her closer, causing her to bump into my chest. Her expression shifted as she registered the reduced distance between us. I continued to gaze into her eyes, smirking.

Unable to maintain the intensity, she looked away, retreating into her comfort zone, her eyes holding a glimmer of past memories. The smile that adorned her face had faded, and her eyes shifted to Liam. It was evident that the combination of ex and alcohol wasn't serving her well. Despite the warmth in her gaze directed at me, it wasn't enough for my satisfaction.

"Let's go..." I whispered into her ear, sensing a loss of control over my desires, the discomfort in my pants becoming increasingly unbearable.

I began pulling her away. Initially, she seemed oblivious to my intentions, following me quietly. However, her resistance surfaced when we reached the stairs, realizing we were leaving the party.

Her tantrum echoed, capturing the attention of everyone around us.

"I don' wunna go!" she began crying, resisting my efforts to guide her toward the hall. "Come on, you're tired," I glared at her, feeling mortified by the scene she was causing.

"No... I'm nat... I wunna..." She pointed back at the dance floor, her voice filled with whining. "Alright," I relented, stopping in my tracks, letting go of her hand, and raising my arms in defeat.

She sat on the floor with her arms folded. "I'm going," I declared, taking steps toward the exit. I knew she would follow me, and indeed, she did. Her desire for me was evident, but her complicated life and past prevented her from admitting it.

Descending the academy's stairs, I walked with haste. She followed, screaming behind me, "Stop, les go back..."

Ignoring her, I continued until I entered the house. She kept following me, persistently expressing, "I wunna danc', Maurilio..."

"If yuh don't stop now. I'll scream,"

I stopped in the dark hall, my brows furrowed. A chuckle escaped me as I threw my head back. The distance between us diminished, the clicking of my heels resonating on the wooden flooring of the house. Her breath quickened, and I gently lifted her chin.

"I can make you scream all night," I whispered into her ears, and she was filled with lust. It wasn't an idle statement; she knew I was not simply throwing words, having heard the gleeful moans of other girls that kept her up for many nights.

My hands, hungry for exploration, went around her waist, gliding over her soft curves, and I tossed her effortlessly onto my shoulder. She attempted to kick through her gown, but it was futile; she had barely any force left within her.

"If you don't stop, I'll toss you down," I warned through clenched teeth.

Pushing open the door to our housing unit with eagerness, I then swung open the door to my room. With a swift motion, I threw her onto the soft bed, and she bounced with the force. I gently caressed the hair away from her face, running the back of my fingers over her features, feeling every curve and turn.

The smooth toughness of her face met a pause when I reached her lips. They felt soft, akin to rose petals, and the desire to taste her overwhelmed me.

Holding her neck, I began pulling her closer; she closed her eyes in submission, the only remaining gap filled with the exhales of our warm breath. The temptation to savor her was strong, the allure of the luxury she had to offer almost irresistible.

But reality struck, I couldn't claim her as mine. At least not yet. At least not while she won't remember a glimpse of tonight. The truth dampened the mood, and I paused.

Pecking her forehead, I left for a shower, seeking relief from the conflicting emotions.

Chapter 15
The Afterlife

"Thank you for your patience, Grissa. I know it has been a week, but Her Majesty Queen Frigga has agreed. Because I had no authority to talk about my experience on the other side."

****

Elora Bates

Some weight died in me. I was in the air, my body upright with no force of gravity acting. My eyes were shut, yet I was conscious of everything, like a dream I knew about but had no control over.

I witnessed the conversation that unfolded in Sherwood's office from a corner. I was talking to Sherwood while Iving and Maurilio stood nearby. Queen Frigga then joined in.

Three departed, leaving only Maurilio and me. His pleading eyes and my cries played out at twice the ordinary speed. Then the blade touched me, and abruptly, my eyes snapped open—the dream was over.

I found myself in a box, my body as light as a feather. Was this my coffin? The box appeared peculiar, and the space I occupied seemed surreal; my feet were not on the ground—I was floating, and so was my hair. Was I in space?

Upon closer examination, the box revealed itself to be something else entirely. It was composed of waves on a microscopic level, appearing as lines moving in a distinct pattern. Through the tiny gaps between these lines, light entered. The front of the box vanished into nothingness, and the light blinded my eyes—perhaps I was facing judgment day.

With no time, the blankness of the room came into sight. It resembled Sherwood's office, only it wasn't because it was waves—holographic waves. Even the furniture didn't quite look real.

A ringing silence filled the space, but I wasn't scared of the unknown.

"Elora Bates, Daughter of Intimus Iving and Scarlett Bates. Welcome to the unfinished," Queen Frigga warmly greeted my curious face.

Taking a step into the air outside the box, I saw her silhouette. "This is it then!" I exclaimed, already resigned to my fate.

Happy was an expression I could use, but that would be an overstatement. Sad was an expression I could use, but that too would not define my current state. I was in a stable state of gratitude, relieved from the strong suffocation I felt while I was alive.

"This is not it," Frigga stated, "The scimitar has not killed you."

I looked at her, my eyes partially hooded. I was standing in what seemed like the spiritual world, and she was claiming I was not dead?

"Remember how Eneas told you, Elora, 'Goodness does not die.'"

"I'm sorry, who?" I asked, pushing my head forward. The name sank in. "You mean the Great Eneas? You mean the Great Eneas spoke to me?" I threw my head back.

"Yes, he even taught and laughed and advised," she said, wearing a vapid look.

My body froze, "What are you talking about?" the words came out calmly.

"Child. Would you like to spend some time with me?" Another voice sounded – strong, gracious, and fatherly.

He entered from the door of Sherwood's office. He was surrounded by a white aura but was not a spirit, he was a man, just like me standing in limbo. His eyes looked oddly familiar, but his face did not resemble any I knew. He was old, the creases on his forehead were evidence of that, and his hair and beard were graying out. He wore round glasses and had a protruding belly.

I hesitated to speak, the aura in the room was strongly mystical.

"Eneas," she called, "I'll leave you to it. Remember to keep up with the rules of this world." The Queen disappeared with a swirl. Eneas? I blinked at the man, squinting. The man claimed to be Eneas raised his right hand toward the ceiling and moved it back and forth, causing it to disappear.

I didn't know whether the ceiling had disappeared or whether he had made the sky appear bright and balmy. Everything was like an illusion here; Reality and Dream were no longer something I could differentiate.

Similarly, he brought up two ordinary wooden chairs and placed a table in between. "Have a seat."

The man pulled on one of the chairs, I followed, and he tucked me into it. I kept watching him, observing his words, and the way he walked; they reminded me of Sherwood.

"Who are you?" I finally asked. "Are you the most powerful being in the world? Are you the great Enchanter?"

"No. I am Eneas, the creator of your world. I am Sherwood, the man that counseled you."

"No, you are not Sherwood." I shook my head, "Sherwood was short and stout, and he didn't look like you."

"Don't you think, if I created your side of the world, then I could create an illusion in that world?"

"Then what of the real Sherwood?"

"The poor man died in his house, due to a gas leak. It was then that I had taken his form. Tea?" He asked, beginning to cause a teapot to appear from thin air. I shook my head.

"Did you know? About me? About my bond with His Majesty…" A shiver ran down my soul in memory, "Did you know about my bond with Maldeus?"

"Yes, I have been given limiting authority to know certain things in that world."

With a face devoid of any expression, questions were just spilling out of me, but Eneas patiently handed me the answers.

"What of… Iving? Did you know…?"

"Yes. Do not be mistaken, child. Iving was a man of good intentions. He would have been a worthy King, much worthier than most I've known."

"Then do you even know him!"

Sherwood remained quiet, sipping the tea in his cup. "Sir, what are we doing here? Is this the end?"

"You have to return, Elora. Your time has not yet come."

I paused, releasing a sigh. "But why? The last thing I did was goodness."

"Sacrifice is the biggest gift for humanity; the world would have collapsed by now without it, and you did your best. Evil is gone, it will return every now and then but for now, it will do. But sacrifices like you will be born. But now for you, it is time for you to feel loved." He again smiled empathetically.

"You must return to be a Queen."

"But it's the law of nature, birth-life-death. There is no rebirth." Then suddenly the idea struck me, "And what of Maldeus? Are you sending me back because of him?" My expression paused, in terror.

"No. Maldeus is dead, paying in the pits of hell, and as far as the law of nature is concerned, it does not apply all the time."

"Then why?" I now deplored.

"Because the decision you make as a Queen will be quite different from those of another woman. Because Ariesque needs a broken Queen, not one filled with positivity and a radiant smile. Because you've got fixing to do."

"I don't wish to go back." His air of superiority did not allow my suppressed emotions to remain within.

"I'm afraid you don't have a choice." "And who, may I ask, decides that?"

"We don't leave, Elora, until our purpose is complete. It has been over centuries; I still linger on the face of the earth so that one day I may come to terms with the evil that bore me."

"That must be terrible." Eneas only smiled back. "And who is this?"

"Hello?" A voice reverberated, *"Hello? Is anyone there?"* It was a woman's voice; it came from outside the office door. Sherwood rose, his eyebrows curved.

"Elora. You must return, close your eyes." He kept his eyes at the door, waiting, anticipating for the voice to be heard again, "The mirror of Mortis is in my office, it is yours now. Summon the soul that wishes to speak to you."

He walked to the door, "Do not leave this room and do not speak of these events in the living world. Sherwood's body will be found, soon."

"Am I dead?"

Maurilio's face flashed before my eyes; I was going to return to him. I closed my eyes. It went black.

I didn't know what happened then, the next thing I knew was that I was in the academy's hospital. My body felt new and unused, but the wound I had… I raised my head to look at my body. The wound on my chest was gone, but the dark mark remained.

My hands were covered in blood, panic gripping me like a vice. Desperately, I rubbed my hands on the edge of the bed, and the smooth, dried blood broke into flakes, falling to the ground in a silent fall. As I tried to comprehend the situation, a feeling of surrealism washed over me—it was over, I reminded myself, but everything still seemed like a trance.

My eyes blurred with tears, and my voice began cracking, choked by the overwhelming weight of emotion. The metallic scent of blood triggered unhealed traumas, prompting me to curl into a ball, hiding away from the harsh reality that surrounded me.

"Elora," his voice echoed, cold and cutting through the haze. My body froze, and my eyes fixated on the source of that commanding voice.

"Elora," the voice called again, but this time, the cover fell off, and my mind played tricks on me, dancing between reality and illusion.

"How are you doing?" The strongest being present caressed my arm, and the events of the limbo came rushing back, grounding my mental state in a semblance of sanity.

A nod was all I could manage. Pushing myself to sit up, I moved my feet into the terry slippers on the ground, instinctively clutching the side of the bed for support.

"I hope you are because this is not the end," the enigmatic figure declared. My head made a sharp turn, seeking answers in the eyes that met mine.

She then added, "He is gone. But his influence still lives." A cryptic statement that left me wide-eyed, grappling with the implications of what had just been said.

She sat down beside me, her hands forming a ball, and then she smoothly glided them apart, revealing what was held within her palm. I watched her movements intently, my eyebrows raised, my eyes fixed like a child awaiting the unveiling of magic. In her palm rested a tiny ball—it looked like a pearl, yet its texture differed; it resembled sea glass in a sea foam color. It seemed dense and slippery, evoking a sense of mystery.

"What is that? A pearl?" I asked, my lips moving after what felt like an eternity.

She smiled and placed it on my palm. "You will know what it is soon. Consume it when under trial," she murmured, rising to her feet with an air of enigmatic authority.

The door banged open, breaking the silence. "Elora!"

The face I yearned to see came into view—his waterline red, his face dirtied, and his hair disheveled. He looked miserable; his hands gripped the door frame, trying to anchor himself in a reality that seemed uncertain. His breathing was haggard, mirroring the tumultuous sea on a high tide.

"Elora?" he called again, his face reflecting shock and disbelief.

He didn't take a step forward, unsure if this was real, waiting with trepidation. I smiled at him, glancing at the Queen passing by. She turned to me one last time, imitating the size of the ball with her fingers, bowed, smiled, and left.

Her actions took place all at once, and I had a hard time realizing the Queen had acknowledged me with her bow. Before I could turn back to Maurilio, my head was buried in his shirt. He stroked my hair slowly, kissing my hair.

I heard sobs; I hesitated. Maldeus was gone, I told myself, and there was no need to live in fear anymore. I wrapped my hands around him, pulling his warmth closer to me.

****

"Your Highness? Do you truly wish the world to be informed of this event? I've observed that there hasn't been any official presentation in the court, and the world remains unaware. Did Her Majesty Queen Frigga actually permit you to disclose this?" Grissa's lips tightened.

"Yes, I don't know why I wasn't allowed to share it at that time, but I am now."

The Queen acknowledged that the entire story might sound like a terrible jest, but it was the truth, and she didn't want to fabricate it. She had met the Great Eneas, she spoke to him, and so did countless others in the academy. She understood that Grissa had a hard time accepting it.

"Do you want to exclude it from the book?" Grissa sounded skeptical. "No," the Queen responded firmly, a serious look on her face.

The writer remained silent at the Queen's reaction, then immediately apologized and chuckled, "I know, right? Why would the Great Eneas speak to someone like me!"

Grissa observed the Queen, neither opposing her words nor completely agreeing with them.

"If there's anything that life has taught you, what would it be?" She attempted to change the topic.

"Life has only questions, no answers."

"What about the Mirror of Mortis? Why was it left for you?" Her eyes avoided direct contact.

"I don't know. I've never found any use for it."

"That will be it then, for today, Your Highness."

There was silence. The Queen seemed to contemplate Grissa's demeanor, concerned about how many more people would be dubious.

That night, while Maurilio was not near her, Elora dreamed again.

I found myself standing alone in a dimly lit room, surrounded by shadows that seemed to dance in the corners. The air was heavily silent, broken only by the distant echo of footsteps. I turned toward the sound of his footsteps, I knew them well.

Click-clock-click-clock.

Always in a rhythm.

I saw a figure emerging from the darkness – Maldeus.

His presence sent shivers down my spine, and the room seemed to close in around me. "Elora," he whispered, his voice echoing like a haunting melody. I felt a strange, I was unable to tear my gaze away from him.

"Why do you resist, my Queen?" he murmured, his eyes gleaming with an otherworldly light. "You hold the power to unlock the secrets of the forest. Embrace your destiny."

I tried to speak, but my words were trapped in my throat. Maldeus approached slowly, and I could feel the weight of his gaze. "You cannot escape the path laid out for you. The Scimitar of Darkness awaits, and only you can retrieve it."

As he spoke, the room transformed. Trees sprouted from the ground, their branches twisting . The air became thick with an enchanted aura like a hallucinogen added to the misty air, and the walls of the room seemed to dissolve, revealing the Garden of Eden.

"Step into the unknown, Elora," Maldeus urged, his voice now resonating from all directions. "Claim your destiny, and Ariesque shall know what true power is."

She awoke with a start, her heart racing, and pulled open the drawer to her bedside table, taking out a hand mirror. She wrote down on a piece of paper, 'A vial of oil,' tucked it neatly into a green envelope, and watched it fly out.

As she anxiously waited, contemplating whether she would ever gain acceptance and if the book was a good idea, a royal servant appeared at the door.

"Your Highness, the oil you asked for," the servant said, watching the floor and handing over the vial.

"Thank you." Elora acknowledged with a nod, and the servant bowed before leaving.

Sitting down, Elora played with the vial in her hand. It had been many years, and now it was finally time to face the truth. She poured the oil onto the surface of the mirror while placing it perpendicularly. The surface of the mirror turned bright yellow, signaling the opening of a portal. She had lied about its use; she was afraid of using it, afraid of the truth that the soul had to communicate.

Slowly, she glided her hand through the mirror until her entire hand had sunk, making a circular movement to call the soul with her fingers. She then pulled her hand out and looked at the mirror in front of her, waiting and waiting. Finally, a man walked into the screen of the mirror, the man she had hoped would not.

Intimus Iving with his indifferent face. The man looked through at the woman before him. "I've waited for so long in the limbo," he said. She had not known that his soul would wait.

"What is it you must tell me?" She avoided his eyes. "The truth," he replied, his eyes twinkling.

Elora said nothing, nor did she try to stop him from speaking, so Iving began to give his side of the story.

"I loved your mother, and I loved you. I met your mother, Scarlett Bates when I was completing my royal studies, final year. She was not in any way different," he paused, smiling. "She had just entered her first year. We met through mutual friends, and it didn't take long for us to fall in love. She was perfect for my imperfection."

The smile on his face then faded, "King Egbert Slayholt in his sixties was ruling at that time, and he was well-healthy and capable. I was a basic officer at first, but great at my job that I was soon promoted until I landed to Chief Officer of the royal army—the highest position. The chief of the royal army usually has the task of training the royal family for battle, and Maldeus was personally trained by me. He spoke his heart to me; his heart was stone since our first meeting.

At first, I believed that it was just the way he'd like to appear to the world, but then he often spoke about things he would do and the changes he would bring if his father died. He would speak of torture and abuse like they were something he was born to bring into this world."

Elora shivered; she could relate to what her father said. It had been over five years since she first felt freedom, and even now, she was getting counseling from the royal counselor. The sessions were intense at first, but now they were less often. Still, the impression that Maldeus left on her was not fixable; the marks would always remain imprinted, and she knew it would influence every decision she made for herself and for the country. She knew, and that was all she could do, 'know.'

"I knew Maldeus would bring about the death of the King if given the chance. So, I ordered the royal security to be doubled, giving the excuse that the royal army had received a threat. The King agreed and was in a tight position; guards accompanied him everywhere. Even the food he ate was tested for poison, he was not allowed to have an intimate relationship with his family without guards.

"Maldeus saw and knew he was in no position to attack. He broke into a terrible fight in the palace during their family dinner, claiming the King to be a terrible father who did not spend time with his family and was selfish to worry only about his life.

The poor innocent King fell into his trap; he drank the night blaming himself and ordered the security to be removed the next morning. He then decided to spend the day with his eldest son, Maxwell, like any father and provide him with what he was lacking," Intimus paused.

"The King's body was found at the dining table. But nobody blamed him; there was not enough proof. It was my mistake; I'd raised the security without telling who the suspect was, and this was a good opportunity for Maldeus to blame it on the cook. The cook was publicly beheaded for his innocence. The Queen knew of her son but was so traumatized by his action that she remained silent. Maldeus took the throne, the same day.

"The Queen and Aristera died the next day, and it was obvious to everyone by now that it was Maldeus who killed his mother and Aristera. Riordian was lucky to survive; he pretended to devote himself to the King and obeyed the King's order becoming a pawn in his game. I was expecting death, but Maldeus welcomed me and gave me the position of Aristera but on one condition."

"Me," Elora looked at her father, her voice cracking.

Iving blinked, "I'm sorry, Elora. As the chief of the army and to-be-Aristera, I had to devote myself to the King and only him."

"But… you…" Tears began flowing, "Gave your own child away, and knowing what he was going…"

"NO!" Iving cleared, "I did not know. Had I known, I would not have. That is the one decision I've regretted till death."

"That was what you regretted?" Elora's face grew disfigured with redness and tightened facial muscles. "Then why were you his favorite till the very end?" She spat.

"I was trying to protect you."

"But the harm was done, the day you gave me away." She composed herself, now speaking with a hardened heart.

There was silence, she swallowed, "My name? Why was it, Bates? What happened to my mother?"

"You must know, marriage is a huge decision in this world. The union ring once formed, gives death as a punishment for betrayal. We were not married when we had you; she wanted to get married and asked me of it, but I pushed her away, placing my royal responsibilities first. I'd betrayed her when you were born. That was the second time I'd escaped death and with the worst payment, her death."

His eyes were wet with guilt.

"But you didn't have to kill her?" she clarified, sobbing.

"I had to, I had to kill James Becile too, he was the chief of the army who knew about you. Anyone who knew was a potential threat to Maldeus. Even his brother, Riordian did not know. This was followed by the death of hundreds of army officers when he decided to wage war against Her Majesty, Queen Frigga. He was completely morally depraved and emotionally, he felt nothing."

He looked at her from the screen, hesitating with his next words.

"I committed another grave deed against you…" Elora squinted her eyes at him. "I placed a visus in your mind, that day during our mind invasion practical lesson."

Her eyes grew wide, realization hitting her. He had gone overboard with her that day; she had lost consciousness for a few moments, and her nose bled, these did not sign of just mind invasion. He planted a micro-chip in her, he had access to her entire memories. Maldeus did not just know; it was Iving who saw and informed him.

She blinked away the hurt, "Is there anything else you must tell me?"

"I love…"

"Don't! You were and are better off dead!"

"I agree."

There was stillness, and by the time she had turned her eyes to the screen, her father was gone.

Chapter 16
The World Sees the Mask, Justice

Maurilio Slayholt 👑

The large, overcast courtroom of the Magaime International Corporation was one place I never expected Elora to be in. Small and deadly trials took place here, but the latter applied even to the royal family, excluding the ruling trefoil of the King, his Queen, and Aristera.

It had been a month since Elora came back to life, and I thought I would finally be able to be with her after all our troubles and difficulties. But it didn't end there. After the King, it was the people—Enchanters—that she gave herself to. When Elora became Queen, Maldeus made her wear an inhumane mask, and the image of that mask now remained imprinted on their minds. They didn't want her here. Elora was going to sit trial today, at this very moment.

If it weren't for King Andronicus' greatness, Elora's crimes would have been for the King to judge. Andronicus' wishes to grant the people a better life seemed to have been imposed badly over us, the current royal family. When King Andronicus realized that Enchanters were being treated unequally behind his back, he appointed the great Scholar Zocia. She was the foundation of this huge corporation that now had an almost equal claim over the people as the King.

Sometimes there are exceptions; Maldeus wanted to overthrow the MIC and was in the process of infiltrating it but could never complete it. It all depends on the King ruling. I turned to look at my father sitting on the King's chair in the courtroom, desperately hoping that he would refuse to sit by this trial and, instead, use his authority and power to shape the decisions of this room. Maybe that was the only benefit of having one of the most powerful staff in the world—the staff of Andronicus; the last of the three-triumvirate staff.

Although deep down, I knew we didn't hold much power today, the courtroom was over-flooded with Enchanters, waiting for a decision against her.

My mother, the Queen, chose to stay in the palace. She acknowledged Elora but refused to stand here in court. They had one stance: Elora must be condemned, unlike my father, who was willing to open an ear and hear while keeping his people in mind. But deep down, I felt he was doing this for me. He was willing to give his ears for me; otherwise, he too seemed to deem Elora condemnable. Do they care about this forbidden affair of mine? Maybe, maybe up until some point, but now their responsibilities were more, and given that, they knew Elora's fate. They must have given up on the possibility of *us*. But I haven't, I will give everything I have until my last breath.

I couldn't rest the past week because nobody knew the truth about Elora. Queen Frigga will not even stand here to give her statement. I violently shook my feet on the ground; they all saw Elora as the Queen who sat beside Maldeus during the killings. It's funny how the diplomats were exempted from the trial. It was my father's decision. He presented an official statement to the Office of Zocia that they were under the influence of Maldeus; that they were coerced and provided his title as King to confirm that they would not be a threat to Ariesque.

My father appointed J. Iscariot from Lacoyara as Aristera. He was among the twelve men who sat at the table with Maldeus, but he always tried to avoid raising an issue. My father believes that appointing someone who knows the system would be more beneficial than appointing someone completely new to the system. His replacement as a diplomat has not yet been found, and so he currently handles both his state affairs and the nation. Why do the people have no problem with this? Given the circumstances, they know that Aristera is among the diplomats, but no one knows which of the twelve is him. Why do they have a problem with my Elora? The diplomats did not commit any crime openly, but they were still at the table of Maldeus rather than dead.

The judge walked in, and the prosecutor and defense attorney followed behind him. The crowd rose except for the King to bow, waiting for the judge to take his seat, the seat of Zocia. This tradition was carried out of respect.

"Bring in the criminal," he said after inspecting the papers on his desk. I bit my lip at the word 'criminal.' Is that what she was now? The guards at the door left, and then she came, and people feared her; there were shrieks, and some even shamelessly pointed their finger at her. I wrapped my hands around myself at her sight. She was cuffed in chains, and with every rushed step, her muddy white gown struck her long legs. Her hair was sectioned in clumps, and her neck was glistening with sweat. The night at the ball on Eromen's day flashed before my eyes. She kept walking to the rough pull of the guards holding her arms.

Elora looked up at the judge before stepping onto the criminal box in the center of the room and taking a seat. She turned her head to the people seated toward the right of the defense attorney; none of them made eye contact, even though their seats were facing her. Among them were Liam Sprague, Bran Becile, Ziva Anson, and an old woman, who wore black. The woman kept wringing her hands and looked at the crowd behind Elora, avoiding her eyes.

"The accused, Her Highness Dowager, Elora Slayholt, wife of late King Maxwell Slayholt, has been brought in on the 12th of March for the murder of Cassiden Anderson, godfather of the accused; Daniel Belier, the former director of Magnifisoul Entertainment; Mia Connor, wife of Logan Harper, diplomat of Criosa; Adam Borysov, 48, Eromen; Kimo Orenstein, 32, Zocian; Angela Petrov Thornburn, governor of Law and Legalities, Office of Zocia.

In addition to these charges, she has also been brought in for partaking in the late King's action against the Magaime community: mass murder, dehumanization, ethnic cleansing, and much more. The accused stands against all values of the Enchanter's communities, and therefore upon one of the foundations of the ministry, which states *'Any accused civilian of the Community that poses a threat to Ariesque shall therefore receive no stand from regal status,'* shall have no request presented from the royal family." Elora continued scanning the people in the room, and her eyes finally fell on me at the 'royal bay.' Her face grew calm. We stared into each other for moments; I begged her to remain strong and that I would be with her through this.

"Does the accused have anything to say?" The judge demanded in his voice.

She blinked vacantly before turning back to him.

"I didn't mean those actions," a light sob escaped; her veil of strength was coming off.

"I… I was abused and tortured and forced to…" She tried to justify, her voice beginning to crack, but she still struggled to keep her hold.

"How so?" The judge demanded.

"How so!" She spat; her face contorted, and the entire courtroom gasped. She clenched the wooden arms of the chair; the judge swallowed before being outstared.

"The act of loving his queen was a facade. I was a dog whose leash was in his hands…" Tears began flowing.

"Can you present the trial with evidence of the spoken?" I watched the judge; he was going to tame to his ways regardless of the truth. He wanted her to be convicted, and it was evident by his tone.

Was this it? I couldn't even spend enough time with her; they seized her two days after she woke. No, I mustn't lose hope, even if this trial was a gone case because if I lost confidence, then what about Elora's hope.

But the truth was, I was a fool to even pray for the slightest chance of winning.

"No… but," She was trying hard. I rubbed the nape of my neck. "Then the statement is invalid."

"I object. I witnessed the actions of the late King toward his wife." I rose; somebody had to do something.

The judge paused, flipping the sheets on his table.

"Hmm… then you, the crown prince, must present your written statement." What if we win? Would Elora ever gain acceptance from this world?

As the trial proceeded, the judge called upon those witnesses who volunteered to comment upon her part in their life or any legit statement that they would like to present that would contribute to her overall crime status.

"I'm sure Elora meant no evil. She's only a child, she's no murderer of my… She was under the influence of Maldeus." The old woman, Mrs. Isabel Anderson, as named, wiped her tears with her handkerchief.

"And what does Mr. Liam Sprague have to say?"

"Elora was a girl who stood up against evil; she would never choose something like this."

I watched Elora smile into his eyes; it was not her usual happy smile.

"I object to these words. These people were kept under the Dowager Queen's good side. Intimus Iving was her father, and Cassiden Anderson was her godfather. Why would she choose to murder her close relations? Why did she not deny the option of killing instead? Of course, she had a choice, but she was too glad to lift the knife," the prosecutor scoffed.

Nobody spoke because the king had risen. The prosecutor's face grew pale, and he refused to look above the table; my father watched him with his face slightly tilted and chest puffed.

He then lightly bowed at Elora, the Queen Dowager, even though he was no longer obligated to do it; a Queen without a King is no longer a queen in this world. She loses her title and her power, and although she remains in the royal palace, she is of no significance.

"Please be aware that Her Highness shall have complete support from the royal family."

It was Her Majesty Queen Frigga's words that keep him here, that lets him give her his support. I know he didn't want to. But he just trusts Frigga and lets her play with the strings for now until he becomes a proper King. And if Frigga thinks Elora is something, then she is according to Father.

"Thank you, Your Majesty, but as you are aware…" The judge leered at the King's superiority.

"Yes, I am aware of the laws. The King shall be in no position to use his power to his advantage in any circumstances that threaten the tranquility of our community."

"Yes… yes, Your Majesty," he agreed with a show of respect. The King sat, and the halted trial resumed.

"The court has been presented with the dagger by the prosecutor that we believe was used to kill Cassiden Anderson. It is also believed that Her Highness may have been involved in the murder of Solomon Sherwood, the late headmaster of Silverstring Academy for Enchanters and Enchantress, and Intimus Iving, late headmaster of Silverstring Academy for Enchanters and Enchantress."

"I rule against this evidence." The defense attorney had finally spoken, but I was beginning to lose my faith in him. "Assumptions cannot be counted as evidence in the court of Zocia as it is well written in her book of laws. Unless Her Highness's magic print has been found positively, the evidence cannot be used against her."

The judge looked more offended than anyone in the room. After flipping pages, he declared his sentence.

"The court of Zocia has not been able to find fault in the Queen Dowager." The crowd made discouraging noises, but a wave of relief spread over me. "There is no evidence to prove the murders, nor the listed crimes that she is accused of. Those that came forward to present their statement stand for the Queen and not against her."

Elora continued to watch the scene deadpan; she was emotionally drained, showing no signs of relief at his statement.

"However," the judge raised his voice, trying to overcome the racket of the crowd.

My heart stopped beating at this moment; my ear sharply opened only to the words of the judge; time had halted.

"The former queen is entitled to banishment from our Ariesque; this is not a form of punishment but instead a measure to protect Ariesque and its people. The court of Zocia will wait, and a voting session will be conducted as in the past." He rang the metallic bell on the table. Elora hung her head in defeat.

My hand grabbed my forehead; they dragged her out, holding the crowd's exit. And she did nothing, said nothing, but silently followed.

"I must see her," father declared to me.

"May I…" I hesitated; mother would have denied me permission if she was here, but my father nodded after carefully speculating me.

"Maurilio, as crown prince, you may never get her because even if you do, Ariesque will never love her."

He didn't realize it, but the instant I heard him, I felt my heart break inch by inch. Why did he say that? His words were not lies, but why didn't he lie to me?

He could have allowed me to live with hope until one day I forget her, until someday I get used to her absence.

We walked through the halls of the building; royal guards formed a cell around us on all four sides.

We reached the basement. It was ancient, never rebuilt; made of stones, and lit by torchlight. A guardian stood at the main gate of the prison, stopping the King.

"I'm sorry, Your Majesty. But I cannot permit you." The man bowed to his hip level, truly regretful.

The King continued to look at him, unwaveringly.

Ariesque will never love her.

The man looked at the King, and then metallic clinking could be heard. His keys came into view, and he unlocked the gate.

"I will remember this favor," the King said and went ahead of me.

I bowed to the man before entering, walking past several doors, and the shadow of our guards leaping in the background of the passageway.

The King stopped before the door that had one of the MIC guardians, who bowed to the King, giving him access to the door. He pushed open the dark cell, allowing light to take over darkness.

Elora was sitting curled in the corner, covered her face. I exhaled at the way they treated her.

Ariesque will never love her.

I have nothing now, nothing to protect her with; she would be better off in the other world without her memories. Happier. Our guards stood behind us, blocking the light to her; she pulled her hands down revealing her lost face.

"Elora," Father said.

"Your Majesty," Elora rose, kneeling on the floor. She blinked at me for a split second but then turned to face the ground. The chains wailed loudly at her movement.

"Rise, Elora," he said soothingly, "I have come to give this to you." He pulled out an object from his pocket that I could not see clearly and presented it to her.

"The Mirror of Mortis," she whispered, surprised.

"You must know what it does, I assume?" "Allows me to talk to souls of the dead."

"I do not know; this was given to me by the Queen of the Forest."

"And what about her? Will she give her statement of me?"

"I'm afraid not."

The faith lingering in her vanished, the glimpse of emotion in her died.

"I shall take your leave," Father left.

I knelt to reach her eye level, "You know…"

"Stop," she cut me off. "It's of no use. This is where it all ends, Your Highness."

"Elora…" The strings to my broken heart completely fell apart.

"Thank you and good luck."

"Maurilio," father called from behind. I glided the back of my hand over her face, staring into her, one last time before leaving.

She wasn't going to listen to whatever I had to tell her, and I could not force her. The steel door shut with a loud bang behind me, and the girl I loved was stuck in there.

Three days later, the decision was made.

"The Magaime Corporation, after considering the statement from its witnesses, from the accused, the random representative of the people, and with all its established proof, has decided to stand by its sentence: the accused, wife of the late King Maxwell Slayholt, Queen Dowager Elora Bates, will be banished from the Magaime community…"

The sound of those words burned me to the ground. This was what the people had wanted.

Elora didn't wish to see any visitors who requested an appointment. She left me; she left our struggle; dividing the pain unequally between us.

****

"She left?" An uneasy look spread on Grissa.

"Didn't you go to see her? On the day her memory was to be erased?"

"No, I was not obligated to."

Grissa pushed back, "Didn't you love her?"

"I did, but that was not primary to me. I am a King by title, but my actions are based on what my people want. Tell me then, Grissa? Am I a King or a servant?"

She scanned the room, searching for an answer that would seem less offensive, and then questioned back, "How, Your Majesty, is that related to your love for her?"

The King looked Grissa in the eye, it wasn't a look of scrutiny or superiority. "My father was crowned King; I was declared crown prince. This meant I had to rush with my education."

"It's no wonder then, how you managed to take the throne in two years…" She folded her arms, smirking. The King tried reading her eyes but waited.

"Would you like to talk about how you came to the throne and Her Highness becomes Queen?" Her lips twisted.

The King, who was standing, placed his right foot on the table, piercing a stare at Grissa.

"Are you hinting that I murdered my father, took over the throne, and married Elora?" His words came through clenched teeth.

Grissa began having second thoughts on her flow of ideas because the next words she chooses to utter could prove to be fatal. Her face began growing white, heat flowed out of her through her sweat.

"No…" she stuttered, the face of the King that she had only seen on display was before her face. "I'm merely asking of… how… how… the late King came to be murdered…" She tightened her eyes shut.

"Woman, why should you doubt your King?" He kept a check on his anger, but he equally seemed like he was in a violent fight.

"The people… they all talk…" she replied, while still not looking. Maurilio's anger subdued, and by the time Grissa opened her eyes to look, he had already taken his seat.

"This makes it imperative then, I must talk about my ascent to the throne. They must know and must never question their King again," he stated. "You are warned, your writing must do well in giving the news."

****

Maurilio Slayholt ♜

It had been over a year, and Ariesque, given all its reasons to celebrate, continued to remain hushed. People died, families broke apart, and this would continue to remain unfixable until a few generations pass.

I walked back to my chamber, glancing at the wall clock before being drawn by the smell of food wafting in my joined chamber. Mom always left dinner on the small dining table; we didn't have family dinners in the palace.

I sat down at the table of my grand brown-gold chamber, self-examining thoughts making their way into my mind. I completed my +2 while remaining in the palace, for two reasons: firstly, to avoid making people feel reserved toward me, and secondly, the academy was going to pause for a few months considering the well-being of the students and teachers. I was the only one from my level who completed it at the earliest, and now, I spent every day doing rigorous work, training to be a King, one day.

I kept pushing my limits, but even with the double workload, every moment I paused, I did not cease to realize how much I've lost, even though I've gained a better world and life.

The palace was silent, and the number of royal soldiers was less. I guess now that the truth of Maldeus' end had settled well, there was no use for security. I always thought that if Maldeus was dead, we would be living a better life, but to be honest, I'm living the same life; I don't even know if one can call it a life.

The palace was always isolated; I barely saw Mother, and Father would never be at home; he had a lot of mending to do after Maldeus's rule. Illegal dealings, joint criminal acts among the three kingdoms, reassuring people that Maldeus was gone, helping open businesses that were lost, joining the MIC to eradicate the infiltration, and building the country's economy that had been affected badly, trying to raise the minimum wage of working citizens.

On the 2nd of March, Eromen's Day, while we were celebrating it on the campus, Moon City was celebrating it on its streets. Maldeus burned the entire street to ashes; five people died, and three were gravely injured. It had been a week since Father took the initiative to rebuild that area of the city.

We each had our kind of trauma, and we each had our way of dealing with it too. Nobody questioned anybody's actions either. Mom would usually keep herself busy but would always reserve at least two seconds of her day to check on my well-being.

I walked to the shower after my meal, the warmth of the water reminding me of Elora's absence, her memories driving the smile on my face.

I will get used to her absence; I must, Ariesque will never accept her.

It's been more than a few months now; the real question was when that day would finally arrive when I'd be able to do the same things, I did in her presence without remembering her.

The royal family and the diplomats are currently undergoing counseling by a royal counselor. This was to create fair, uninfluenced decisions. Elora was something I never spoke to anyone, not even the royal counselor, and maybe that was why she stayed, because some wounds are better when left untouched.

I made every thought leave through my mouth except hers, and deep down in my heart, I knew I was scared to let her go.

I never want to be King. Stories tell great tales about a King, about how rich and well-off they were, and even though I was rich, I will not be well-off. I am bound by the very same laws that my people are bound by. As Slayholt, we keep a very low profile even with a regal status.

Perhaps, at the end of the day, the only relief I could derive was from the softness of my bed, a reminder that someday my life will also end in comfort, and the struggles will go away.

Another day and maybe another chance, I pulled the curtains; that was what my therapist asked me to do the first thing in the morning, draw the curtains and admire the beauty of life. I had to make it to Martial Arts class, so I walked to the main dining hall, my shoulders aching from yesterday's class. The palace had a much better look of a home; most guards were off, but it looked way out of place when I realized that all the guards were off, no guards at the dining hall. Father must have really decided to remove the palace security.

I picked up sandwiches from everything on the table; they're the best go-to food when you don't want to sit and have a proper meal. But how could I sit at a table again after Maldeus?

I began coughing, having swallowed into the wrong pipe. "Water!" I called; the servants were missing too! What was the occasion for such an absence from royal workers? I poured water into a glass, settling the choking feeling.

After leaving my bag of clothes on the chair, I began to look around, walking into the door at the corner of the room—the kitchen, but it was bustling with orders and noises from the loud clanking of metallic pots.

"Your Highness, is there something I can do for you?" The kitchen chief called from the right end side; he had a loud voice and was sweating from all the orders he gave.

He came toward me without any delay, tilting his head. "Anything special or out of order today?" I tried to sound casual.

"No, not really. Is there a problem?"

I shook my head, leaving the kitchen undisturbed. So, there was no special occasion that I could have forgotten about. I started walking toward mom's chamber, the curiosity of change getting the better of me. A sudden sound stopped me dead in my tracks. I pushed the door to her room.

It was empty; the window was open. It must have been the wind. Letting out a breath of relief, I turned to leave. Mother must have left for business; she did that sometimes, but she'd always leave a note to me.

It was surprising that she hadn't left one this time.

Then I heard it loud and clear, the slap of bare feet on the tile, choking sounds, and the struggle for breath. I ran toward the source of the sound, into her bedroom, but there was nobody in sight.

The sound became clearer. I ran to the opposite side of the bed in the room. Blood on the floor.

"Mom," I called out to her. She raised her hand toward me, simultaneously pressing her throat, which was draining blood.

My eyes remained fixed upon her, and my knees fell on their own. What happened?

"Help!" I screamed, at the top of my voice, pleading for someone's presence. "King..." Her strangled voice came out "They..." She was struggling to remain conscious.

"Mom!" I shook her in my arms, "Mom! Help! Please, someone..." Her breathing grew slow, her eyes partially closed.

"Ari..." The soul in her had gone.

I heard footsteps, but they were late.

"Your Highness," they shuddered at the sight. My contorted face yelled at them.

"Get a doctor now!" Tears rained down, "The King. Secure him."

I kept much patience for this day; the dawn of justice would quench the thirst in me for revenge. It has been a month since the incident took place.

A sharp knock on the door to my chamber sounded.

"What is it?" I asked, sipping tea and looking out through the window, admiring the glory of the day.

"The Minister of Magaime has sent you a letter."

The royal servant placed the letter on the sofa table and left.

I laid the teacup back on the saucer on the windowsill and picked up the letter, knowing its contents. It was an official statement of the discussion held two weeks back during my meeting with Aniket Neger, the Minister of Magaime Corporation.

The Magaime Court of Justice had received an official notification from the Royal Court of Justice on the 15th of July, proposing to hold the trial against the heinous crime committed toward the royal family.

As per Statement 3 of Royal Rights, the Magaime court of justice will step back, provided that the royal court of justice takes the consequence of the act upon their shoulder.

The trial of the following:
1. Former diplomat of Lacoyara, Aristera – J. Iscariot
2. Diplomat of Criosa – Logan Harper
3. Diplomat of Largus – Andrus Dimos
4. Diplomat of Aerilon – Russ .A. Terrel
5. Diplomat of Bilthor – Dolion Bacia Sephtis

6. Diplomat of Prielvar – Duncan Blike
7. Diplomat of Oscaet – Berube Johnson
8. Diplomat of Godin – Samuel Zagan
9. Diplomat of Scapular – Ambrose Flitcher
10. Diplomat of Herlo – Neal Preston Carr
11. Diplomat of Nortovor – Peter Archerion
12. Diplomat of Hakeon – Cement Sorel Batista

Would be conducted on the morning of August 3rd at 10 am, in the presence of an official witness from the court of Zocia.

There are two copies of this contract; you are requested to sign and return a copy.

I signed both copies and re-sent one back to the MIC, leaving for the trial. They had granted permission from their side late, but I was already ready for this trial. I collected all the evidence, got it tested, and knew who was guilty of what crimes. Today was the day of sentence declaration.

I flipped my cape, taking my seat on the Regal Justice seat—the Justice of Andronicus. The throne has been preserved since then, but required restoration was done wherever and whenever needed. The seat was stiff and hard, made of gravel with ancient carving. The courtroom, on the other hand, was modernized with an open roof. I struck the staff of Andronicus, one of the triumvirates, onto the stone floor built around my seat, eyeing the twelve captivated Enchanters with their masked faces.

The court servant pulled each of their masks off, revealing the faces of those guilty and those innocent, pushing them to kneel on the ground before me. I represented power today and sat with my staff to remind my people that regardless of the face I choose to display to the public; I am the rightful owner of Ariesque and the very laws built upon it.

All shall bow to their King when required regardless of their hesitation. I would turn into a heartless King that knew no mercy when it came to justice. Justice that the people refused to give equally, throwing Elora away to banishment.

The sowa bearer introduced the criminals and their crimes to the gathered. The evidence was then displayed to the crowd of people, the knife used to stab my mother, the DNA analysis of a strand of hair found in her room, and the statements of the royal guards stationed outside the meeting room when father was meeting with the diplomats.

The accused were then allowed to give their final statement before their sentence. I sat, silently listening, eyeing every tiny facial expression they gave off while speaking—the diplomats who spoke with guilt, the diplomats filled with pride, and those who did not seem to be part of this act.

After they spoke, the court servant brought a piece of paper upon which I would write my final judgment; the trial was halted, causing the silence to break apart. Light chattering began, then turned into heavy conversations, while I was inking the paper.

An hour later, the court servant declared silence, and by the time my feet touched the ground, a silence of dread had already occurred. I lightly tapped my staff on the stone, and a sowa bearer walked toward me, holding it near my mouth.

"I, Maurilio Slayholt," I turned my eyes to the crowd to declare a fact, "King of the Enchanter community and the sole judge of this trial." A look of abomination spread on my face for both my people and the criminal before me. A deadly reminder that I am not weak in my decisions despite the difficult times of my life.

"Declare the consequence of this trial as such… the diplomat of Criosa—Logan Harper, the diplomat of Prielvar—Duncan Blike, the diplomat of Bilthor—Dolion Bacia Sephtis, the diplomat of Nortovor—Peter Archerion, the diplomat of Godin—Samuel Zagan, and former diplomat of Lacoyara, Aristera—J. Iscariot have been found to be guilty of the accusation and have willingly taken part in the murder of…" I paused, taking a deep breath, "The late King and Queen and the attempted murder of their new King. They are sentenced to be immediately executed this moment."

Through my peripheral vision, I saw some of their eyes grow wide, but I avoided looking at them, terrified, because if I saw their eyes, I might see a little of Elora and change my sentence. And even though Elora was a murderer, they are murderers of free will.

The executioner with the sword walked to the first diplomat, the diplomat of Criosa while the sowa bearer warned the people of the sensitive scene about to take place and that they had a total of a few minutes to leave the site or bear witness.

The diplomat of Godin, Samuel Zagan began crying when he saw the executioner hold the sword against the neck of the diplomat of Criosa; he was to meet the same fate.

I struck my staff against the gravel and blood splattered against the ground, the head rolled on the floor, and the diplomat of Herlo's screams mingled with the horrified noise of those remaining in the crowd. The executioner repeated the act five more times, I then watched the last man kneel before his death, a victorious grin spread on his face—J. Iscariot, before his head was chopped off. The headless bodies of the diplomats were then taken offsite; they would be handed over to their families for a proper respectful burial along with the dead people who lived a good life; as King, this was my form of forgiveness.

J. Iscariot confirmed that my decision was not all too cruel. The disguise he wore before my father of a good man was the biggest deceit I came to terms with, especially when he tried to protect people the most, during Maldeus' reign. He was the man who devised this plan of tranquilizing my mother and then killing her, and he was the man who fearlessly struck my father with his power sword.

The remaining six people were terrified even to make eye contact; they were drenched in sweat.

"As for the diplomats of Largus—Andrus Dimos, Scapular—Ambrose Flitcher, Hakeon—Cement Sorel Batista," their faces went red.

"They are to receive lifelong imprisonment since they were coerced to take part in this act." Even though a look of relief appeared, they did not know what was waiting for them in the Black Heart Correctional Center.

"Diplomats of Herlo—Neal Preston Carr and Oscaet—Berube Johnson have not been found guilty of this crime. They are innocent but were aware of this performed act. For sheer negligence, they are to be immediately dismissed from their position. Furthermore, they are banned from working in the royal court and the Magaime International Corporation," I paused, swallowing thickness. "The court has terminated."

Those not dead were indirectly pronounced a death sentence.

I began taking my steps away from the seat; my peripheral vision saw the guards bow to me at the door to the back room, but I was lost in numbness.

****

"On returning to the palace, I suspended my work for the week. It was going to be just me and some privacy. I didn't want to be who I was; I didn't want to make rough, difficult decisions for the nation, and it was at that moment in the depth of my loneliness that I realized being King had its privileges."

"Own privileges?" Grissa tilted her head. The King smiled cunningly, and a glimpse of the young Maurilio appeared on his face.

"That's all I will be telling you. Time's up, you see," he pointed at the clock that showed the passing of three hours since 1 pm.

Grissa pressed her lips together, suppressing the emotions she felt, and then let out a breath of disbelief.

"I shall… take your leave then."

She rubbed her neck, rising toward the door.

"Oh and Ms. Grissa, make sure you do not display the King in any way to be vulnerable."

The look of a king appeared back.

Chapter 17
Bran Becile's Secret

The next meeting Mr. Leo—the scheduler could appoint was with Bran Becile, The King's secretary. Grissa had to move to the province of Prielvar to meet him from the province of Lunare, without any prior notice.

"You may ask him when you meet him, I'm merely fixing appointments." That was all he informed her.

Bran Becile was no significant figure, politically speaking, only having to stand beside the King during his decisions. The frown on her face made it obvious that she was not pleased with having to move to another place for an ordinary man when he was supposed to be with the King back in Lunare.

She entered a tower – The Royal Office of Prielvar that could fit a maximum of sixteen floors. Grissa discovered that working in a royal court was not as bad as she believed earlier; the tower was luxurious, light panels marked the wall behind the reception, and the tiled desk extended several meters.

The employees wore a uniform but even the cleaners dressed as though they worked in the royal palace. The casual seating area of the lobby was covered with navy blue carpets paired with couches and armchairs.

It seemed too much when she watched one of the cleaners begin cleaning a spotless table and then attempted to perfect her cleaning, by working on a dot of grease that refused to go.

The receptionist who was busy attending a call hooked the telephone. "Good morning, how can I help you today?" She was formally trained to even greet people with a smile on her face because the bags under her eyes said otherwise.

"I'm Grissa," she raised her eyebrows, informatively and then continued after a pause, "I have an appointment with Mr. Bran Becile, I believe."

"Oh yes… yes… Just a moment."

She opened a drawer, pulling out a paper. "You are requested to sign the undertaking before meeting him."

"An undertaking?" Grissa squinted at the paper.

"Yes, it's just a formality. Being the King's secretary, insider information must not leak out."

Grissa scanned the paper. "The undersigned is also required to perform any necessary action without free will…" She looked at the receptionist and then back at the paper. "This constitutes a legal binding, and the undersigned will be held accountable to face further legal action should the contract be broken from their terms."

She stopped, re-reading the terms, and then stated, "Does everyone have to sign this?"

"Apparently, yes. Even I am subject to legal action if inside information gets disclosed to the public from my hands, including drinking the praeterious if I get fired or terminated, and I believe that is the action mentioned to you too."

"I hadn't had to do so for His Majesty, the King himself then…?" she rubbed her chin, "Are you sure you're not scamming me?" Her question sounded genuine.

"No… no," the woman chuckled. Grissa kept tapping the pen forcefully onto the desk before resigning to sign it.

The receptionist then asked her to follow her. They entered the bronze lift, and she pressed the topmost floor button, the 16th Floor.

"15th is the diplomat's office," she randomly informed, trying to eliminate the discomfort.

Bran Becile, as the secretary, had the topmost floor. *So much for only a secretary's pose,* she thought to herself. The receptionist pushed the double door after knocking twice. "The moment you enter the door, you will find your answer, but the moment you exit, you will lose it too."

Grissa took her first step into the largely unoccupied office.

"Good morning," the man's voice echoed around the room.

"I'm Bran Becile," He flipped a page, writing something and then flipped the next, only throwing occasional glances at Grissa.

"Grissa," she replied, slightly overwhelmed by his presence and the atmosphere of the room.

"Sit," he gestured to a comfortable chair in front of his desk.

Grissa took a seat, her eyes still wandering around the room. The office had an air of elegance and sophistication, with dark mahogany furniture and gold accents. The walls were adorned with paintings, some of which seemed to depict historical events. He stopped whatever he was doing when he felt like Grissa hadn't moved from where she was standing and looked up at her, who was unresponsive, her eyes glued to the fireplace, lost in the mesmerizing beauty of the dancing swan carved out of the steel fireplace gate built into the wall.

"Yes, I too find such things amusing." The man smiled; she shook at the sudden interruption.

Grissa took quick paces toward the desk. Bran observed her for a moment before speaking. "I heard you had quite an interesting meeting with the King. How did it go?"

Grissa shifted her attention back to him. "It was… informative. He shared some personal stories, and I got a glimpse into the complexities of his role as a king."

Bran nodded, "Yes, being the secretary, I often get to witness those complexities firsthand. The burden of ruling a kingdom is not a light one."

"I can imagine-" Grissa almost replied. She stopped dead in her words, and her eyes grew wide. Her eyes fixed on the paper he was working on.

Bran Becile glanced to either side, confused before following her eyes to the paper, the blue ink on the black and white paper where he had just signed.

"Oops!" He played, "Secret's out!"

Grissa looked up at him and then at the paper and then back at him and then at the nameplate on the table ''Bran Becile—Royal Secretary', she scanned the room and then bowed.

"Your Highness, I'm sorry, I did… I… not… thought… know." She stuttered with random hand movement.

"Rise Grissa, I do not look forward to such formalities. I hope you'll understand, too."

She nodded; her eyes still fixed at the place where Aristera had signed the paper.

"Please have a seat," he then added hastily, like he was a busy man. More busier than the King himself. "And call me Bran." There was silence, Grissa pulled out her notebook, still looking unsettled by his identity.

"Let us begin with your friendship with the Queen. What do you have to say regarding that? What was it like when you found out she was queen?"

Bran eyed the woman who appeared uncomfortable, but this was not new to his sight. She would soon forget his identity, like the countless who forgot.

"I first spoke to Elora only because I was bored and alone. How we turned out to be friends remains a mystery. She always drew me to her; there were many rumors back in the academy of us dating, but none of them were true… The day I found out she was Queen was… a few days before level two."

****

Bran Becile 🕯

I lack energy, having spent it on traveling. We had just returned from a mini vacation in the other realm, and this is not my type of vacation. Even though it has been three months, a lot has changed—Moon City is like it never existed, the people are always hiding in their homes, lest they face the royal guards marking their rounds.

There was a 7 pm curfew time declared by the King, and no matter the emergency, nobody could move out. But people chose to abandon the streets even before the sunsets. I decided to complete my +2, even though Mom asked me not to return. I didn't want to be someplace where I wouldn't be able to be myself; magic defines me, and I've missed this place so much—the strong iron-like smell in the air, the home-like spell it casts over me, and without a question, Elora, and Ziva too.

I can understand Mom, why she's terrified and concerned. She lost her marriage at a young age, and having first-hand experience with the King's capabilities, she wanted to keep her child safe. I've asked her countless times to remain in the other realm with her brother, where we spent the vacation, but the idea of leaving her child in a desert while living next to a waterfall with a safe and sound life did not fit her idea of life.

"Have you heard the news?" Mom asked, willing to share the latest gossip she heard from the neighboring flat.

I placed the big black carry-on bag onto the floor of the hall. We lived in a good two-room apartment at the far end of Moon City, so the destruction of the main street did not go unseen by Mom. She had spoken to me, her brother, and even his wife, during our gathering on night about the dead black smoke rising to the sky, being terrified and all alone at home.

"What!" I asked, vexation grabbing me, pulling me back to reality. We had to travel through three terminals before we could get to our province; teleportation can drain your energy. They made big changes to the port station, so now we could not directly arrive from the other realm to Prielvar, where we live, or Largus.

But that was not all; intra-teleportation also had problems, like we could not move from Criosa to Prielvar; it was closed. So when we entered Criosa, we had to teleport to Aerilon and then to Prielvar. If that even makes sense because Maldeus too never made sense.

"There's a queen," she stared wide-eyed. "The King has finally decided on marriage. Perhaps, now maybe, he will be a changed man."

"A queen?" My response was automatic once her statement had sunk in. "Unaware is unlike you," she smiled while squinting at her discovery.

I ignored her, concerned because the king had just married. Who would want to marry him? He is all fleshless and pale and old, as the papers depict.

He was planning something, but there is a strong possibility about what Mom said; maybe he did have a change of heart and decided to forgo his previous ways. How did Mom ever manage to forgive him?

She nudged the folded newspaper at my arm, breaking my thoughts away. I unfolded it, pulling the paper a little away from my eyes.

'His Majesty Declared Marriage'

A large picture, clicked at a height, captured two unclear figures standing on a raised platform. The woman wore the usual white wedding gown, and the king was in his black traditional royal suit, embroidered in real gold. The photograph was taken during their marriage vow, their left ring fingers entwined with each other. The woman looked at the ground instead of the King; this could not possibly be a love marriage.

The King Declared marriage yesterday without any prior notice or invitation to any royalties or diplomats. The King's unexpected decision has struck the nation as chaotic, but this decision continues to be a point of celebration throughout the nation. While the King has declared a ban on all forms of entertainment except the papers, the Queen has not made her appearance to or addressed the nation as is the usual tradition.

The King addressed the nation as such: "My Dear Citizens, it is with much pleasure I declare to you, my Queen. Queen Elora Bates, (17/E) who shall be my company all through my life and ruling."

This… this, my eyes, what did I read? Elora? Who? Surely, there isn't just one Elora. I scoffed at the idea, but 17? Eromen? The King's marriage, especially to someone named Elora Bates, hit me on a personal level. The air seemed to thicken as I struggled to process the information, my mind grappling with the implications of this union. What did it mean for the people, for the nation, and, more importantly, for me? The newspaper offered only glimpses, leaving me yearning for more information. It had sparked a myriad of questions within me, creating a void of uncertainty.

****

"I'm not sure if this question is appropriate." Her voice sounded hesitant. "Ask away, it is for me to decide if the question is appropriate or not." "As Aristera, you…deemed the Queen to be innocent, despite murder during her trial. What was on your mind? Elora, your friend or the nation?"

Aristera exhaled, a minor smile playing on his lips. "Well, that's inappropriate up to a certain extent. You will not be able to quote Aristera in the book because, firstly, that is not what you will write. Secondly, to answer your question, I was not Aristera when I professed her innocence."

Grissa hesitated before responding, "How do you mean? Do you think that Her Highness was rightly punished for her crimes then?"

Aristera paused, "No. Do you know the crimes she committed, murder? Does that crime sound forgivable to you?"

Grissa's throat bobbed, "So…"

"So, I think she was not punished justly. But I can't give a say here because she did not commit it out of free will."

"She did have a choice…"

"Yes, a forced choice. A do-or-die situation is never a choice."

"Did you ever try to find out? Why she chose to be Queen?"

"I knew for a fact that Elora would never make that decision, but now and then, I would rethink. I realized that deep down, Elora was well capable of craving power. She loved the idea of being above everyone."

"So, you're saying that there is a possibility that whatever the Queen has laid bare up until now could be false?"

"No, that wouldn't make sense now, would it? Because the facts stand somewhere. I am merely assuming for which there is no proof."

Grissa thought, agreeing, "When His Majesty, the King declared to bring back the Queen to this world, he mentioned to the community that this decision was not just his, but of Diplomat Ziva Anson, Diplomat Liam Sprague, and you. What was the actual deal behind this?"

****

Bran Becile 🪶

We were waiting in one of the meeting rooms of the palace; it was unusual for us to be summoned here, and the wait itself was going overboard. Ziva and Liam Sprague were also present, the clicking teacups playing a tense tune in the room. There was no prior notice, just an immediate meeting called by the King.

After several minutes, the clacking of shoe heels on the tiles could be heard, and Maurilio finally entered the room. The crowd rose.

"Do not panic. I've called this meeting not as King but as friends."

"Maurilio!" Ziva glared, "You should have mentioned that. Calling two diplomats and your secretary within the palace is not something not to panic for. I thought something had gone wrong,"

"ZIVA! Don't address the king in such a manner," Liam rebuked her with hidden unease.

Maurilio shook his head at Liam, indicating that such conventionalism was not required.

"Then what is it you called me too for?" Liam asked, "I don't remember us being friends for a very long time."

"And that is not what I called to discuss today," Maurilio made his statement, "I hooked this meeting to talk about Elora."

"Elora?" I asked. The name that never came from his mouth came smoothly and without hesitation today—three years later. "What about her?"

"I want to bring her back." He did not hesitate again, showing how much he had thought this over.

"What!" Ziva brought her head forward. Liam chuckled, "Good one!"

The King stood at our ignorance.

"Oh, so you mean it," I clarified in the end. "Very well, so."

Something was growing in me, and it wasn't pleasant; I clenched my teeth. "But you'll be going against the community."

"Yes, I am powerful enough to bring war upon anyone that denies me," he replied haughtily, gliding his tongue against his lower lip.

"You're willing to break war for a girl you love! And you call yourself king!" I took a step forward.

I've seen Elora in the other world; she's doing fine, living an ordinary life without chaos. Bringing her back is beyond an option; I cannot allow that to happen.

"No, Bran. That is not what I meant… but how about you tell me what the real problem is here," he folded his arms and tilted his head, trying to get a clearer view of my expression.

My rapid breathing came to slow down. He was right; I did not care about the community.

"There's no problem," I flatly said. He was the King. I was wrong to think I could argue here. He continued to look at me, waiting for a reply.

I glanced at him before looking at the floor, sighing.

"I've been watching her since the year she left, and Elora seems to be doing fine… and bringing her back…"

"I understand, Bran. But I promise, she'll be happy with me, not just fine."

I remained silent; this argument was not in my favor. Maurilio has come determined, not for a discussion.

"Why tell us of this decision?" It was Ziva.

"I need your support. The community will be less likely to lash out at this decision if it is a joint one. I need you to convince the higher authority, convince anyone willing to see a better future." His eyes were pleading.

"Liam, you're silent." Ziva pushed him, even though his silence was justified given his past relations with Elora.

"I don't understand the entire story. It's either I'm not following well, or my head is filled with hay. MIC made her banishment an official statement, so how are you going to go against the community's wishes to bring her back?"

"Liam," the King said with solemn silence, "Do you know why the MIC was formed?"

The silence continued, while we all looked at his face for the answer. "To protect the interest of the community."

"Yes, Maurilio, but I don't see how this is valid here…" Ziva sighed out; she was beginning to get frustrated too.

"The King's words are law," he counter-stated.

A large pause because it still didn't make sense. Even if Elora did come back here, what about the people? They don't seem to be open and accepting, and they wouldn't want anyone that had any association with Maldeus.

"So, you're just going to bring her back. The law says that the royal family cannot protect any threat to the community."

I looked back at him wide-eyed, "Unless you decide to abolish that foundation!"

"No," he chuckled, with a humored look, "I'm not going to abolish the foundations of our community that protects my people. They were created by my ancestors."

I continued to look at him, not understanding his words, "The law does not apply to the King and the Queen and Aristera; provided the King authorizes."

Silence.

"You want to re-crown a dowager who was married to your uncle. A dowager that the community claims to be one of the reasons for their painful life," my lips formed a thin line.

"Why else did you think I wanted to bring Elora back?" he questioned me back.

Liam broke our conversation, "Of course, this matter does not just concern the royal family and the people. The MIC must be considered. The moment you declare that Elora's banishment is lifted, the MIC will hold a meeting. You must have a reasonable explanation to convince them, to allow Elora to enter, and being King, you may be exempt from the law but Elora, being a dowager, is only a citizen who had a royal status but continues to remain a threat to the nation. You are in no position to bring her back."

"I am going to declare her Queen before she returns. I'm going to bring a Queen back, not a citizen or…"

"That way, being Queen will give her authority to stand over her identity of a criminal that being a dowager, an ordinary citizen cannot,"

"That is bloody brilliant," Liam said, his mouth partially hanging. "Why Elora?" That was all that came out of my mouth.

"Because it's Elora," he replied, his eyes twinkling.

"There is one great issue…" Ziva said with a straight face, "Elora has had the union bond formed, and even though usually, once the partner dies the bond ceases to exist. There have been cases of unexplainable death when the widowed partner re-marries and the worst of all is that Elora was associated with dark magic when this bond was formed. It could relapse and kill her."

****

"You confound me, sir. Sometimes, you stand for Elora, and sometimes, you believe she did not receive her punishment justly. Why do you have two sides?"

"As Aristera, I am in my rightful position to stand in favor of the country, and that is my foremost priority. But in places where the country has nothing to do with my decision, I stand for what is true. Over time, there has been a role change; Zocia, who was the King's advisor, now solely supports the people, and the role of Aristera is that of an advisor and second ruler.

"I cannot show partiality to the people of Ariesque by deeming Elora to be innocent because she was not. Murder is not innocent. Of course, she was compromised, so bringing Elora back was not a bad decision for the country. She was no threat to the country. She was a threat only in the presence of Maldeus."

"I see, sir, why you are Aristera. Indeed, wise like how Sherwood, Eneas if it's true, called you."

"You wouldn't remember any of Aristera."

Her eyes suddenly began searching the room, "I won…'t re….member?" Bran looked at her and opened the drawer simultaneously. "Praeterious, hasn't anyone told you… Oh, dear… It's not something to linger upon now; you've got just this one meeting."

Grissa remembered the receptionist saying something about it but hadn't paid good attention, thinking about the undertaking sheet.

"That is all, Mr. Becile," Grissa said gravely.

Bran made a sharp nod before lifting the telephone on his desk, "Danika, please come in."

The receptionist hurriedly walked into the room and was then informed to proceed with the security checking, which included reviewing Grissa's notes and taking out anything that pointed at Aristera or his identity, redoing the notes, and inspecting her belongings.

Danika called for help, and the two ladies began examining everything on a large inspection table placed behind the door that Grissa hadn't noticed earlier.

"How is your writing coming along?" Bran asked, trying to calm the impatience in her by making small talk. Grissa glanced at him before returning her sight back to the table.

"It's going fine. I've almost completed it. Just got to interview His Majesty one more time and Ziva Anson." Her head turned back at the sound of flipping pages.

She watched the two ladies roughly handle her belongings while not wanting to go through the procedure.

"Why are you interviewing all of us?"

Danika then read through her interview notes, erasing and redoing whatever was possible, and then placed each page individually within a machine, making the binding of the book hang.

"I want to make the people realize that whatever Her Highness has spoken is true by verifying the story with you all."

Grissa straightened herself up, facing forward unable to watch her hard work change its form in the hands of a stranger.

"That's wonderful," he smiled, "it's a pity, though, that we're all diplomats or royal workers."

"There's only so much that can be done. I did want to interview Bexley Weber, currently working in the illegal department of the MIC, and Orson, the main headmistress of Silverstring. But then, I realized that they wouldn't be able to be of much help given that the Queen's close friends themselves have unsure opinions about the past."

"We're done!" Danika finally called from behind, proud. "That was fast," the writer raised her eyebrows.

"Yes, practice makes perfect. You should know," Bran answered, pulling open his drawer and bringing the vial to her sight. He opened the lid and dropped a piece of paper with Aristera's signature, pulled a strand of his hair, and allowed it to dissolve into it.

"That should do. I've lost over 100 strands of hair just for this purpose," he chuckled, trying to ease her discomfort.

She looked hesitantly at Bran and took the vial, shutting her eyes and drinking it all in a gulp.

The vial slipped through her hands, falling to the floor. She fell back on her chair, unconscious.

Danika swiftly picked up the plastic vial from the floor and placed Grissa's belongings back onto her lap.

When Grissa woke, she blinked hard, slanting her head. "I'm sorry! Did I just sleep? In between our interviews?"

"What are you talking about? We were just talking…" the man acted perfectly.

"I'm sorry then, where were we, Mr. Becile?"

The man looked around the room for an answer, "You asked me if I were single…" he blurted.

"Nonsense," the woman laughed, looking suspiciously. "I'm already seeing someone… That was a terrible joke."

"I apologize, then," Bran smirked.

"I remember, I was about to leave. Thank you very much."

Chapter 18
The Pearl of Echo

"Mr. Becile has updated me on the story, but how did you even come across a loophole to bring Elora back, Your Majesty?"

"Loophole?" The King questioned her. Lines grew on the writer's forehead, but the King smiled.

"I had given up on the idea of Elora. I thought life was finally settling for me, but she was always there somewhere in my mind, flashing before my face at random times. I never truly loved anyone before Elora; I slept with many but never loved." He paused, "Please do not write that part."

Grissa gave an empathic nod.

"During all my years until the death of Maldeus, I was alone. My people saw Maldeus from afar, but I was with Maldeus. I spoke to him, I saw his actions, his desires, and the thoughts that he spoke out.

"The best interest of the people was to suffer in silence than die a long torturous death, a death that would wipe them from existence like they never existed. To me, Elora was the only person I could see my reflection, and I wanted to give her all the love and support that I couldn't get." The King huffed a breath, walking to the table to pour a glass of water for himself, but the moment the writer saw him raise the glass jar, she rose.

"Your Majesty, allow me..." She started, not having a chance to serve the King. He pulled on the front panel of his suit.

"Grissa, I can do ordinary tasks." He sipped and then placed the glass, with a light thud, on the wooden table.

"How did you convince Her Highness to return? I heard you declared her queen here before you could even propose to her."

"I declared her Queen after; I knew she would come, but I almost failed."

****

Maurilio Slayholt ♜

I stood before the brown wooden door to Elora's apartment; beyond this barrier was Elora. My emotions overwhelmed me—she was here. She lived here. I finally had my chance, an opportunity to fight for her.

It took me over a month to prepare myself for the disguise I was going to present to her. I held my breath, trying to make three confident knocks.

Would she still be the same Elora I knew, or would she be different? The door clicked, and I refused to blink. Bran had seen her, but I hadn't seen her face for a long, long time.

A woman came into view—it was her. A few noticeable changes: she looked messy, but the smile she wore showed she was doing okay. She watched my expressions wide-eyed, but I couldn't be more formal before the woman I knew. I took a swallow, returning to the present before this whole ordeal got messed up.

"I was told you're looking for a roommate."

She too swallowed her facial expression and opened the door wide. "Welcome. Home." She didn't hesitate. I almost began speaking to introduce myself, but I was taken aback; my eyes blinked at her openness to a stranger.

"Oh, yes. I've been desperately looking for a roommate for the past three months, and I'm due on one and a half months' rent since my last flat mate left. Everybody that contacted me later declined the stay because somebody told them this place was infested with roaches. I mean, who would spread such a stupid rumor…" She slashed her hand at the idea.

It was Bran; such ideas usually get generated from his brain.

She spoke about the rent and made me familiar with the house. It was small but more than enough for two people. It had two decent bedrooms, a joined kitchen to the tiny hall, and a bathroom. The apartment seemed old, and the wooden flooring creaked in certain areas.

It hadn't been cleaned in weeks; my shoe caught up in stale chips, cereals lying at the corner of the kitchen table. There was dried gravy on the kitchen counter, and the dishes lay piled in the sink.

The pale-yellow walls and orange sofa sheets made the flat look uglier than it was. The blue-tiled bathroom, however, looked like it was cleaned occasionally.

"Does someone else live here?" I asked, expecting a 'yes' even though Bran hadn't mentioned it to me.

"No, it's just me…" She smiled brightly.

I paused; Elora used to love being tidy. She was a perfectionist to the point that I would find her cleaning spots in our housing unit where the cleaning nymph or satyr hadn't gotten to.

Then after Maldeus happened, she grew untidier; she would sometimes require motivation to even get small things done. I'm surprised that she retained that habit and didn't go back to being the Elora I first met.

"That's my room." She pointed to the first room next to the kitchen, "and that would be yours… that is if you still like it here and would…"

"Let's negotiate then, shall we?" I cleared her doubt. This place was untidy, and I doubt people left because of the false rumor that Bran had leaked. Had it not been for Elora, I would have already left too. It didn't seem to be in good living condition, and it was pathetically maintained by her. I would have a lot of fixing to do if I shifted here.

"7 am is my bathroom time,"

"Dinner and laundry duty every alternate time. Two months' rent deposit."

"The same goes for dishes and cleaning," I added. "Knock at my door before entering, too."

"You can't bring anyone over, without prior notice."

"Well, I work from home, so I occasionally have to have some people home." "Oh, what do you work for?" She realized.

"I… I… I…" I stammered at the sudden question, looking at the magazine on the dining table, "I'm a freelance worker."

She raised her eyebrows at me, "As long as it's not drugs… or illegal business. I guess you're good to go?"

It didn't take long before an entire month had vanished, I spent most of my time at home with the first week doing maintenance work after calling the owner. Elora worked at a travel agency, dealing with customer queries and issues, and setting statistical and financial records.

She was doing two jobs at once in the same company but was being paid the same minimum wage. She barely complained about it, but we had grown close enough. I gave her a shoulder massage last Tuesday after convincing her I used to work as a massage therapist.

"Freelancers are all-rounders," I added, and she chuckled like we knew each other for a good long time.

During the time I spent with her, I found her to be a different... Some things were still unchangeable; she continued to struggle emotionally, pretending that all was well. I would sometimes find her crying to sleep or struggling to breathe in her sleep at the memories that made it to her as haunting dreams.

It was at these times that I would use my magic to enter her mind and remind her of me. They say; Subconsciously, our bodies know what they need. I wanted her to remember me, but to fall in love with me on her own. I would not manipulate or push her on me. Meanwhile, I fell in love with her all over again.

Even though I stayed in my room with the excuse of freelance work, I would write letters of instruction to Aristera to carry out all the tasks that required my attention.

But there were two times I had to return to Ariesque, it was for the meeting between the three kingdoms and secondly to declare my absence to the public under the cover of going for surgery for appendectomy. I was trying to keep things as discreet as possible because I didn't want an uproar to take place while giving full authority to Aristera to carry out my decisions. I trust him very much, and for good reason.

Another two months or so passed. Elora and I were good friends; we'd spend the weekends watching movies or trying a new restaurant. Whenever I was loaded with work, she would push dinner into my room, or sometimes take over my part of the household chores, get me something on her way back home, and even do my share of the monthly shopping.

Sometimes I would wait down outside her office with hot coffee, just to watch her. But for her, it was like her burning soul, soothed at the sight of me. It was those little things we did that made me feel like we were almost dating. The look in her eyes convinced me that she was starting to fall for me.

Then on a fine autumn evening, when the leaves were yellowing, I was cherishing a cup of hot tea. Elora was in the kitchen, and I watched her under the pretense of watching television hooked on the wall immediately after the kitchen area.

Even though her hair was tied in a bun behind, the red streak fell gracefully on her face, and she was lost in her world kneading the flour dough, bits of wet flour stuck to her hair. The door opened; I turned around at the unexpected intruder.

"Elora!" he called, not noticing me.

"Gabriel," she awed widely, running into the arms of the man dressed in army attire.

The man then noticed me, "We have guests," Elora turned to me, her face turning pale. She licked her lips, nodding.

"Nice hair, where did you get it done?" He asked me, my contact broke from Elora.

"Far away," I half-smiled.

He held Elora's waist, pulling her to the seat beside me. My feet began bobbing, are you married? Everything was beginning to shatter all over again. She played me badly; feelings of repulsion were beginning to take over me.

"What did you do to the house, Elora? It looks more like home now."

She chuckled nervously. He kept drawing her toward him, and she kept pushing away.

"Gabriel, this is my roommate. Maurilio." Her eyes wandered at ground level. Really? Were we just roommates?

"Your what!" He sounded demanding, moving his hand away from her waist.

"My roommate," Her voice grew timid like she was now standing before Maldeus.

"Who?" There was space between them, now; physically and emotionally.

"Hi, I'm Maurilio Slayholt. Elora's roommate." I declared, stressing on roommate with a feeling of betrayal, I extended my hand toward him.

"Hi," he returned the handshake with all his muscles into play, "I'm Elora's lover."

I could feel the heat leave my body through my breath at the word lover, it sounded as indecent as the man claiming it.

He turned to Elora, "We need to talk. I'd like to know why I wasn't aware of this and mostly, why is the roommate a male," he sized me up and then walked into her bedroom.

Elora glanced formally at me and followed him, and while they were in there together, I waited in the hall—went to the kitchen—checked for food in the refrigerator, and cleaned a spotless table, constantly keeping one eye on the door of her room.

I didn't want them to be together, I wanted her to be with me. I spent a lot of my time waiting without even knowing, and now I'm tired. Why is it that whenever I try to give myself a chance, she's not there?

Maybe, coming here was a mistake; maybe I should have just rather listened to them—my endless trail of thoughts was broken with the sound of breaking glass. I'm going to kill him if he touches her.

I pushed the door open like I owned the place. Elora was cowering in fear, squatting in the corner—crying. The ceramic vase from the decorative table at the corner of her room was on the floor shattered into pieces. Water marked the wall and dripping onto the floor, pooling at the edge.

Without thinking twice, I pushed the man back, locking him on the wall, my forearm pressing against his neck, and declared with clenched teeth, "You. Need. To. Leave."

"No!" Elora yelled back, and I turned to her, puzzled. She rose, her fierce red eyes piercing me, leaving me dumbfounded. Did she turn blind too, after coming here?

"You need to leave. You are the wall between us."

My fist loosened around his shirt and so did the muscles of my face. I looked at the shattered glass and then at the man, taking a step back; squinting at her, begging that she did not mean it.

"Leave! Don't you dare interfere in my life! Again."

I've had enough; I would leave, not just the flat but that part of the universe, returning to mine. I shall not return to her; she didn't want me. She was different now; way better, and she hurt me. I was only a playdate in her life.

Weeks passed; I asked Bran to clear my belongings from the apartment. And now, I was sitting in a meeting with Queen Frigga and King Rayan.

"Maurilio, your kingdom has been dumping a vast amount of Hterion," It was the waste remains of an illegal plant.

"Noted," of course, the criminal must have thought this would never come to my notice, but I will be making sure that this illegal business of theirs comes to an end.

"A lot of Monojacinth is forming in the ocean…" Rayan spoke, "The last time that happened, one of your men died," he warned me.

Monojacinth was named after its appearance of the gemstone jacinth, but as beautiful as it sounds, it was the deadliest bullet in our world. The bullet only had to meet a single drop of blood in the body and the person would be on the floor, looking through memories of their life that come before they stopped breathing. Its poison spreads like electricity in contact with water, fast and deadly without any known cure.

"We cannot currently figure out who it is or why but we're working on an anti-poison."

"You have lives… in your hand."

I slammed my palm onto the desk; Rayan pushed back. "You think I don't know that?" He spat.

"Maurilio," Frigga called me, "I would like to speak with you." I jutted my chin, nodding without breaking eye contact.

"Let's end the meeting here." I finished.

King Rayan apologized to me before leaving. I sighed; I crossed my line today. I was not doing okay; I was having a hard time breathing.

"Elora knows Frigga made a statement without any emotional consideration." My sight began turning blurry. "It's okay, Maurilio." Not king, not child, not anything but Maurilio. The very true identity of me. She placed her weightless hand on my shoulder, taking a step closer.

I pressed my fingers onto my eyes, sobbing. I was almost beginning to get used to her absence, a part of me just wanted to hear it from her; that she was happier without me.

It took several moments and then, I asked her, "Why are you speaking about Elora?"

The duties of a king are not ordinary responsibilities that I could abandon for a while and wait for her, so that she can realize that she needs me.

"I may look like the most superior being in the universe, but that is not me. I follow the orders of the one true superior being whose identity cannot be revealed to a mere mortal." There was a long pause; more than words were conveyed. She continued, "I gave her a gift. Yes, she was given a chance in life, but that was not it. She remembers, Maurilio."

I didn't know whether I was hurt or worried; words struggled to come out.

"I gave her the Pearl of Echo."

"Does the Pearl of Echo exist? No being has heard of it."

She smiled, comforting the darkness in my eyes. "No logic can ever define life."

"So, she was wearing a pretense?"

"She was wearing what she believed to be her identity."

"WHICH WAS PRETENSE." My voice was hard, not superior.

"Look through her, not at her, Maurilio. Sometimes when one has spent a lot of time in chaos, chaos begins to define their life. I rest here." She said and rose, walking to the door, turning one moment to say, "She wants a home."

Frigga's identity was no surprise to the world. She was a spiritual being, but today, I saw the heart of a human in her, quite comparable to my mother. My mother was not wise but was understanding and had an answer of her own to every question.

I tried not to overthink the matter, but every time she looked at me, she saw me; Elora saw me. I rose, a strong determination in me; she was not beginning to love me, it was that same love.

I want to only know the reason why she lingered on me knowing that she was already in a relationship with Gabriel. I want to know why she gave up on the idea of us and chose him. I will return, but only to confront her and ask her whether she ever truly loved me; I may seem desperate but that didn't matter because I was.

I want to be able to live in peace without any doubt, knowing that Elora has managed to create a life of her own without me and that she willingly chose it. The memory of when she first saw me years later flashed before my face. She knew, damn this! I should have known from her reaction.

I knocked on the door, drenched due to the thundershower. My clothes dripped water; a cold breeze ran down my skin from the window in the corridor. She opened the door and stood staring at me, concern etched over her face.

"Come on in, you'll catch a cold," she suddenly cried, running to fetch a towel and offering it to me.

I took it, watching her lie, "I was wondering where you went; someone came and claimed you moved out and took your belongings. But that is yours to deal with. You must let me know in advance if you want to terminate your contract, I…"

"Was it Bran?" My words were laced with hurt; she sucked in the air, realizing something was off and looked at my face for a hint of what I meant.

"Ah, yes, I believe that is who he is."

"I want to terminate my contract," I said, nervously.

I was scared to confront her. What if she was happy? What if I was just a lingering feeling in her from our past, the spur of the moment?

She stood there, shocked, her eyes widening with disbelief, "What? Why? Did something happen? Are you not comfortable here?"

"No, it's not about the place. It's about us."

"Us?" she questioned, confusion etched on her face.

I nodded, "I can't be here pretending everything is normal when it's not. I can't just be your roommate and act like we're strangers. It's hurting me, Elora."

She stared at me, silent for a moment, as if processing my words. "What do you mean?"

"I mean, I can't stay here while you are with someone else. I can't watch you with Gabriel. It's tearing me apart, and I can't pretend it's okay."

I kept silent, watching her every move, waiting for her to reveal the truth, but she said nothing.

She looked down, biting her lip, "I never wanted to hurt you."

"It's not your fault. It's just the way things are."

She walked up to me, her voice almost a whisper, "I never wanted to hurt you." Her voice broke. She grabbed my shirt. "Please don't go."

"Elora, it doesn't matter. I can't stay here or…"

"Or what…?" She begged.

"Or stop pretending and come back home," I finally managed, my voice barely above a whisper.

She stopped dead, blinking hard at my words, searching for a way to divert her answer. But it was too late; her mask had come off. Without denying, she walked toward the large window opposite her room, folded her right leg, and sat on the windowsill. She seemed to empathize with the earth outside.

Green light flashed across the screen, and drops struck the window roughly without care. She continued watching out like she didn't hear me because her face had no expression at all.

I begged before her one last time, "Please," I said, "Come home… come home, to my world," and she turned to watch me again with those empty eyes.

"Three years since…" she paused like it all happened yesterday.

"In these three years, I've tried everything, but 'home' was not something I felt. And your offer is tempting but so was his, and now I feel empty to death."

I remained silent; she continued, "He snatched so much away from me. I thought I would never be open to feeling again. The switch of life was hanging in the middle and then Gabriel came, and I was beginning to forget…" She traced the edge of the window with her fingers, carefully marking its borders.

"Are you happy with him? Is he what you truly want?" She kept quiet, "Answer me, Elora, I will leave this instant if you confirm it."

She nodded; my eyebrows twitched. I turned, making my way to the door. "He made me happy. He really did." I stopped, listening to the melody of her voice one last time. "But then you came…"

"I'm sorry…" My voice cracked, "I shouldn't have."

"Then I realized the difference between love and happiness. And then Gabriel came back, and I was confused."

"And now?" I glanced at her through the corner of my eyes.

"I can't see anyone but you. But…"

I bolted toward her, knowing what was on her mind, grabbing her hand, "I am true and so are my words." The desperation was evident in my voice.

"It may be, but your world is not. This is my sentence. Unless you stay here with me."

She rose, some form of hope brightening up her body. I shook my head slowly, even though my heart bore strong resistance.

"I cannot abandon my people."

She fell back onto the windowsill, an excuse to avoid my eyes.

"Then why are you here?" She whispered words of strong disappointment.

"Be my Queen."

Even though it was a statement, it came out like a question. She turned to look at me, her lips so upturned that it seemed to have lost the argument before it could even begin.

"A dowager re-marrying. A criminal taking over the country," she scoffed. "It's your experience speaking, Elora. Come home, I promise you. We. Will. Try."

"Experience is what makes a person, Maurilio. I just don't know…" She cried out of exhaustion, "Give me one reason…" She begged. "Just one and I will not question you, I will return."

"Because you love me. Because you're still here, arguing with me, asking me for a reason, desperately trying to 'want' to return."

****

"Now, that was touching. I guess this is where I'll end it with you," She smiled heartwarmingly.

"It was nice having you interview me!" The King extended his hand formally, and Grissa gladly took the shake.

Chapter 19
What Is Happily Ever After?

"How would you describe your relationship with the Queen at the moment?"

"We are good friends, but we try to keep things as professional as possible."

The woman with the blue streak spoke, freckles all around her nose, and her skin glistening.

"And what was it like when you came to know that Her Highness was the woman Maldeus had chosen as his Queen?" Grissa spoke to her with the utmost respect among all that she had previously interviewed.

"I was just like any other person out there; I thought she wanted to be Queen. I had this idea of her solely based on evidence."

"Evidence?" The writer asked, wanting to hear more than just statements.

"Yes, like entering Imperium even though she was an Eromen, getting the gold power mark, marrying the King who is known for his notorious deeds. This all made her seem power-driven, and the truth is, she was. If you placed love and power before the young Elora, she would have chosen power."

"But power has nothing to do with anything here, or does it?" She asked.

"Yes, people tend to align facts based on how well they fit the idea, not based on how true the idea is. Nobody told us anything about her circumstances. Bran was the sole person who stood up for her name even though she was Queen; Bran knew something was not right…"

"Why do you say this?"

"Because Bran would spend the most time with her; he knew her inside-out. They were like couples only they weren't."

"You are the first woman diplomat, and it is a great honor for me to be seated here."

Grissa's words were as genuine as her expression, "Is there anything you would like to tell the public? Or maybe tell us what it was like when Elora returned from the other world?"

"When Elora was declared Queen by His Majesty, the only way the nation decided to approach this issue was by causing an uproar. The MIC had sent a notice to His Majesty, blaming his uninformed decision. There were huge protests before the King's palace.

But the plan went on as it was decided; the union bond was formed in the other realm, and it was then that Elora returned to be officially crowned here. But the palace was invaded the night before her crowning, and she was placed at gunpoint. The chief of the royal army handled the problem, but security was tripled in the palace, and Elora had a guard watching her that night. It must have been the most chaotic Crowning Ceremony throughout history.

The ceremony went through with much difficulty, and the charges of a criminal on her head were taken down. Nobody dared to attack or talk bad about their new Queen. And I think it is for you to tell me whether Her Highness has gained acceptance or not."

"Indeed, she has," Grissa joined in the proud smile, "I understand you have been busy recently, and I have only a few hours, but would you like to tell me that despite having your distance from Elora within the academy, the two of you have managed to keep your friendship at its peak."

****

Ziva Anson

"It's an emergency. All students are dismissed to go home," professors announced at equal distance, rushing the students. There was chaos in the academy; people were running in the middle of the night. What was happening? I looked around, searching for Bran or Elora. Something had gripped me from within; never in the history of the academy has an episode like this taken place.

"Spiritual beings are waiting at the entrance of the academy. Abandon your belongings and leave."

"Elora!" I called through the noises.

"Ziva!" Bran called me, turning me by the shoulder. "It's Elora. She's nowhere to be found."

"Please, don't wait, leave now. This is an emergency!" Danbud yelled at our faces, and before we knew it, we were at Silverstring Station departing to go home; nobody's parents were at the station.

"Let me drop you home safe," Bran insisted, drenched in sweat. We left for Prielvar, Norhall, Street 318, Villa 3. Bran saw me off, waiting until the lights to my house were switched on, and then waved me goodbye from the window.

"Ziva, it's midnight. What are you..." Mom began pulling her nightgown together.

"I don't know. There was an emergency." I tried to calm my shaky voice.

The next morning, the morning Lodestone appeared earlier than its due date.

'Her Majesty Queen Frigga Claims the King's Death'

****

"It was that day when the story of Elora's death and life came out. Nobody knew the reason; we all pointed to dark magic, and I believe that was the reason that led to her banishment. Even though I gave my statement about Elora, standing for her in court.

I was not with her; I merely stated my experience. I realized I had wronged her years later and didn't object to His Majesty's decision to bring her back. I wanted a chance to make things right, and I got it."

"That is all then, Ms. Ziva Anson..." She rose but seemed hesitant. "Would you... umm... would you... if you could sign an autograph for me?"

"Oh, ME?" Ziva asked, looking shocked. Grissa nodded, excitedly.

"You've been my inspiration for the past two years." She almost squealed.

Ziva looked out of place at that comment, she forced a smile, "Thank you, I guess."

Epilogue
One Month Later

"I have compiled two books. One consists of the exact details of the events as spoken; this one includes all the intimate conversations, and the other speaks only of the important details of the story," she pushed both the books on the table so that they glided toward the King, sitting at the opposite end, after skating past Ziva Anson, Bran Becile, Liam Sprague, and Elora Bates.

"Depending on the book you wish to be published, please sign the last page, which has the undertaking with all your names mentioned. The undertaking will allow the public to know that these are your actual true words," she rose, slinging her bag over her shoulder, "and whatever corrections are required, send it to us."

She bowed to the gathered and then bowed to the King, giving a final glance at Liam before leaving, closing the door after her.

The tension in the room ceased, "I think we're something... Maurilio," Liam smiled dreamily.

"I still haven't wrapped my mind around the fact that we carry out the nation's decisions. We were just ugly teenagers back then..." Bran chuckled.

"Bran, you know the best part of this was when she asked me for my autograph. You should've seen the look on my face."

"But I always saw you, Ziva, to be someone great in the future but not you, Bran. You turned out to be Aristera, and that's crazier," the Queen mocked.

"And you turned out to be Queen, Elora."

"Since we're all here, what if we go out for dinner... and catch up..." Maurilio began, looking at everyone in the eye.

"Maurs darling," Bran played, "Why are you hesitating as King?" Maurilio looked dumbstruck while the rest of them giggled.

"I'm pregnant."

There was immediate silence; all eyes turned to Elora. Maurilio's eyes grew wide awake.

The wooden surface of the door struck, and a man brought the daily paper. "Your Majesty, there is news," his face was blank, placing the paper on the desk.

Maurilio took the paper; his face turning pale, he swallowed. "What is it, Maurilio?" Elora asked.

"Her Majesty Queen Frigga declared her death."

Dear Readers,

You have made it to the end of this Book. Thank you for accompanying me on this journey. Please leave a review on Goodreads, or hit me up.

Instagram: *alishh_sequeira05*
Email: *alishhsequeira05@gmail.com*